Rakes Who Make Husbands Jealous

Only London's best lovers need apply!

The League of Discreet Gentlemen has only one priority—providing the women of London with unimaginable pleasure. The secrecy demanded is expensive, but satisfaction is definitely guaranteed!

The League pride themselves on knowing *everything* about desire. But they're about to discover that whilst seduction is easy falling in love can be very hard indeed…!

Don't miss this incredible new quartet by dazzling Mills & Boon® Historical Romance author

Bronwyn Scott!

SECRETS OF A GENTLEMAN ESCORT
(Mills & Boon Historical)

AN OFFICER BUT NO GENTLEMAN
(Mills & Boon Historical *Undone!*)

A MOST INDECENT GENTLEMAN
(Mills & Boon Historical *Undone!*)

LONDON'S MOST WANTED RAKE
(Mills & Boon Historical)

AUTHOR NOTE

Meet the League of Discreet Gentlemen, a group of men who have dedicated themselves to women's pleasure! The *Rakes Who Make Husbands Jealous* mini-series is a collection of stories about Victorian male escorts who are exceptionally good at their jobs. These are not your standard petticoat-mongers— these are high-class, highly talented escorts, gifted at helping a woman remember her beauty and her value.

The League is headed by Channing Deveril, who has masterminded this group of men as a way of secretly thumbing his nose at matchmaking mamas and the marriage mart. But what started as an underground rake's game has now evolved into something more organised and serious. Every woman in London knows all she has to do is drop a request in a certain mailbox in town and her wish will be granted. Every married man wishes he knew if the League was fact or fiction.

In Book One readers will meet Nicholas D'Arcy, a gentleman's son down on his luck. The League is a chance for him to piece the family's finances back together. He's risen to the heights of notoriety for his skill as a lover in London Society—until one evening an assignment goes wrong and he's packed off to the country, where he is forced to come to grips with who he is and face the demons of his past.

Books Two and Three are Mills & Boon® Historical *Undone!* eBooks, with stories about League members Jocelyn Eisley and Captain Grahame Westmore.

The series finale is Channing Deveril's own story, in which he meets his match in Lady Alina Marliss. You may recall her as his special holiday guest in FINDING FOREVER AT CHRISTMAS. Will this signal the end of the League? Read the series and find out!

Stay tuned at my blog for updates and giveaways at www.bronwynswriting.blogspot.com

SECRETS OF A GENTLEMAN ESCORT

Bronwyn Scott

First published in Great Britain 2014
by Mills & Boon, an imprint of Harlequin (UK) Limited,
Large Print edition 2014
Harlequin (UK) Limited, Eton House, 18-24 Paradise Road,
Richmond, Surrey TW9 1SR

ISBN: 978 0 263 23966 9

Harlequin (UK) Limited's policy is to use papers that are natural,
renewable and recyclable products and made from wood grown in
sustainable forests. The logging and manufacturing processes conform
to the legal environmental regulations of the country of origin.

Printed and bound in Great Britain
by CPI Antony Rowe, Chippenham, Wiltshire

Bronwyn Scott is a communications instructor at Pierce College in the United States, and is the proud mother of three wonderful children (one boy and two girls). When she's not teaching or writing she enjoys playing the piano, travelling—especially to Florence, Italy—and studying history and foreign languages.

Readers can stay in touch on Bronwyn's website, www.bronwynnscott.com, or at her blog, www.bronwynswriting.blogspot.com—she loves to hear from readers.

Previous novels from Bronwyn Scott:
PICKPOCKET COUNTESS
NOTORIOUS RAKE, INNOCENT LADY
THE VISCOUNT CLAIMS HIS BRIDE
THE EARL'S FORBIDDEN WARD
UNTAMED ROGUE, SCANDALOUS MISTRESS
A THOROUGHLY COMPROMISED LADY
SECRET LIFE OF A SCANDALOUS DEBUTANTE
UNBEFITTING A LADY†
HOW TO DISGRACE A LADY*
HOW TO RUIN A REPUTATION*
HOW TO SIN SUCCESSFULLY*
A LADY RISKS ALL**
A LADY DARES**

And in Mills & Boon® Historical *Undone!* eBooks:
LIBERTINE LORD, PICKPOCKET MISS
PLEASURED BY THE ENGLISH SPY
WICKED EARL, WANTON WIDOW
ARABIAN NIGHTS WITH A RAKE
AN ILLICIT INDISCRETION
HOW TO LIVE INDECENTLY*
A LADY SEDUCES**

†*Castonbury Park* Regency mini-series
**Rakes Beyond Redemption*
***Ladies of Impropriety*

and as a Mills & Boon® special release:
PRINCE CHARMING IN DISGUISE
(part of *Royal Weddings Through the Ages*)

Did you know that some of these novels are also available as eBooks? Visit www.millsandboon.co.uk

For Ro, because everyone should seize their day.

Chapter One

London, June 1839

If Nicholas D'Arcy had been a less extraordinary lover and his partner, the lush red-headed
Lady Alicia Burroughs, more discreet, her husband would not have discovered them. But 'less'
had never been an adjective to describe Nick, any
more than 'discreet' was an adjective one applied
to Lady Burroughs, who was currently voicing
her appreciation of his abilities with enough vocal
skill to impress an opera diva.

Lucifer's balls! The whole house could hear
her. Why stop there? The whole neighbourhood
probably could. It was only by a stroke of luck
that Nick caught the rapid thump of angry boot-
steps surging up into the hallway just as Lady
Burroughs took a breath beneath him before she

climaxed. The climax was beautifully done, one of his best, and all screaming aside, the stunning Lady Burroughs was worthy of it, laid out across the bed as she was. Her auburn locks cascaded over the bed's edge, her head thrown back, throat exposed, neck and back arched as he thrust into her. She was breathing hard and, deuce take it, so was he. He'd managed to get fairly worked up about this, too. Lord Burroughs didn't know what he was missing, but he was about to.

'Alicia!' the man's voice boomed down the hallway.

'It's Burroughs!' Alicia sat up with a gasp and a believable amount of panic, enough to make Nick start worrying in earnest. He had—what? Ten seconds? Maybe fifteen? Burroughs was heavily built and not the fastest runner. Maybe he wasn't even running, just walking quickly. There'd be time for trousers, but nothing more.

Nick leapt from the bed and grabbed up the discarded trousers. He thrust in a leg, hopping around on one foot while he tried to simultaneously gather up his shirt and coats. 'You said he was gone until Monday!' Nick hissed, piling his shoes on top of the messy pile in his arms.

'Oh, hush, will you? You don't want him to hear you. Hurry.' Alicia sat in the middle of the bed, a sheet drawn up modestly over those creamy breasts of hers.

Nick glanced around the room. There was no time for this window and her door was certainly out of the question. 'Does the dressing room go through?' If he was to be caught, it wasn't going to be by a pompous ass of a man who couldn't keep his wife in his own bed.

With a wink to Lady Burroughs, he was off, sliding through the dressing-room door with two seconds to spare and into the connecting room just in time to hear Lord Burroughs roar, 'Where is he?'

In your room, you old windbag, Nick thought with a chuckle, but he had to think fast. This would be the first place Burroughs would look. Even Burroughs wasn't dumb enough to realise the only way out was through the dressing room. Nick dashed into the hallway and opted for another room on the garden side of the house. He sidled in and closed the door softly behind him. He was safe for now. He set down his bundle of clothes and put on his shoes.

'Millie, is that you?' a voice called from the antechamber. Nick halted in midmotion, one shoe on, one shoe off. He grabbed his clothes and raced for the window. He was too slow. An older woman in a dressing gown emerged from the little room before he was halfway across. The dowager countess!

She was going to scream. Nick could practically see it climbing up her throat. He had to silence that scream and he had mere seconds to do it. He did the only thing he could think of. He strode two paces towards her, swept her into his arms and kissed her. Most soundly, too, and damn it all if she didn't kiss him back with a little tongue. The dowager countess—who would have thought it? It was arguably the most pleasant surprise of the evening because afterwards, she cleared her throat and said, 'Young man, you'll want to use the window. I think you'll find the trellis quite stable.' Then she winked at him. 'It's been used before.'

Good Lord, did Burroughs have any idea what went on in his house? Nick thanked her and wasted no time. The last thing he needed was for Millie the maid to show up. He'd have to kiss her, too. But that would be better than Burroughs, who Nick could hear throwing doors open as he barrelled down the hall. Again it was down to a matter of seconds between discovery or escape. Nick tossed his clothes down first and stuck a leg out to test the rung.

'Come back any time you like,' the dowager countess called after him. 'I have the gardener keep that trellis well maintained. He thinks it's for the roses.'

Nick merely smiled and climbed into the darkness as Burroughs knocked on his mother's door. The dowager would have to live with her disappointment, Nick decided. He wasn't coming back to the Burroughs town house for quite a while.

The rest of the escape was easy after that. He found his way out of the garden and, after he'd travelled through the warren of back alleys, he stopped and finished dressing. He was safe for the time being, although safe was rather relative. Alicia Burroughs wasn't exactly a soul of discretion, as he'd noted earlier. It would only be a matter of time before Burroughs knew it was him.

There was going to be hell to pay for this. Nick tucked his shirt tails into his trousers. His name would be all Burroughs would know, though. Responsibility for tonight's débâcle began and ended with him. There must be no connection to the agency, no threat of exposure to the League of Discreet Gentlemen, the organisation to which he belonged and which, by virtue of its name, had to remain discreet at all costs. People didn't mind doing business with a highly capable gentleman escort, but they *did* mind others knowing about it. If word of the organisation and what they did got out, every last one of them would be completely ostracised.

Nicholas began to walk. He wasn't ready to go back to Argosy House, the league's headquarters. What would he tell Channing? The league's founder would be so very disappointed in him. Discretion was the code the league lived by. To break it meant the worst kind of ruin. It would be the end of the Gentlemen, the end of the very good money he made, the end of a lot of things, not the least being the end of him; Nicholas D'Arcy, London's most outrageous lover. Women paid enormous sums for his skill in bed. They stuffed jewels in his pockets to find out just how outrageous he could be. And because he needed those jewels and those extraordinary sums of money, he encouraged it. Who was he if he wasn't Outrageous Nick?

Nick kicked at a pebble on the pavement. To be fair, he probably encouraged the attention for darker reasons than money and the notoriety. Sex was about all he was good at. Thank goodness he'd been able to turn his one skill into a marketable talent. More than that, he thanked goodness he'd met Channing Deveril, who'd made his success possible. Otherwise, he'd probably still be bumbling around as a clerk in a shipping firm on the docks, making too little to offset his family's financial needs.

Now, thanks to his reputation, he was able to send decent sums to his mother. He was able to write fabulous letters to his two sisters about the glittering parties he attended and all the latest fashions without making it up. Of course, they didn't know what he did for a living, only that he was now a man of business. Thanks to his brother's poor health, they would never know differently. There would be no chance for them to come up to London and see the reality, for which he was eternally grateful. A broken brother was bad enough. He couldn't break his mother's heart, too.

The milkmaids were starting their rounds when Nicholas climbed the front steps of Argosy House, nominally no different than any of the other houses along Jermyn Street quartering bachelor gentlemen of means. All the other windows on the street were dark, but lights still burned here. The boys would be up for another hour or so, reliving their evenings and then they would all retire.

A passing milkmaid gave him a flirty smile. 'Good morning, Master Nick. You've been out all night again.'

Nick swept her a bow and blew her a kiss. 'Good morning, Gracie.' He knew all their names, every milkmaid, every vendor that claimed Jermyn Street as their venue. Women especially liked that sort of thing.

Gracie waved a scolding finger at him. 'Don't you try any of your gentleman's tricks with me. I'm wise to all of them,' she teased. 'Besides, I've heard you've been up to no good.'

Nick was tempted to ask Gracie what she'd heard, but she'd already picked up her pails and moved down the street, her saucy hips swinging. Worry picked at him. Had his contretemps at Burroughs's already made the rounds? He stepped inside Argosy House to the sound of raucous male laughter spilling from the drawing room. He smiled. There was comfort in knowing the routine, of having expectations about what one would find when one came home. This was the only home he had now, the only place where he felt comfortable. It had been a long time since he'd felt that way about his real home.

Inside the drawing room, seven men sprawled carelessly on the chairs and sofas. Cravats were undone, jackets were off, waistcoats unbuttoned. Snifters of brandy in varying states of emptiness sat at their elbows. These were his colleagues of the past four years, the fellow members of the secret league.

Jocelyn Eisley spotted him first. 'Ho, ho, Nick my boy, you had a close call tonight. We were starting to worry.'

All heads turned towards him. Whistles and applause broke out. 'You'll be the talk of the broadsheets.' Amery DeHart saluted him with a half-drunk snifter.

'Three cheers for our man, Nick.' Eisley cleared his throat and leapt up on to an ottoman in a graceful move for one so big. 'I feel a poem coming on to commemorate the occasion. It's not every night one of us pleasures a lady with her husband in the house.'

There was a collective, good-natured groan. Nick took a seat next to DeHart on the sofa. Eisley's poems had become one of their traditions.

'A limerick, Eisley,' Miles Grafton called out. 'A dirty deed requires a dirty poem.'

'Here, here!' the chorus went up.

'All right then.' The big blond called for attention. 'I give you my latest creation.' The big blond's baritone resonated with enough dramatic flair for Drury Lane. 'There once was a man named Nick who satisfied women with his prick. How women did swoon when Nick did moon. He was the envy of every man in the room.' He gave an extravagant bow.

'Aren't we all?' Amery put in more loudly than necessary. 'We're the rakes who make husbands jealous.'

'And thank goodness for that,' Captain Grahame Westmore said darkly from his corner by the fire. 'If the men of the *ton* did their duty properly, we'd be out of a job.' A former cavalry officer, Westmore was private, as private as Nick was himself. Of all the men present, Nick knew the least about him.

'Well, what do you think?' Eisley stepped off the ottoman. 'Is it my best yet? I'll recite it at White's this afternoon and, by dinner, my little ditty will be repeated in every Mayfair drawing room—discreetly, of course. You'd better lay in another order for those French letters you like, Nick. Your popularity will soar. They'll call it "Nick the Prick".'

'They're calling it "In the Nick of Time", in the papers, according to my sources,' a sombre voice said from the doorway.

Nick winced. He didn't have to look up to know Channing Deveril, the league's founder, had heard the news already. It seemed quite a few people had heard if milkmaids and journalists knew. He'd hoped for a little more reprieve.

'Close call tonight, eh, Nick?' Channing's blue eyes met his.

'Only close, though.' Nick shrugged. Maybe Channing wasn't too upset. It was merely an occupational hazard. After all, it could happen to anyone.

Channing managed a half-grin. 'We can all be grateful for that. Come to my office and we can speak of it more privately and decide what to do.'

Nick's good spirits sank, replaced by a wary sense of caution. 'What is there to decide?' he asked, settling into the chair opposite Channing's polished desk.

'What do with you, of course.' Channing eyed him as if he were an idiot. 'You may have gone too far tonight.'

'You can never go too far.' Nicholas laughed, but Channing did not.

'I'm serious, Nick, and you should be, too. This won't blow over. Burroughs will know it was you.'

'I prefer *suspect*. He doesn't know it's me, not for sure,' Nicholas amended.

Channing cocked an eyebrow in disbelief. 'You're deluding yourself. With limericks like "Nick the Prick" and drawings labelled "In the Nick of Time" floating around London like so much flotsam?' Channing had a point there. 'Besides, I don't think Alicia Burroughs wins any awards for secret keeping.'

Another point in Channing's favour. A rather valid one, too, given tonight's display. 'The agency won't be implicated,' Nick put in, hoping to soothe Channing's feathers.

'My worry is not for the agency alone. I worry for you, too, Nick. I don't want there to be a duel.' Channing opened a drawer and pulled out a folder. He pushed it across the desk. 'That's why I have a new assignment for you.'

Nick scanned the document inside with a frown. 'Five nights of pleasure? In the countryside? Is such a thing even possible? It sounds like a unlikely juxtaposition to me.' Nicholas D'Arcy pushed the letter back across the polished surface of the desk with obvious disdain, his dark brow arched in sceptical disapproval of such a proposition. He was a London man. The city was his preferred environ with its refined women. There was nothing quite as fascinating as a city woman with her fashions and perfumes, her sharply honed repartee on a myriad of cutting-edge subjects and her bold overtures. In sum, a London woman was someone who knew what she wanted on all accounts. But a country woman? Lord spare him. 'It's really not my speciality, Channing.'

Behind the desk, Channing quirked a blond brow in answer to his darker one. 'And provoking duels with cuckolded husbands is not mine. If I may remind you, the league's mission is a woman's pleasure *without* the attendant scandal. Duels, my friend, do not fit our code of discretion. You need to get out of town and let the rumours settle. You know how London is this time of year. There will be another scandal within the fortnight to retire this one, but not if you're here reminding everyone with your presence. Until then, I have no wish to see you on the receiving end of a jealous husband's pistol.'

'Nothing will come of it, I promise,' Nicholas protested. 'Burroughs has no proof.' It had been a near-run thing though, getting out the window in time. 'He couldn't have seen more than a shadow.'

Channing played with a letter opener. 'Yes, well, what he'd like to do to that shadow is all over London. Was anything left behind? A shirt stud? A boot? Anything that could link you to the scene?'

'Nothing,' Nicholas replied vehemently. 'I never leave anything behind. It was a clean getaway, I swear.' A getaway that involved kissing the dowager countess. Still, it had been clean in the end and that was all that mattered.

Channing gave a short laugh. 'You and I have somewhat different interpretations of "clean getaway".'

Nicholas put a dramatic hand to his heart in mock play. 'You wound me.' In truth, he *was* a bit insulted Channing even had to ask. He was one of the best Channing had when it came to the more carnal pursuits of their organisation. Not every woman came to them looking for physical pleasure —some came simply looking to make a splash in society, perhaps raise a little decent notoriety for themselves to win back a husband who had strayed too far or taken them for granted too long. But there were those who *did* come looking for the intimate pleasures that had eluded them thus far in life. That's where he came in. Nick hoped Channing would overlook that aspect of the letter.

'The potential scandal notwithstanding, I'd still send you.' Channing set down the letter opener and fixed with him a stern blue-eyed stare. 'The woman in question is looking for physical fulfilment and *that* is indeed your speciality.' So much for overlooking it.

'But not in the country,' Nicholas argued. He was losing this fight and he knew it. He could feel his grounds for refusal slipping away. 'It's a poor time for me to be gone from the league.' He gestured to the date on the letter. 'Almost a whole week in the middle of June? That's the height of the Season. We already have more requests than we can handle.' It would absolutely *kill* him to miss the entertainments: the Marlborough Ball, the midsummer masquerade at Lady Hyde's Richmond mansion, which was that week, to say nothing of the summer nights at Vauxhall with its fireworks.

Channing remained unfazed by his line of reasoning. 'We'll manage.'

Nicholas pressed onwards, running roughshod over the implied refusal. 'You could send someone else. Jocelyn or Grahame? Miles or Amery? Didn't DeHart say he enjoyed the country? He was an absolute hit at the last house party you sent him to.' He was *not* going to the country. He avoided the country like a saint avoided sin.

'Everyone is busy,' Channing said with finality. 'It has to be you.' He gave a winning smile, the one that charmed men and women alike into doing whatever it was Channing required of them. 'Don't worry, Nicholas, the city will still be here when you get back.'

What could he say to that without saying too much? There were things about his life even Channing didn't know. Nicholas drew a breath. 'The letter says she'll pay handsomely. How much?' He knew the question signalled his concurrence. Still, better to retreat the field with polite acquiescence than to be routed from it with a direct order.

'A thousand pounds,' Channing announced quietly.

Nicholas gave a wry smile. He'd do just about anything for a thousand pounds. Even face his demons. There was no question of *not* going and they both knew it. That kind of money ensured his acceptance from the start. 'Well, I guess that settles it.' In a moment of insight, he appreciated Channing's effort to at least let him think he could argue the situation.

'I expect it does. Now, go pack your bags, I've arranged a post chaise for you. It leaves at eleven. You'll be there in time for tea.'

Lovely, Nick thought with inward sarcasm, but he could see Channing was set on this. There'd be no getting out of it, so he played that old mental game: it could always be worse, although he wasn't sure how it could be. Well, he supposed it could have been for longer, it could have been for the entire month.

Chapter Two

Sussex, England

Annorah Price-Ellis had a month to live. *Really*
live. She could feel it in her bones and it wasn't
the first time. She'd been feeling it creep up on
her since April and here at the last she was powerless to stop it. The inevitable was going to happen although for years she'd been in denial. Now
it—even at this late point she couldn't call it by
its rightful name—stared her in the face, a big
red date on her mental calendar.

Of course, she'd sought help. The experts she'd
consulted all concurred with the same diagnosis.
There was nothing left for her to do but accept *it*.
Such news had forced her to make concessions
and, along with concessions, preparations as well,
which was why she sat in her sunny drawing

room at Hartshaven on this beautiful June afternoon, prettily dressed in a fashionable new gown
of jonquil muslin, looking her best and waiting,
an odd occupation for someone for whom time
was running out.

Annorah glanced at the clock on the mantel.
It was nearly four. He would arrive any minute
and her nerves were entirely on edge. She'd never
done anything as daring or as final as this. As
that damnable red date approached, she'd thought
long and hard about what her final acts would be,
what pleasures she wanted one last time. She was
rich. She had piles of money. She could afford
anything she desired: Paris, the Continent, beautiful clothes. In the end, all that wealth wouldn't
save her. She couldn't take it with her without
condemning her soul to a certain hell. So the
question had loomed. What did she want? In her
heart, it hadn't been that difficult a question to
answer.

She was thirty-two, at least for another two
weeks, and past her prime by at least a decade.
She didn't feel it. She hoped she didn't look it.
She had very little to show for the last ten years,
at least not when it came to the things a woman

should have at her age—a husband and children. She'd been close a few times. Once, she'd managed to get her heart broken and another time she'd cried off, unwilling to risk a second heartbreak, or maybe it had been the lack of such a risk. After that, she'd retreated to Hartshaven, withdrawing from society a little more each year until it had been ages since she'd set foot in London and longer still since she'd taken an interest in anyone or anyone in her.

It was a lonely way to live. What she did have, however, was a beautiful estate in the country and piles of money to keep her company. What she lacked in social currency, she more than made up for financially. In terms of creature comforts, she had everything a woman could want, except a man. That was about to change. In a few moments, a man was going to come down the drive. She'd ordered him from London much as one orders a gown, and if she had misgivings about such a process it was too late now.

Annorah mentally went over the carefully drafted letter she'd sent one last time, every word committed to memory.

Dear Sirs,
I am looking for a discreet association with a
man of breeding and manners. Must be clean
and well-kept, an informed conversational-
ist—in other words, educated—and enjoy the
quiet of the countryside. Will pay handsomely
for five nights of companionship.

She'd taken three days to draft those few lines.
It seemed like the letter should be longer for her
efforts. She hoped the agency would know exactly what she meant. The small advertisement
she'd seen in a magazine suggested the agency
was very good at reading between the lines and
knowing precisely what was required in any
given situation. Still, those meagre four lines
were the most audacious words she'd ever written.

'It's time, Annorah. Stop being such a goose.'
She felt her courage start to flag. If not now,
when? She knew the answer to that. Never. If
she wanted to know the mysteries of passion before it was too late, she had to take matters into
her own hands. So here she was, waiting for her
birthday present to arrive; the perfect man—one

who wouldn't break her heart, who wouldn't pretend to love her for her money, one who would understand what she wanted was a temporary liaison in which she could experience the joys of the flesh without the regrets.

Five nights of pleasure should be enough. Then she would reconcile herself to her fate, a fate the best of England's legal minds had assured her she could not avoid: Marry by her thirty-third birthday and keep her estate and wealth intact, or should that fail and she remain single, the estate and much of her fortune was forfeit to the church and other charities. The house would become a school and she'd be left with a cottage and a comfortable portion to live simply, but not grandly. Gone would be the days of fine gowns and the option to do anything she wanted.

Either way, she stood to lose her life the way she knew it. Marriage meant her fabulous wealth went to her husband. Remaining unwed meant it went to the church. Last time she checked, neither of those parties was her. In response to her demise, she'd gone shopping and purchased an outrageous number of dresses and all the necessary accessories, including a man to go with them.

Gravel crunched on the drive and her pulse quickened. Out of the window, Annorah caught sight of a chaise pulling up in front of the steps before it was lost from view, blocked by the large semicircular stairs leading to the front door. One could only see the drive fully if one was standing at the window and Annorah did not want to be that obvious.

Her butler, Plumsby, appeared at the doorway. 'Miss, your guest is here. May I say he is quite handsome for a librarian?' She'd not been able to admit the truth to her staff for fear of disappointing them. Instead, she'd professed a desire to catalogue the library one last time, an inventory list of sorts should she opt to leave everything to the school.

'Thank you, Plumsby. I will be right out to meet him.' Her pulse began to race, her thoughts latching on to Plumsby's last words: *He was handsome.* She played out how she wanted to greet him in her mind. She would be modern and sophisticated. Annorah took a final look in the mirror on the wall to make sure her hair was in place, her face free of any errant smudges. She took a deep breath and stepped out into the hall, suddenly feeling overly bright in her jonquil muslin against the muted blues and Italian marble of the hall. But there was no time to change now, no time to slip away on the backstairs unnoticed. He'd seen her.

Annorah smiled and swept forwards. 'You're here. I trust you had a pleasant journey?' She clasped her hands tightly at her waist, hoping to hide her nerves, but she could feel a blush creeping up her cheeks. Handsome didn't even begin to cover it and she was already at a loss for words. He'd think she was a bumbling idiot. One minute into their association and her power of speech had failed her.

Tea! Her mind grabbed the idea. 'Plumbsby, have tea brought to the drawing room. I can see to our guest from here.' As soon as the words left her mouth, she knew she had erred. 'Forgive me, I'm getting ahead of myself. Here I am ordering tea before we've even had introductions. I'm Annorah Price-Ellis.'

She stuck her hand out for him to shake in a businesslike manner, but he took that hand and bent over it instead, lips skimming knuckles, eyes holding hers as he took her gesture and turned it into something more than a greeting. Under his touch it became a prologue, a promise. 'Nicholas D'Arcy at your service.'

At her service. Annorah swallowed hard. He was here and he was gorgeous! Dark-blue eyes looked up at her over her hand, riveting and intense in their regard; black hair roguishly pulled back to reveal high-set cheekbones and the most perfect mouth she'd ever seen on a man; a thin, strong upper lip, a slightly fuller lower lip, full enough to invoke a certain sensual quality, full enough to make a woman want to trace that mouth with her finger.

Good lord, her thoughts were running fast! They'd barely met and she was already tracing his mouth in her mind. Annorah recalled her manners soon enough to fumble through an awkward curtsy, only to wonder if that was the correct response. Did one curtsy to such a man? But that was just it. What sort of man was he? A gentleman down on his luck or a bounder in fine clothing merely apeing his betters? Perhaps she should curtsy simply to preserve the façade and why not? This was her fantasy. She could play it any way she wanted.

What she couldn't do was stand around the hall, staring like a looby. Years of good breeding finally caught up with her in a single thought: *now* she could get them in to tea and everything would resolve itself. Tea would take some of the edge off her nerves. There would be a natural progression of questions to ask: Did he take cream? Did he prefer sugar? Would he like a cake or a sandwich? It would ease the transition into conversation and give her a sense of starting to know him.

Annorah gestured towards the wide doorway on her left and said in what she hoped were sophisticated tones, even if the message was slightly repetitious, 'Plumsby will have tea set up for us in the drawing room. You can take refreshment and we can discuss business.' Surely that was the appropriate next step. It would be best to get the particulars out of the way before things progressed much further.

Nicholas D'Arcy's blue eyes twinkled, the edges crinkling up delightfully as he smiled. He leaned in with a conspiratorial air, his body close enough for her to catch the scent of him—the sweet hay of a fougère mixed with the tang of lemons, quintessential summer. '*This* is business?'

Suddenly it was hard to think. She was vaguely aware she was rambling on about clients and contractors and negotiating the parameters of association for both their sakes. A gentle finger pressed against her lips.

'There's a lovely summer day waiting for us outside, Annorah. Why don't you show me the gardens? We can talk while we stroll.'

'Will it be private enough?' Annorah hedged politely. Talk about their arrangement outside where they might be overheard? She hadn't exactly been truthful with the staff when she'd told them about her visitor.

'We'll put our heads together and whisper.' His eyes were laughing again as he offered her his arm, a very firm arm encased in blue superfine, another reminder that his clothes and bearing were immaculate. His dark head lowered to hers until they were almost touching, his voice quiet at her ear. 'Besides, I find the risk of discovery adds a certain spice to even the most mundane of outings, don't you?'

'I will have to take your word for that, Mr

D'Arcy.' A delicious tremor shivered through her at the very notion, tempered only slightly by the reality that the man dressed in expensive blue superfine, fashionable buff breeches and highly polished boots was definitely not a gentleman at all.

'Please, call me Nicholas. My father was always Mr D'Arcy. Shall we?'

How quickly she'd lost control of the conversation. It was something of a marvel, really, how smoothly he'd taken over. He'd been standing in her hall for a handful of minutes and already he was assuming command. He didn't even know where the gardens were and yet they were heading out of the bank of French doors as if he'd lived here his entire life. She'd not expected him to show such ease. She'd expected to have the upper hand. This arrangement was to be conducted entirely on her grounds, literally and figuratively. When she'd sent her letter, she'd assumed a modicum of security in knowing he was the guest and she the host. But now it was clear those roles could easily become blurred.

The gardens restored her sense of balance. He asked questions, pausing now and again at certain flowers to comment on their blooms, and she answered, feeling more in control, once more the host.

Nicholas halted at one flower. 'Ah, this one is very rare indeed. A rainforest iris, if I'm not mistaken? Very wicked, is it not, with its stamen jutting straight up from the bloom?'

Annorah blushed furiously at his less-than-veiled reference to a man's phallus. 'All flowers have stamen, Mr D'Arcy.'

'Yes, but not all of them have stamen that are so blatantly displayed. Take this delicate pink blossom over here. The stamen is neatly shielded by the petals closing around it. But not this fellow.' He gestured back to the iris. 'He's a bold one, sticking straight out from the flat bowl of the blossom, tall and proud for all to see.'

'Flowers are hardly sexual beings, Mr D'Arcy.'

'You don't think so? I must respectfully disagree. They are perhaps the most sexual, most promiscuous...' he stopped here to arch a dark brow her direction, emphasising promiscuous '... creatures in the living kingdoms. Think about it—they pollinate and cross-pollinate with multiple different partners every day, all for the purpose of casting their errant seeds to the wind with nary a care for where they land.'

Social protocol demanded she put a stop to such ridiculous conversation, but she could not bring herself to do it. He had the most pleasant of voices, a sibilant tenor that caressed each word, creating decadent images with his sentences. If he could turn her legs to jelly with talk of botany of all things, chances were rather good that this voice of his could make any subject seductive. Still, she should try to maintain a civil face to their interactions. 'Mr D'Arcy, this is hardly a decent subject for discussion.'

'I insist again that you call me Nicholas,' he chided her gently. 'And to be blunt, you didn't invite me here to be decent.'

It was a well-timed comment. There was no better opportunity to bring up the nature of their association. They'd begun walking again, leaving the phallic iris and the flower garden behind. They were further from the house now, wandering down a tree-lined alley towards a roman folly in the distance. Their privacy was complete. For a moment it crossed her mind he'd manoeuvred the conversation in that direction on purpose.

'No, *Nicholas*, I didn't bring you here to be decent. But neither did I bring you here to indulge in a sinful gluttony of an orgy either.' This was where her directness ran out. She was no retiring wallflower afraid to speak her own mind. She'd charted her own course in life thus far, but this was new conversational territory. She'd never once expressed such feelings, such *desires* to anyone before, let alone a handsome man who stared at her with the full attention of his eyes.

Of course she had his full attention! She gave herself a stern admonishment. This was his job. She should be worried if she didn't have it.

'I understand,' Nicholas answered solemnly, covering her hand in a comforting gesture where it lay on his arm. 'What have you told the servants?'

'I've put it about that you are here to assess my library collection. It's quite extensive and it hasn't been catalogued since my grandfather had it done half a century ago.'

The grin he flashed filled her with satisfaction. She'd thought long and hard about the ruse she'd use to welcome a visiting male into her household. 'Very nice, Annorah. You painted me with the sheen of a scholar, a bookish sort, which will certainly allay suspicions that I have ulterior motives for your person. You've given me a project that requires me to closet myself away with you daily and, best of all, you've given me the perfect reason to be seen escorting you about the countryside. No one would expect you to keep your guest all to yourself.' He winked. 'I know how country folk work; a newcomer is cause for excitement and must be shared.'

Annorah felt herself blush under his praise. They turned away from the folly and headed back towards the house while he continued.

'As for us, Annorah, we will not speak of such arrangements again. You and I are to dedicate ourselves to becoming friends. We cannot be bothered with anything as base as a business transaction.' He wrinkled his nose in a show of humorous distaste that made her laugh.

'All that aside, though, we must be serious for a moment.' He turned and faced her, bringing them to a full stop, the house in view over his shoulder, a reminder that when they returned to it the ruse would begin in truth. The point of no return began at the garden's edge and her body trembled with the knowledge of it.

He took both her hands in his, his grip warm and strong, his gaze sincere. 'We are about to embark on a wondrous and intimate journey together, Annorah Price-Ellis. I am honoured to share that journey with you. It will change us both. You have no doubt given it much thought, but I must ask one last time—are you ready? Is this what you truly want? You're not forced to it in any way either implied or explicit?'

This must be what it's like to stand at the altar and look up into the eyes of the man you love, knowing he feels the same. The thought had come to her out of nowhere and without reason. She knew logically he must be compelled to ask for one last show of consent. She knew, too, that there was nothing about love or marriage or altars behind his request. But that knowledge did nothing to dispel the impression they were taking vows of a sort, pledging themselves to one another, even if only for a short time. After tonight, he would always belong to her, always be with her in a way no other person would. For the rest of her life, she would carry a piece of Nicholas D'Arcy in her soul, as her first and perhaps only true lover.

Annorah nodded, her voice quiet in the still of a summer's late afternoon. 'I am ready.'

Nicholas raised her hands to his lips. 'I am, too.' He gave her a reassuring smile. Perhaps he'd heard the tremor in her voice. 'Rest assured, Annorah, I know exactly what you want.'

Chapter Three

She wanted the wedding night, the honeymoon; the pleasure of lovers learning one another for the first time, savouring one another in both body and mind. It was one of the more difficult scenarios to enact. The trick was to create an intimacy that went beyond the physical without exposing oneself to feelings. He dealt in sex, not intimacy, by preference.

Up in his room, Nicholas opened his valise, the one piece of luggage he'd not let the footman assigned to act as his valet unpack. Nicholas surveyed the tools of his trade with a contemplative sigh, laying them out on the dressing table in his room like a surgeon preparing his scalpels and saws: the tiny glass vials of scented oils, the expensive imported sheaths from France made of thinnest lambskin, the silk ribbons, the soft feathers. Often, he used them as much for him as his clients. All were designed with one goal in mind: physical pleasure. They were his insurance that he could please even when he wasn't all that interested in a woman. With the right woman, though, they could be extraordinary.

There was no question of delivering the physical adventure Annorah sought. The other, the sharing of a mind, would be more difficult. He was a guarded person by nature. Drawing others out had been an early acquired skill of his. It had served double duty as a means of learning others and as a means of protecting himself. When people were busy talking about themselves, they had little time to wonder about him.

Nicholas tucked the items into a bureau drawer, carefully hidden among cravats. Librarians did not carry feathers and ribbons with them. He smiled. A librarian? That was a new one. He'd pretended to be a lot of things before, whatever his clients needed. In the process, he'd become an adept chameleon. In this line of work, a person did a lot of pretending, which wasn't all bad especially when the fantasy was better than a reality full of debt and worry and even guilt.

There was no place for those feelings here. He pushed those thoughts away and shut the clasp firmly. His mental efforts would be better spent planning his strategy. He would not need these tools this evening. She was not ready in spite of her words to the contrary.

He'd sensed her nervousness from the start, as if she couldn't believe someone had actually answered her letter. He'd touched her immediately and often after that, bowing over her hand with a kiss, keeping a hand on her at all times as they strolled. She'd been skittish and he'd feared she might change her mind, a prospect he could not afford now that the money had been mentally allocated in his mind by the time he left London.

He understood full well the power of touch to ensure acceptance. In his experience, people were far more likely to do what he wanted if he touched them while asking. By the time they'd returned to the house and he'd garnered her pledge, she'd started to thaw.

Not that she was cold or that she wasn't pleasantly disposed towards him. He'd seen the race of her pulse when she'd sighted him in the hall. He'd noted the blush on her cheeks in the garden when they'd discussed the iris. She knew very well the way of things. But the codes of decency had been drilled into her head over the years and, as much as she wanted to cast them off ever so briefly, it was proving to be more difficult than she'd likely anticipated. Well, he could certainly help her with that. What he really wanted to know was why? Why had she written the letter?

Nicholas moved to the bed and stretched out his long form, tucking his hands behind his head. He had two hours before dinner and he needed to use them to think. He mapped the evening in his head like a general before battle. Tonight's arena would be the dinner table. That was easy enough. There were myriad ways to stroke the stem of a goblet, to cup its bowl, to eat one's food and drink one's wine that stimulated sexual interest, all the while talking, drawing her out, getting her to relax, to think of him more as a man than a machine who'd been sent to fulfil a need.

His goal tonight was twofold. For her sake, he wanted to dispel any sense of artifice about their association. For his, he wanted to figure out what had driven Annorah to write such a letter. More than that, why had such a letter even been necessary?

A request of this nature was not made idly. He thought of the pistols packed in his bags and ran through the usual reasons. Was this an act of revenge on her part? Would there be people who would resent her decision? It would not be the first time a woman had tried to avoid an unwanted marriage in this way. These arrangements were seldom straightforward.

The letter itself had been unremarkable. He'd studied it line by meagre line on the way here. There had been little to offer in the way of clues. The line about enjoying the countryside had made him laugh at the irony. The word quiet was a bit more insightful. What did it signify? Was she a recluse? Did she actually *prefer* the solitude of the country, unimaginable as such a concept was? Simple deduction made that an easy scenario to discard. It was hard to imagine a recluse, someone who deliberately shunned the company of others, requiring a conversationalist. Upon arrival, he'd been proven correct. He had to discard that notion even if the logic hadn't fallen short. She might have been nervous, but she wasn't a recluse.

Nick considered another option. Had she been forced into seclusion? Was she someone who had been abandoned to anonymity? Someone craving human contact? Perhaps that was too extreme. Sussex was hardly the ends of the earth. It was a mere five hours from London. Surely a woman with a thousand pounds to spend on five nights of pleasure could afford to come to London if she so chose.

That was the other thing that niggled. Motive. London had its own plans for women possessed of a fortune. It was called the Marriage Mart and it would certainly resolve any penchant for intimacy by providing an heiress with a husband; especially London in June. The city was teeming with men looking for money and marriage. It called to mind the line from the Austen novel his female acquaintances were so fond of: 'A single man in possession of a good fortune must also be in want of a wife', or something like that. In this case, a *woman* in possession of a fortune was an odd thing indeed without a husband.

If she was not naturally reclusive or forced

to seclusion, that left option three: she was in the country by choice. Of all the scenarios, this was the most mysterious. Why would anyone choose the countryside if they didn't have to? Why would someone choose to engage in paid intimacies with a stranger when a potential marriage awaited just five hours down the road?

There were only so many reasons a rich woman would refuse London and none of them was good, especially when the major reason would have been looks and that was clearly not the case with Annorah. He could rule that out.

Ugly would have been a problem for him. It was a selfish, petty wish, he knew, but he was used to beautiful. Most of the women who could afford him hadn't been ugly. They'd merely been curious about what should have been theirs by right of marriage, something a conscientious husband should have provided Fortunately, Annorah Price-Ellis had turned out to be attractive with a quiet, understated beauty. She'd drawn his eye immediately, a splash of colour amid the elegant austerity of the entry hall.

She had struck him as a nature goddess when they'd strolled in the garden. He'd used the time to take in her features: the soft curve of cheek giving her face a delicate cast, the sharp mossy green of her eyes, reminiscent of a rich field of summer grass, and the wheat blonde of her hair, which argued to be the colour of wild honey when wet, a hypothesis he wouldn't mind testing. There'd been curves, too, beneath the muslin with long legs, narrow waist and a high, full bosom. No, Annorah Price-Ellis was definitely not a hag. Which only furthered the mystery. How did a lovely, rich woman arrive at this point?

There was only one way to find out. Nicholas rang for the valet. It was time to dress for dinner and tonight he wanted to give his *toilette* thorough consideration. The man assigned to him was a young fellow named Peter, who had some talent for the job, if not experience. If the valet thought it was odd for a librarian to linger over his *toilette*, then so be it. In the end, the two of them turned him out quite finely in a dark evening suit, paisley waistcoat of rich lavenders and blues and a well-tied osbaldeston knot in his cravat that had taken only two tries.

Nicholas dismissed Peter and took a final look in the mirror, checking to see that the diamond stick pin in his cravat was exposed enough to catch the light, that his coat was smooth across the shoulders, that his hair was neatly tied back with a subtle black ribbon. Longer hair might not be the trend preferred by society in the ballrooms, but it was amazing how many women loved it in the bedrooms.

Satisfied with his appearance, Nicholas closed his eyes and drew in a breath. Let the seduction begin. No matter what ghosts the country raised against him, he could do this. He would make love to Miss Price-Ellis as if everything depended on it. Because it did.

He was waiting for her in the drawing room, having followed the gentleman's dictate that no lady should have to remain alone in anxious anticipation for a guest's arrival. He was casually posed, elegantly dressed, the dark evening clothes a marked contrast to the white of the marble. A pre-prandial drink, partially consumed, dangled negligently in one hand, his gaze fixed on the windows and the display of green gardens beyond. He turned at the sound of her entrance, the quiet click of her low-heeled slippers and the soft whisper of skirts giving her away.

'You have a lovely home. I was just admiring the view.' The hand holding the glass gestured towards the long windows to indicate the gardens, but his eyes held hers, suggesting he was appreciating another view entirely.

A delicious shot of warmth spread through her at the frank assessment. She'd spent an hour agonising over which gown to wear before summoning her maid and deciding on the lavender chiffon. Apparently the effort had been worth it. 'Thank you. Hartshaven was designed to be appreciated. It was meant to be a showcase for beauty.'

'It certainly is.' His smile deepened, exposing the dimple at the left corner of his mouth.

Good lord, could he turn every comment into a veiled compliment? What could she do but forge ahead and take it all in her stride? Annorah moved to the window and motioned for him to join her. She tried to redirect the conversation on to more neutral ground, ground that would be less likely to leave her feeling flushed and so focused on the night to come that her tongue was tied. 'My great-grandfather had the initial gardens laid out by Kent and Bridgeman.'

'I recognise the styling.' He stood close at her shoulder. She could smell the faint undertones of his cologne; the lemon and fougère creating the scent of a summer fantasy, perfect for a night like this. She did not think a man had ever smelled this good. She was so intent on smelling him, discreetly of course, that she nearly missed his conversation.

'I've had the good fortune of visiting at Chiswick House. Burlington's gardens are exquisite, as are yours.'

Chiswick? That grabbed her wandering attention. Annorah couldn't resist a sideways glance at her companion. Chiswick House was the domain of the Earl of Burlington. Nicholas D'Arcy, whoever he was, ran in vaunted circles if he was calling there.

He caught her glance before she could look away and smiled. 'Surprised?'

'I hardly know you. I think anything would count as a surprise at this point.' Her tone was sharper than she had intended but she was grasping for any point of defence now. Hardly knowing him was not stopping her pulse from racing, or her mind's apparent desire to hang on his every word. When she'd begun this, she'd counted on logic to protect her from any depth of emotional response. That strategy was clearly going to fail.

'Touché.' He reached for her hand and tucked it through his arm, his touch igniting little jolts. 'We'll rectify that over dinner.' He nodded in a direction past her shoulder. 'I think your butler is ready to announce the meal.'

Plumsby cleared his throat, drawing her attention for the first time. She'd been so riveted on Nicholas she hadn't noticed his arrival. 'Dinner is served.'

'I've had Plumbsy lay the meal out in the informal dining room,' Annorah said, glad to have something of proprietary to say. She was sounding less and less like a hostess with every minute, which was not how she'd imagined this interlude. When she'd pictured it, she'd cast herself in the role of the sophisticate, taking the lead in their encounters, commanding every social nuance. It was easy to see the flaw in her reasoning against the black-tie *élan* of his town bronze. She hadn't half the polish he had. Annorah hoped her dining room did.

The room did not disappoint. It looked out on to the back veranda and the staff had set it to perfection. Of course, they thought it was a business dinner to discuss the library, but they still wanted their home to look its best. And it did. The rose shades of summer twilight filtered through the panes of the French doors, bathing the cream walls in dusky hues, but it was the table in the room's centre that drew all eyes. Two tall white tapers stood like sentinels in their silver-candlestick holders atop pristine white linen, flames flickering an invitation. A bowl of yellow roses from the garden sat between them on the round table. In complement to the yellow roses, her favorite Wedgwood pattern of blue flowers was laid out in two place settings with slim goblets and silver. Cold champagne rested in a chilled bucket.

Two footmen seated them and Plumsby removed the covers, presenting the meal, but that would be all the service she required. She'd already made it clear to Plumsby they meant to dine casually, serving themselves from the dishes on the table. Plumsby had protested, but she'd argued all the fuss for one guest was hardly worth it. Since that guest was a 'librarian' there to do a job, Plumsby had eventually conceded the point.

'Shall I?' Nicholas reached for the bottle of champagne, uncorking it in a deft movement with the merest of pops. He poured the glasses and turned his attention to the chicken, applying the same dexterity to carving that he had to champagne. Effortlessly, he filled their plates with roasted chicken and salad greens. Gentleman born or not, he was skilled in the art of the dining room, offering her the best of everything the table had to offer. It made him all the more intriguing, all the more mysterious. What sort of man kept the company of Chiswick House, dined with the manners of a well-heeled peer and found himself at a socially retiring woman's table under these circumstances? Goodness knew with looks and manners like his he would have been welcome anywhere.

'A toast, Annorah.' He raised his flute. 'To summer evenings and new friendships.'

Their glasses touched in a satisfying chime of crystal against crystal. She sipped and let the cold liquid run down her throat. She loved champagne and could certainly afford to drink it every night, but it seemed a sin to drink alone—although in retrospect it seemed a very *small* sin compared to the one she'd commit tonight. She groped for something to say. Perhaps she should have spent as much time thinking of conversational topics as she had selecting a dress. She'd never learn anything about him at this rate. She had to try. Annorah settled on the one topic that came to mind.

'Are you an aficionado of gardens, then?'

'I'm an aficionado of many beautiful things, gardens among them.' His hand slid idly up and down the stem of his goblet. On another man she might not have noticed the gesture. With him, she could hardly pull her eyes away.

'What else do you admire?'

He smiled. 'I admire *you*, Annorah.'

She looked down at her plate, flushing. She hadn't blushed this much in years. Perhaps her social skills were more out of shape than she'd thought. 'You are not required to say such things. Besides, you hardly know me well enough to come to any sort of conclusion.'

'Do you think I don't mean it? I assure you, I

do. I've spent the afternoon being treated to this lovely home and I beg to differ with your assessment. An estate is often a reflection of its owner. You can tell a lot about a person by the state of his or *her* surroundings. I sense there is a story in you, Annorah, and I would love to hear it. How is it that you've come to be here?'

She met his gaze with a sharp look over her champagne. 'Is that the polite way of asking how I've reached the august age of thirty-two alone?'

Nicholas laughed and leaned back in his chair. 'What a prickly creature you are! Are you always this cynical? Since we've sat down to dine you've accused me of being insincere with my flattery and when I have *sincerely* enquired as to your history, you believe me rude. You present me with quite the conundrum.'

Oh, lord, she had. He was right. She'd been so worried about playing the decent hostess and at the first opportunity she'd performed poorly. She studied her half-eaten meal, gathering her thoughts. 'I must apologise. I have little experience at this.'

He leaned forwards again, this time capturing her hand where it lay on the tablecloth. 'No apology necessary. I find conundrums refreshing.' He winked. 'Have some more champagne. It will help and perhaps we'll try again.' He was tracing sensual circles in the palm of her hand that were both relaxing and stimulating.

No man had ever touched her as he did or so often. She'd been intimately aware of him since his arrival: the casual touch of her hand on his sleeve, the feel of his hand at her back, all of it legitimate. Gentlemen touched ladies like that all the time. *She'd* been touched like that, but not with these results, not with a pleasant warmth spreading through her, a tingling heat filling her belly and lower. Oh, no, most certainly never like this.

'Now, Annorah, tell me your story. I want to know how you've come to be the queen of all this.' He poured more champagne with his free hand.

'I grew up here and I never left, not for long anyway.' She took a sip from her glass. He was right—the champagne did help. She hardly ever talked about her family. It had been a good family once, but it had fallen due to time and circumstance, leaving her with a legacy that was about to end soon, a situation she was rather loath to recollect, a potent reminder that she was about to lose all this unless she sold her soul in marriage to a man she didn't love.

'Why?' He coaxed with his voice, with his touch, with the sincerity of his gaze. Even the room conspired against her, the candlelight creating intimacy in the deepening darkness.

'Because it was home, and the people I loved were here. Hartshaven hasn't always been an empty house.' She had not meant to talk of herself or to reveal so much that couldn't possibly matter, that had no bearing on the job he'd come to do. But once started, she couldn't help herself.

The stories fed upon themselves, encouraged by Nicholas's laughter and the occasional nod of his head. She told him of her family: her grandfather and grandmother, her parents, her cousins who had come to visit in the summers. She did not tell him of her aunt. Her aunt had no place in happy stories.

Those summers had stories of their own: days of roaming the meadows, fishing in streams and endless games of hide and seek in the gardens. The memories leapt to life as she talked. Merry ghosts of the past peopled her stories: the laughter of her cousins shrieking as they ran through the gardens; the patience of her grandfather teaching them to fish in the cold river. Everything was alive again—messy and vivid, and she was alive with it, no longer sitting at dinner with a stranger, but with a man who'd become a friend in a very short time; a friend she didn't know much about, but a friend none the less.

'What happened?' Nicholas poured the last of the champagne. Dear heavens had they drunk so much already or had they been at the table that long?

'What always happens. We grew up and time moved on.' The merry ghosts she'd conjured receded. The candles burned low. 'I would give anything to have it all back. What about you? How have you arrived at this point?' The question was bold. That was the champagne talking, but it had been talking all night.

'I think the future holds infinite promise.' Nicholas drained his glass and set it aside with a sense of finality. He rose and held out his hand to her. 'Come with me.'

Annorah set her glass down slowly, all her

thoughts coalescing around his words and what they meant. This was it! He would lead her upstairs and bed her. She rose and took his hand somewhat woodenly. Now that the moment was upon her, the impending act suddenly seemed an empty conclusion to the fullness of their conversation and the friend was a stranger once again, the spell broken.

Chapter Four

He was losing her. The intimate magic of champagne and candlelight had not enthralled her enough to let go of her reservations. It wasn't that he had misjudged their effects, but rather the power of them. They hadn't lasted very long. Already, Nick could see the magic strings starting to come undone, leaving her free to revisit her doubts, her choice in inviting him here. He had thought to take her upstairs, now he opted for the terrace, fresh air and starlight.

She fanned her cheeks with her hand and gave a little laugh once they were outside. 'I fear I've broken one of the cardinal rules of socialising.'

Nicholas gave her a slow smile, enjoying the flush of her cheeks. 'What rule is that?'

'The one where I'm supposed to let the man do

all the talking. More to the point, I'm supposed to let him talk about himself through skilfully questioning him and drawing him out. It's the first rule a débutante learns. If a girl can't flirt, at least she can listen.'

Nicholas threw back his head and laughed up into the night sky. Her candour was absolutely refreshing in the most surprising of ways. 'Hardly! I enjoyed your stories. I think this is one of the most enjoyable evenings I've had in years.'

'Isn't it, though?' The sharp stab of cynicism brought Nick up short. She was watching him, her moss-green eyes narrowed in contemplation. The entire spell had come unravelled. He would have to weave a new one now from whole cloth.

'I beg your pardon?' Nick feigned a quizzical look, although he knew very well what she was asking. If she was going to be so bold, she'd have to own to it.

'You know what I mean. Dinner, the stories— it was all meant to draw me out. I think it was very clever of you to use a simple débutante's trick against me.'

She was far smarter than his usual client or else far less pliant. This was going to be a challenge.

She had all but accused him of feeding her a generic line. Nick reached for her hand, tracing idle circles on the back of it. 'Trick is a harsh word, Annorah. What makes you so sure it was a ploy rather than the truth? You're a very enjoyable woman to be with.'

It was true. He'd liked watching her come alive as she told her stories, as she talked of her childhood. It was a childhood not unlike his own and he glimpsed wildness in her as she spoke. It was a wildness well contained and it made him wonder what had happened to see such a commodity so carefully fenced and penned. He wondered, too, what it would be like to see that commodity unleashed, the fences down.

'I'm a very suspicious woman to be with,' she rephrased. 'Especially when it comes to someone taking an instant liking to me.'

That someone being male, Nick would wager. There was hurt behind her words. Omitted parts of the story told over dinner were starting to emerge. 'Some people have a natural affinity for one another, do you doubt it?'

Annorah gave him a look that practically

shouted her opinion on the subject. 'Some, perhaps. Not all. Not most.'

She was challenging a lot of his assumptions tonight. He'd not expected his country conquest to be a prickly, worldly, beauty. He'd expected this to be easy. He could see it was not going to be that way. For a while at dinner she'd forgotten all that. He could make her forget again, but he was going to have to work for it.

Nick raised her hand to his lips and took a deductive stab in the dark. 'I'm not a fortune hunter, Annorah. I'm safe and you're safe with me. I'm not most.'

She shook her head. 'I invited you here to fill my head with flattery that I knew would be false from the start. You might be worse, I think—'

'Then don't think,' Nick interrupted swiftly. Her thoughts were not headed in a direction conducive to romance. He cupped her cheek, running a gentle thumb down the line of her jaw. 'You didn't bring me here to think. You brought me here for pleasure.' He began to intersperse his words with kisses, starting at her jaw and moving to the slim column of her throat. 'There's no shame in pleasure, Annorah, no dishonour in desiring it. Pleasure is a human enough condition.' His mouth was at the base of her throat, his lips over the pulse beat. She was starting to melt again. He caressed her with words, with kisses, feeling her body come alive as he intended.

He took her mouth then in a decadent dance of a kiss. Slow and savouring, his lips were in no hurry to leave hers and there was languorous exploration; there was tasting and teasing, duelling and heat. He brought her against him, letting her feel the planes of his body, hard and sure through his clothes. The press of his hand at her back urged her closer, coaxing her to meld into him, convincing her this was heaven and earth all in one.

Nick knew the moment he had compliance. Her arms went about his neck, she arched her head back and he murmured against her exposed throat. He asked once more, in husky tones redolent with desire, 'Come with me.'

This time she came. He was careful to maintain contact, careful to keep her hand surrounded by the warm, comforting grip of his. It should have worked and it did up to a point. It worked all the way up the stairs, down the hall to the third door on the right, which he knew to be her room, and then it stopped working. For her at least.

His body was surprisingly primed for what should lie ahead. There would be no need for his usual 'assists', as he liked to call them. It was no small matter to call up stimulation at a whim. But tonight it had been easy, the only thing that had been, in fact. From the moment he'd seen her in the delectable lavender chiffon with its high waist and low-cut bodice gathered beneath her breasts with ribbons designed to maximise the effects of its cleavage, he'd had no problems in that regard. The gown fit her curves to perfection as had the candlelight, although she had not flaunted it as one of his London women would have.

He reached for the door handle, ready to usher her inside and follow, but she stalled him, her hand covering his, her eyes honest and perhaps a little sad when they met his. 'I'm sorry, Nicholas. I don't think I can tonight.'

He smiled softly and placed a kiss on her cheek. 'Perhaps I could convince you. A massage by candlelight, perhaps? We have all night, we can go slowly.' It would be a delight to linger with her, no fears of angry husbands bursting through the doors.

'No,' she said more firmly, stepping away from him to establish distance. 'You're a very attractive man, Nicholas D'Arcy, but you are still something of a stranger. I think anything else we do tonight would be nothing more than a mistake. I, for one, would rather wait and hope for better.'

She turned the knob and slipped inside, leaving him alone in the hall uncomfortably aroused and wondering how was he going to turn off what she had so unwittingly turned on. When he'd contemplated this evening earlier in his chambers and laid his strategy, he'd never envisioned he'd be spending it with only his own hand.

But here he was, aroused both physically and mentally. Nicholas undressed, not bothering with nightclothes or a light. With any luck he'd find relief and then sleep shortly afterwards. He lay down on the bed and took himself in a loose fist, running his hand the length of his cock in long fluid motions, starting slow and then increasing his speed as his need grew. It didn't take long. He hadn't thought it would and he did feel a measure of relief when it was over, but only a measure. He reached for a towel and waited for sleep to follow.

His mind would not cooperate. There in the darkness, his brain was alive with thoughts, darting here and there on tangents and considerations, all of them on the same subject: Miss Annorah Price-Ellis. Had she gone to bed unsatisfied as well? Even now was she rethinking her choice? She had not been immune to him. Had she gone to bed, too, forced to find her own satisfaction? Now that would be a perverse irony indeed, to have them both just doors away, pleasuring themselves instead of each other. It would have Channing and the boys in stitches if they knew. He would never live it down.

Neither would he live down her comments in the hall. *A mistake? She would wait and hope for better?* Those were two things a woman never thought about sex with him. Nick fluffed his pillow and rolled to his side in search of a more conducive position for sleep. But it turned out to only be conducive to further examining the wonder that had struck him earlier. What had happened to tamp down her wildness?

He felt a surprising affinity for Annorah Price-

Ellis. Her stories had struck a chord of memory in him. He, too, had such memories of country summers full of laughter and play. He, too, had felt their glaring absence when they'd come to an end. More than that, those stories offered him insight to her. He'd seen the reckless flame of her youth come back to her as she told those stories, a flame that was all but extinguished now. In that way they were alike as well.

She thought her life was over, that nothing would ever happen to her again. Life had occurred and the best days were behind her. The reasons for that conclusion were unclear. She had been careful to hold a little something back tonight even with his prodding. He understood, too, that she'd created a safe harbour inside that reality. There was comfort for her in knowing what to expect.

He knew that particular comfort. It was something of a shock to discover that beneath a surface of differences, he and Miss Price-Ellis shared a fundamental similarity. When he'd come to London and taken Channing's offer to help with the agency, he'd known he was giving up certain hopes and expectations.

Channing did not ask him to give up those ex-pectations. There was no official relinquishing, but he knew how society worked. Once he was committed as an escort, he'd have his own niche, but he'd never truly belong. He'd never be mar-riage material. What decent woman would want a man such as him for a husband? That meant no family of his own, something he'd taken for granted right up until the day his father died. Now, he had a brother, two sisters and a mother counting on him. There'd been no question of setting aside his dreams to support them through whatever means possible.

He wondered what Annorah had set aside that had brought her to this moment. What had hap-pened in her life to make her think life as she'd expected it to be was over? Did she really believe it or was there a flicker of hope that somehow it could still be different? After all, he was here, a veritable wolf in the den of her security, poised to threaten that very fabric through her own in-vitation.

By the time the sun rose, Nicholas had decided this seduction could be going better. He had not slept well in spite of the excellent accommodations and the relief he'd provided himself. Annorah's rejection had kept him up most of the night. Nicholas scrubbed at his face with his hands and took in the sunrise from the little balcony of his room. The east-facing room afforded a view of the rolling lawns leading to the stables and carriage house.

From here he could just make out the dark figures of grooms and horses going about their morning rituals. He had forgotten how early life began in the country. In London he'd just be getting to bed—his own bed anyway. Like as not, he'd have already been in someone else's. That was another item bothering him this morning. He'd spent the *entire* night in his own bed.

Strategically, he had to admit Annorah had made a sound decision to defer coupling. She might have treated him as a welcomed guest, and for a time at dinner as a close friend, but it was still at the fore of her mind that he was actually a guest who was paid to be here. There would be no pleasure for her if she couldn't get past that. She needed to see him as that close friend she had imagined at dinner, as a temporary but sincere companion, if she was to find the joy she was looking for.

She'd not been unaware of him. If anything, she'd been too aware: of what he was here to do and of her part in bringing him. She *had* to go through with it. He could see the internal debate he'd hoped to stem in the garden still being waged behind her hazel eyes. So he'd poured her more champagne, coaxed stories from her and to some extent it had worked. When he had kissed her, there had been moments when she'd forgotten he was a hired service. He'd felt her body come alive, felt her mouth move beneath his. He needed to create more moments like those. She was more than capable of them. How to do it?

Nicholas rested his elbows on the balcony railing. The day promised to be fair and warm, a perfect summer day. *Summer.* Pieces of Annorah's stories from the evening flitted through his mind. The summertime, the stronghold of her wildness, perhaps the last preserve where what remained of it still roamed free. An idea started to take hold. Nick smiled to himself. He knew exactly what to do. It was time to get dressed and do a little rummaging.

Chapter Five

There was a man in her house! It was the first thought that came to Annorah upon waking and it stayed lodged in her brain while she dressed. How could it not? Apparently everyone was fixed on the idea of a male presence at Hartshaven. It was the first piece of news her maid imparted. Her guest had been up at first light, exploring the stables, looking for something and ordering the gig for a tour of the estate later.

Her maid, Lily, slid her a sly glance as she laid out one of Annorah's pretty new morning dresses. 'It seems odd a librarian would want to see the outside of an estate.'

'It will help him understand the place,' Annorah offered vaguely, suddenly thoroughly engrossed in the contents of her jewellery box. She didn't need the staff questioning his presence too much.

'Well...' her maid went back to laying out the clothes '...he's certainly a handsome one. We were all commenting on it last night. Don't see too many handsome librarians.'

Annorah looked up from the box and gave her maid a polite but freezing smile, meant to halt the conversation. 'There's a first time for everything. I trust we won't embarrass our guest with too much probing while he's here.'

Now, if only she could live by those rules. There was a man in her house and she wanted to know everything about him. He was handsome and charming and when he looked at her, when he flirted with her, when he'd kissed her, it had become difficult to remember he didn't really mean it, that he was just doing his job. Her inability to accept that had created a dilemma for her last night she'd been unable to resolve.

Part of her had clearly been ready to melt for him and engage the fantasy in full; those looks, those lines were for her alone, that he didn't run all over London saying the same things to a different woman every night. *You're an enjoyable woman to be with... I think this is one of the most enjoyable evenings I've had in years.* She had been willing to believe his words, every last one of them. That scared her. Her feelings had been thoroughly engaged once before to disastrous results. She had to be careful. She didn't want to walk down that road again—it was one of the reasons she'd hired Nicholas in the first place: physical pleasure without mental attachment. Now, that was being called into question. She could lose herself in him, the way she'd lost herself more than once before, only to be fooled by false affections in the end.

And yet that was the other side of the dilemma. If she kept her distance and reminded herself he was just doing a job, she didn't know if she could go through with it. She was not a person who believed intimacy could be a job. Intimacy had to be more than a daily chore. It had never been work for her parents, who had lived and died together. She'd promised herself years ago it would never be work for her either.

Somewhere, there was a middle ground and she needed to find it. Perhaps seeing him in the morning light without the added benefit of moonlight and champagne would bring the balanced perspective she needed to let herself move forwards.

It only took a moment to realise the morning would bring no such thing. When she arrived downstairs, Nicholas D'Arcy sat at the head of the breakfast table, turned out in summer driving gear, carefully pressed trousers and polished boots, his linen pristine, looking as elegant as he had last night. He looked up from the two-day-old newspaper and smiled. 'Good morning.' It might possibly be the nicest good morning she'd ever heard. The only one better would be to hear those tones on the pillow beside her.

'You're an early riser.' She caught herself too late. His sense of naughty innuendo was wearing off on her.

'I can be.' He gave her a wicked smile, not letting her ignore the implication. 'I had a few things I wanted to take care of.' He set aside the newspaper and gesture to the chair next to him, motioning for her to sit.

'Missing town already?' Annorah nodded towards the discarded newspaper. She seldom read the papers. It didn't matter to her how out of date they were. It would matter to a man like him, though, yet another reminder of how different they were. She was a country mouse to his citified bronze. How was she ever to feel at ease with such a sophisticated man?

'Just keeping up on the news.' He rose and went to the sideboard. 'Would you like eggs?'

She nodded, a bit amazed he was fixing her plate. 'Sausage?' he asked, keeping up a steady stream of conversation while he assembled her breakfast. 'I explained to Cook we'd be touring the grounds and that we'd need a lunch. I made arrangements for the gig to be ready at ten. We'll want to set out before it gets too hot.'

He presented her with breakfast and a sudden, unexpected rush of tears stung her eyes. It was perfect. She would have eaten whatever he served, even if it had been a plate full of eels, so touched was she by the simple gesture. Maybe there was no middle ground. Maybe she should just give over to the fantasy.

'I could have done that,' she managed to choke out. The plate, the picnic, the gig. She could have done all of it. She'd been making her own arrangements and decisions for years.

'Of course you could have.' He sat down again. 'That's not the point.'

'You're not here to wait on me,' she protested between bites of shirred eggs. But it was a half-hearted protest at best. Had breakfast ever tasted this good? Her usual breakfast was more of a pro forma ritual, something she had to do. This morning, however, she was aware the eggs were hot, the sausage was spicy, the toast was warm and the butter was melted.

'Let me worry about what I'm here to do and not do.' Nicholas took his seat again.

'I'll change after breakfast so I don't keep you waiting.'

He knit his dark brows together in exaggerated consternation. 'Why change? You look lovely in what you're wearing.'

'It's not a driving dress,' she argued, but again with little heat. A carriage dress would be much warmer wear and less comfortable than her morning dress in cool white muslin sprigged with tiny pink flowers and who was there to see her?

He leaned forwards, resting his chin on his

hand. 'No one is likely to see us. Why don't you send your maid for a hat and gloves and call it good?' He rose and held out his hand, giving her no chance to refuse. She couldn't very well go with him *and* go back upstairs to change. He'd left her no choice.

Nicholas had been a whirlwind of efficiency that morning, a fact she realised once he allowed her a moment to appreciate the details of their departure. He had her settled in the gig, hat, gloves, light wrap and all, within minutes, pointedly deflecting her questions about what was strapped to the maid's seat in the back with a laugh, saying only, 'You'll see when we get there and not a moment sooner.'

He leapt up beside her on the narrow seat, a seat really made for one-and-a-half people instead of two, especially if one of them was a full-grown man with long legs. He picked up the ribbons and clucked to the horse, a sturdy chestnut she often used for short jaunts, and they were off, jouncing along at close quarters, an effect which was not lost on Annorah. She tried vainly to keep her thigh from touching his on the small seat, but the more she tried, the more he made sure his leg took up the space until she had no choice other than to let her body relax alongside his. Perhaps if she said something?

'You're doing that on purpose.' He might truly be unaware of it after all. But her mind laughed at her. He knew very well what he was doing and so did she.

'Doing what?' They hit a bump in the road and his leg brushed hers.

'That.'

Nicholas laughed, the sound filling the empty road around them. 'It's a small seat, Annorah, where do you propose I put my leg? Besides, I don't think it's an unpleasant sensation, merely a new one.' One she feared she could get used to, like breakfast plates and just as easily.

Everything was easy with him. He hadn't even been here a day and already he'd insinuated himself into the routine of her life. He'd done it so well, in fact, that there was an undeniable sense of rightness in having him beside her, almost as if they'd known each other for far longer.

'It's all right to like me, you know.' Nicholas slid her a sidelong glance, his intuition catching her off guard with its accuracy. 'It would be better if you did, actually.'

'How did you know that's what I was thinking? Do you read minds?'

'I read bodies and lifestyles. You've been independent for a long time, too independent if you want my opinion. You aren't used to having people look out for you.'

'You're wrong there. I have servants.'

'It's not the same. I mean someone who looks out for you voluntarily, without being asked.'

'What does that have to do with liking you?' Annorah shifted on the seat, wishing there was some way to put distance between herself and this interview.

'Everything. Your independence has made you cautious of others.' He guided the horse around a sunken spot in the road.

'Stop thinking of me as another hired servant and start letting yourself like me, Annorah. There's no harm in it.'

He might be right but it didn't stop her from feeling defensive. 'You are not my friend.' She shot him a look to see how he'd take the pronouncement.

'No, I'm not. I'm much, much better.'

'I can trust my friends,' Annorah said staunchly.

He arched an eyebrow. 'Really? Then answer me this. Why have you been alone so long?'

Annorah fixed her eyes on the road. She was *not* going to answer that out loud. *Because people hurt people. Intentionally or unintentionally, the result was still the same and she simply couldn't go through it again.* What her aunt and a long string of suitors had done to her for the sake of money was unforgivable.

'We all have the lives we want, Annorah. Nothing will change that until *we* do,' he said softly.

Nothing except calendars and legally binding documents. It was on the tip of her tongue to challenge that statement. No matter what she did, everything *was* going to change in a matter of weeks and she still hadn't decided what to do. Annorah pushed the thought away with a hard mental shove. She'd promised herself she wouldn't think about that while he was here. This was her last escape from reality. Her obligations weren't supposed to intrude during these last days.

The cry of a hawk overhead broke the silence.

Nicholas bumped her shoulder with his and pointed to the cloudless sky, impressed with the sudden intruder. 'We don't see many of them in London.'

Annorah looked up. 'They live in the hills. There's a whole family of them that have been here since I can remember.' She smiled. 'When I was little, we used to pretend to be hawks. We used to pretend we could fly.' She gave a little laugh. 'That's silly, isn't it?'

'Not really. I had a kite when I was younger. I used to fly it and wish for the same thing.' He smiled back at her, taking his eyes from the road long enough to meet her gaze, letting the sweetness of a childhood memory remembered pass between them.

'I can hardly picture you as a little boy.' It *was* difficult to think of this perfect man as a rambunctious scamp, running about the countryside in short trousers flying a kite.

'Why not? I was adorable.' He pretended mock hurt.

She gave a slight shake of her head. 'It's just that you're so well put together; your clothes, your manners, you seem to always know what to do and what to say. I can't imagine you not always having been this way.'

Nicholas laughed. 'My mother wouldn't describe me that way. I assure you, I had my share of scraped knees and less-than-pristine moments.' He winked and said with exaggerated seriousness, 'I had a mother, too, just think of it.'

The conversation had become easier after that. They talked of the plants they passed, the wildflowers that grew along the side of the road, the fields and the crops, until he turned off and brought the gig up beside the wide grey ribbon of river to a place where it pooled into a swimming hole beneath the shade of an old oak tree.

'I haven't been here in ages.' She looked down at him, instantly suspicious as he came over to her side of the gig. 'How did you know about this place?'

Nicholas shrugged and swung her down, letting his hands linger at her waist, his grip strong and confident as he held her. 'I asked around. Your master of horse said this was a good spot for a picnic.' Nicholas moved to the back of the gig and began to unpack, revealing at last what he'd stowed away. 'I hear it's a good place to fish.'

Fishing poles! Good heavens, she hadn't seen the fishing poles for years, not since her grandfather had passed away actually. She hadn't even been sure the poles were still around. Part of her assumed they'd simply found their way into other hands—perhaps a groom or two who'd gone fishing on a day off and had kept them, or perhaps some boys in the village had borrowed them. But here they were, looking as able as ever. He held out a pole. 'Are you game?'

Annorah shot a quick glance at his boots, noting their high polish and expense. Water would ruin them. 'You have to go *in* the water to fish.'

Nicholas gave her a wink. 'I'll let you in on a little secret. I plan on taking them off. How about you? I don't think those half-boots will fare any better.' Nicholas sat down on a big boulder by the river and tugged at his boots. He tossed them aside. 'Here's another secret. I plan to take off a lot more than my boots.'

Dear lord, he meant it. Annorah's mouth went dry as he pushed up his trousers and began rolling off his socks, revealing well-muscled calves.

It was ridiculous to be aroused by a man's legs, but she rather doubted most men had legs like his; so perfectly turned with a sculpted bulge of muscle and tanned, too, not a pasty white. It suggested extraordinarily good health. Here was a man who knew how to take care of himself, whose body was not padded and moulded into a false representation of its true physique. There was no artifice here.

No, absolutely none, she affirmed a moment later. Off came his jacket, just to reinforce the point. The thin linen of his shirt hugged the breadth of his shoulders and tapered into the waistband of his trousers, calling attention to the trim line of his hips.

'Well? Stop dawdling, Annorah.' Nicholas stepped into the river with his pole. 'We don't eat until we fish.'

Right, just as soon as I get my jaw shut. She was being ridiculous.

He tossed a fishing pole in her direction. 'Unless you're too scared?'

That did it. She'd been more than an able fisher in her day. Annorah set to her boots with a flurry of efficiency. Boots and stockings were off, the skirts of her dress hiked up with the help of a hair ribbon. 'I can outfish a man about town like you any day of the week.'

Nicholas grinned. 'Then get in here and do it.'

Chapter Six

Her toes touched the water and the years fell away. How quickly it all returned to her! Her body had not forgotten a single thing. Annorah cast her line with a fluid back-and-forwards movement, revelling in the thrill of the motion as the river took her fly and pulled it into the current. She revelled, too, in the knowledge that Nicholas was watching, approving.

'I must have been thirteen the last time I did that!' she called over the gurgle of the river, her self-consciousness slipping away with the water.

'Very nice!' he called back with a mischievous look that said he wasn't to be outdone. No sooner had she thrown her line than he threw his in a side cast, the fly landing with a quiet plop on the water.

'Show-off!' Annorah retorted with good humour. 'That's not bad for a man about town.' She caught a suspicious movement in the water to her left. Fish! She quickly reeled in her line. A basic cast would have been sufficient, but she couldn't help a little showing off of her own. 'Watch this.' Annorah flicked the line back and forwards and back again for a sharply executed false cast.

It became a competition after that. He answered with a side cast. She came back with a roll out. He executed a double haul. She threw a flawless reverse. On it went until they were laughing and wet, their clothes far beyond damp.

A fierce tug on the line claimed her attention. 'I've got one!' Annorah shouted, the excitement of the catch seizing her. She began to reel in her line, but the current and the weight of the fish conspired against her. She took an involuntary step towards the centre of the river, planning on retrenching, but her fish had other ideas. He tugged. She slid. Her bare feet ploughed the soft mud of the river bed. Annorah wrestled with the rod. The pole began to bend. 'You're not getting away from me, you little bugger!' She was going to need help.

No sooner had she thought it, than Nicholas

was there, his hands closing over hers, his body coming up and around her from behind, lending her its strength. 'Tut, tut, Annorah. Such language from a lady. I wouldn't have guessed.' He chuckled in her ear. She could feel the heat and muscle of him through his soaked shirt.

'Pull with me, I think we've got him.'

They tugged and reeled, laughing and stumbling in the current, his body there to steady her. At last they landed that fish, a huge river trout. 'Enough to feed two.' Nick dragged the fish up on to the bank and flopped down beside it. 'I say we save it for dinner.'

'What about lunch?'

Nick grinned and pulled out a gutting knife. 'You've shown yourself to be the better fisherman between us. You go get a pair of fish for lunch and I'll see to this fellow here.'

'I'll race you!' Annorah laughed and waded back in. Her dress was soaked. It hardly mattered how wet she got now. But it was a race she was happy to lose.

By the time she'd returned with her creel full of fish, Nicholas had a camp of sorts arranged. A blanket was spread out in front of a small fire, a spit already set up over the flames. The day was warm, but the heat was welcome against the chill of the river and the damp of her clothes.

Nick skewered the fish and she busied herself laying out the rest of the picnic items with one notable exception. 'You meant it about no fish, no food, didn't you?'

Nick flashed her a grin as he bent over the fire, his wet trousers tight over his buttocks. 'I never lie.' He removed the fish and slid one on to a plate for her. 'We wouldn't have starved. There was bread and wine.'

'Hardly a meal,' Annorah shot back with a laugh. She sliced bread for him. He poured wine for her. There was an easy rhythm in the simple tasks. She wouldn't have thought slicing bread could be intimate, but here by the fire, with their catch roasting, it was.

'Oh, there's worse, I assure you.' Nicholas settled beside her on the blanket, looking entirely too attractive with his wet hair falling in his face, his shirt undone to reveal the muscled chest beneath, a beautiful bronze to match his legs.

'Like what?' Annorah bit into her fish. She

flicked her tongue to catch the juices dribbling down her chin.

'Lutefisk. It's a Norwegian fish soaked in lye for a particular taste.' Nicholas made a face.

'Wherever did you eat that? It sounds terrible.' Annorah laughed. She'd been doing a lot of it since yesterday and it felt good. It made her wonder if her world had been so very silent before his arrival.

'I lived with a Norwegian family when I first came to London. How about you? What's the worst thing you've ever eaten?'

'I don't know.' Annorah pushed a hand through the tangle of her hair, thinking. 'Oh, yes, I do!' She smiled suddenly, the memory coming to her. 'I sneaked into the kitchen one afternoon, determined to make a cake. Let's just say it didn't turn out.'

Nicholas's eyes danced. 'In my experience, icing can save a lot of doomed projects.'

'Not this one.' She finished her fish and set aside her plate. 'What shall we do next?' She was feeling relaxed and perhaps a bit euphoric. It was surprisingly easy to be with him—yet another easy thing to add to the list: easy to laugh with, easy to talk to, easy to be with. She was just about to conclude anything would be easy with him when he came up with his next idea.

'I'm going swimming. How about you?'

There was nothing easy about that. Swimming would be complicated. Annorah drew her knees up and hugged them. She used to love to swim, but that was before she grew up and swimming was ruled as something ladies didn't do. A lady couldn't very well swim in her clothes, which made the activity lewd *and* public. 'The water will make my skirts too heavy.'

Nicholas grinned wickedly. 'Then take them off.'

He was going to have to debate with her about it. Nicholas heard the regret in her voice as if she was merely making the appropriate answer. Well, he'd see what he could do about that. He rose from the blanket and shrugged out of his shirt. It was perhaps not as gracefully done as it might have been. The shirt was wet and it stuck to him. He threw it on a hanging branch and his hands went to the waistband of his trousers.

'What are you doing?' Annorah's voice barely

disguised a gasp of excitement mixed with trep-
idation.

'I'm taking off my trousers. I don't mean to
swim in them,' he called over his shoulder.

'What *do* you mean to swim in?'

'In my altogether. You could swim in your chemise if you preferred,' he suggested.

'I couldn't.' Annorah hesitated, biting her lip.

'Then take it off, too.' He pushed his trousers past his hips and kicked them off, leaving
only his smalls; a concession to her modesty. He
turned around and Annorah blushed, her gaze
looking everywhere but at him.

'Don't tell me you're embarrassed by my natural state.' Nick spread his arms wide from his
sides and sauntered towards her. He couldn't resist having a bit of fun. If he'd learned one thing
about her this afternoon, it was that she could be
teased—the wildness inside was very much alive
once she let down her guard. He rather enjoyed
getting past that guard, as he had in the river.

'It's not that.'

'It isn't? Then is it perhaps that you're embarrassed about your natural state? I think your natural state would be quite lovely.' He reached a

hand down to her and tugged, letting the teasing fade from his voice. 'Come on, Annorah. It's just the two of us. You've been eyeing that swimming hole since we got here. You know you want to.' *You want to do more than swim and if you'd look at me you'd know I do, too.*

He had her on her feet and then he had her in his arms, kissing her; her throat, her neck, her lips. She tasted like wine, her body all compliance beneath his mouth. A soft moan escaped her. His hands worked the simple fastenings of her gown. He hesitated before pushing the dress down her shoulders, giving her one last chance to back out. If she resisted now, he'd let her. But she didn't. He smiled to himself. Sometimes all a person needed was a nudge.

Then they were running, her hand clasped in his as they took a leap into the swimming hole. They hit the water with a splash and he let out a yelp. Good lord, it was cold! Nick surfaced and shook the water from his hair. He watched Annorah emerge, her hair a sleek pelt neatly slicked back from her face by the water's efforts. She was laughing and trying to catch her breath.

'You should have warned me!' she sputtered. 'It's colder than I thought.'

'*I* should have warned *you*? It's your swimming hole!' Nick splashed her for good measure. She yelped and dived beneath the surface, disappearing for a moment before he felt her pull on his legs and he went under. Oh, he was going to get her for this!

She was waiting for him under the water and he gave chase. He caught her and pushed them both to the surface. She gave an undignified squeal and he kissed her hard on the mouth. 'That's no less than you deserve, wench, for dunking me.' He was too breathless to be serious. Her arms were about his neck. His hands rested on the narrow span of her rib-cage just beneath the swell of her breasts, the thin linen of her chemise outlining the dark press of her nipples. The wet fabric offered no protection, but plenty of provocation. Her head thrown back, she was enjoying the thrill of the moment. Even in the chilly water, the sight of this woman finding pleasure in their play made him hard, *genuinely* hard. No artifice or tool, or amount of concentration on his part, had conjured this.

In those precious seconds Nicholas felt one fundamental truth rock his body. He was alive! The power of the summer's day, the potency of his body's response fired in his blood, sending its message of life thrumming through his veins. It was a moment and a sensation he had not thought to reclaim. He'd not felt like this since he was seventeen and desperately in love, or what passed for love at that age, with Brenna Forsyth, the squire's daughter. What a heady summer that had been!

When he looked at Annorah and saw those hazel eyes dancing with the same emotions; he knew he wasn't alone in this perfect moment. To share it with this woman he'd known for such a short time was almost overwhelming. She was nothing like his London women. She was extraordinary.

Annorah's lips parted, her head tipped slightly to one side and all thoughts of summers past were driven away. The tip of her head was the only warning he had. She was kissing him. Softly, gently at first, pulling on his lower lip with her teeth, tracing the contours of his mouth with the tip of her tongue. It was quite possibly the most honest kiss he'd ever received and he revelled in it.

'I've wanted to do that since you stepped into my hall,' Annorah whispered, tracing his lips with a finger. 'You have the most sensual mouth for a man.'

Nicholas laughed. 'Why, thank you. Do you know what I've wanted to do?' He didn't give her a chance to answer. He swept her up into his arms and carried her ashore, giving her little screams of surprise no quarter. He deposited her on the blanket beside their fire and followed her down, propping himself up on one elbow.

'*This* is what you've wanted to do?' Annorah teased. But he could see the action had excited her. The pulse at the base of her neck beat a fast tattoo. 'You've wanted to carry me dripping wet out of a swimming hole.'

'Oh, yes.' He gave her a slow smile and drew a lazy finger down her breast bone, resting his hand on the flat of her stomach. 'You were a spot of vibrant colour in the hall, dressed in yellow like a daffodil. I thought then that your hair would look like wild honey when it was wet and I could hardly wait to find out.' He held her gaze.

'I was right. It is the colour of beautiful, thick honey. Close your eyes, Annorah.'

He kissed her mouth and worked his way down, kissing her throat, her neck. Wet fabric clung to the curve of a breast and he took it in his mouth, nipping and suckling. He moved over her, feeling her body rise against him, her hips arching up to him as a little moan escaped her lips. He had his mouth at her belly, her chemise pushed up, her skin bare as he feathered her navel with a gentle breath. His hands bracketed her hips as he steadied her for his next foray, his thumbs at the juncture of her thighs, his mouth pressing a kiss to her mons.

She jumped a bit at the extreme intimacy of the contact. 'Nicholas?'

'Shh. Keep your eyes shut, Annorah,' Nick coached softly. 'It's all right. You will like this, I promise.' He blew against her furrow, as he had her belly, and looked up long enough to see a smile take her mouth. He kept his voice low, a whispering caress. 'That's right, Annorah, let go. This is for you. Get lost in the moment.' He licked the secret pearl of her flesh and felt her tremble as the initial sensation of such contact took her. She tasted of salt and desire on his lips and his body was tense with a rising want of his own. But that was for later. Here, by the fire, with an afternoon of pleasures behind them was just for her.

He cupped her with his hand, working her swollen pearl with his thumb. She was rising fast. She pressed hard against his touch, searching instinctively for the satisfaction that waited on the other side of this. Her breath came in gasps; she was working hard for it. She wasn't far now. Then she was there. He watched the achievement sweep over her. Her back arched, her hips bucked against his hand. Her head was thrown back, all that honey hair spilling about her, a sob on her lips full of amazement and wonder at the miracle of climax.

An urge to capture the moment took him unexpectedly. This had happened before numerous times. He'd brought this particular pleasure to women beyond his count. But this was a new variation on the old theme in some immeasurable way he couldn't define beyond the simple fact that it *was* different.

Annorah opened her eyes and he took up his

old position, propped on his side next to her. Her eyes weren't dreamy or faraway as he'd expected. They were sharp and alert. Suddenly, he feared the first words out of her mouth. He didn't want those words to be: you were worth every pound. He didn't want to talk about what had transpired at all. He simply wanted it to be. Other lovers, *real* lovers, didn't lie around and dissect the interlude afterwards, analysing the performance.

Annorah raised a hand to his face, brushing back a strand of loose hair. It was a delicate gesture, perhaps a trifle hesitant once she realised what she was doing and the familiarity attached to it. Her first words didn't disappoint. 'Thank you for today. I haven't had this much fun for ages.' She gave one of her delightful little laughs. 'I've been saying that a lot. It sounds trite, but it's true. I can't quite recall the last time I had this much fun as an adult.'

She paused, a delightful furrow appearing between her brows as she studied him. 'Why do you suppose adults stop playing? Why would society decree such a thing? I can't imagine it makes anyone happy.'

'*We* don't have to stop, Annorah.' His voice was

quiet—he was unwilling to shatter the wondrous intimacy that had sprung up between them. The world was still around them, interrupted only by the murmur of the river and the occasion chirp of the birds.

She gave him a wry smile. 'Shall we be rebels?'

'I think you are already more of a rebel than you realise.' He traced a swirly design on the flat of her abdomen. 'You've defied convention, Annorah Price-Ellis. You're an heiress who has escaped marriage, a woman who has defined the terms of her existence according to her own wishes. In our world, that is rare indeed.'

She warmed to that thought, a slow smile replacing the wry one. 'I like the sound of that. I am a rebel.' They laughed together in the warm afternoon. She was extraordinary. His earlier use of the term had not been exaggerated. She was a unique woman, living under unique circumstances. He thought if anything neared earthly perfection, her life was it. And yet, she wasn't perfect. He knew that already. She had a sharp tongue and a streak of cynicism. Those were certainly not the qualities of perfection, nor were they qualities acquired from living a perfect life.

She had her mysteries, but she'd opened to him today. Part of him wanted to congratulate himself on a brilliantly designed strategy. He'd played this just right. Part of him didn't want to think of today as another tactical manoeuvre. He wanted today to exist on its own merits because he'd enjoyed it, too.

'Should I take the rebel home?' he asked reluctantly when the laughter and conversation subsided into a lull.

'No, I'd like to stay awhile longer.' They were both whispering now in an attempt to hold on to the magic.

Nicholas rolled over on his back and pulled her to him, nestling her in the hollow of his arm where shoulder met chest. 'I'd like that, too.' He meant it. Perfection was hard to come by and when it was available, it was usually in small moments. Today had been surprisingly full of them and he was loath to let go. It had been full of spontaneity. He'd planned the outing in the hopes that coming to river would help her relax and get past some of the restraints holding her back. But he'd not planned on the casting competition, or playing tag in the swimming hole. He'd certainly not planned for the remarkable set of feelings that swamped him now as they lay here.

The outing was notable also for what it had lacked. For the first time in seven years, he'd been in the country and not been swamped with the memories. Then again, it was easier to hold the ghosts at bay in the summery light of an afternoon with a woman lying in his arms. Maybe only storms provoked them, his more cynical side argued, the side that was determined he'd never forget every detail of the night the life he knew had slipped away and he'd been helpless to stop it.

Chapter Seven

The last of the late afternoon slipped away, giving ground to a stunning evening while Annorah soaked in her bath. The wide windows of her room were open, catching a cooling breeze and providing a delicious contrast to the warm water. She sank low into the lavender-scented bubbles, eyes closed. She wanted to savour the afternoon, wanted to commit it to memory.

It was an afternoon full of pictures, peopled with images of Nicholas: Nicholas rolling up his trousers; Nicholas wading into the stream and daring her to join him; Nicholas, muscles flexing as he cast his line. There were more intimate images, too: Nicholas standing before her in his smalls, completely at ease with his nudity.

And why shouldn't he be? He'd been magnificent, beautiful even.

It was a beauty that went beyond his physique. It was there in his laugh, the dance of his eyes, the way those eyes would lower just before he kissed her, and it had been infectious.

She'd felt alive, too. In his arms, she'd been vivid and real, living out loud. He saw her in an entirely different light than the men she was used to and she'd thrilled to his interpretation. She found it freeing actually. He had words for her that she didn't have for herself. Annorah ran over the phrases in her mind like the beads of a rosary: her hair was wild honey; she was a rebel. He'd called her beautiful in the most decadent way possible. *I think your natural state would be quite lovely.* She'd been called beautiful before, by less honest men who saw only her fortune or by more shallow men who saw only the pretty tailoring of the latest fashions.

The Annorah he saw *would* hike up her skirts and fish in rivers, *would* later take off those skirts altogether and swim nearly nude with a man. And—oh, yes—the Annorah he saw would indeed give herself over to the wicked, intimate pleasures they'd explored on the picnic blanket. Even now, her body quickened at the memory.

The woman he saw was who she used to be before she'd chosen exile over excitement, disappearing over disappointment. She'd liked that woman once. She'd almost forgotten her. It had been good to discover her again today. The whole day had been about discovering, about living.

Annorah pushed up in the tub, dislodging the bubbles. If today had been about living, what had the last several years been about? *Not* living? The disappearance of the other Annorah was proof it had been. The past five years had changed her and perhaps not for the better.

After the last disaster of a marriage proposal, she'd barricaded herself away in the country ostensibly so she could live life on her own terms. But she'd long harboured the suspicion that her choice to retreat was about something more. That it was her attempt to protect herself from her own fatal flaw: choosing the wrong man. It had happened both times a gentleman had come up to scratch. First with a viscount's young heir and then more awfully with her aunt and uncle's neighbour, Bartholomew Redding. In between there'd been countless young swains who had tried their luck, but none had left her more than lukewarm for their affections. They'd not been a threat.

Only in hindsight had she been able to see the similarities between the two that had mattered. Both suitors had been wild in their own ways; willing to flaunt convention, willing to use people for their own ends. The young heir had not been clever, merely mean. What might have initially looked like sharp wit was a thin veil for remarks that bore the stamp of cutting cruelty. She'd met him early in her come-out, her own skills of discernment not fully honed.

He'd been visiting, which had been a nice way of saying he was on a repairing lease until he was received back into his father's good graces after some messy business with debts in town. He'd wooed her most thoroughly, someone having given him wind of her fortune. She must have looked like a miracle to him. She might have capitulated to him when the offer came, too; he was handsome and witty, albeit often at other people's expense, except for a note at the eleventh hour from her uncle's sister in town offering full disclosure of the man's true character. It hadn't bothered her aunt and uncle unduly, but it had bothered her. She had declined the offer, much to their chagrin.

It was a pattern that would be repeated over the years until Bartholomew Redding had finally succeeded in driving her out of her aunt and uncle's home and out of society. If this was the nature of man, she would find a way to live without it. He'd been the worst. He had good looks, a certain charm and he'd been comfortable. He'd not roused her young passions like the viscount's heir, perhaps, but she'd felt at ease with him; they knew the same people, the same lifestyle. He was a neighbour and not too old to make a good husband. Thirty-one, perhaps. But it had been a ruse. He'd been no more above compromising her for her fortune than anyone else. She'd not trusted the others, but she'd trusted him and that had made his betrayal all that more hurtful when it came.

Nicholas wasn't either man— She had to stop herself there. The other suitors had been the wrong men. But that didn't make Nicholas D'Arcy the right man. He was *supposed* to be the right man. It was his *job* to be the right man. He had to be accountable. A thousand pounds said so.

She had to stop her thoughts again. She didn't want to think of Nicholas as a chameleon changing colours to fit his surroundings, to be what any woman wanted him to be, even if it might be true. She didn't want to remember this day as an elaborate play enacted on a stage where Nicholas had pretended to like to fish, had pretended to want to kiss her, to pleasure her, or where Nicholas hadn't meant a single word of the rosary she'd strung together. She needed it to be real. She needed him to simply be hers, nothing more.

Annorah understood that she'd invited Nicholas D'Arcy not so much because she craved carnal knowledge of a man, but because she wanted to live again, one last time to be the woman she wanted to be and not what the world had made her. Sex was merely a symptom.

The tantalising smell of cooking food wafted up from the kitchens and through her open window, restoring her optimism. She smiled. It had been an incredible day. Supper was still to come and the night after that.

Lily entered, carrying a pile of thick towels and a box. Annorah sat up in the tub, her curiosity piqued. It seemed an odd thing for Lily to bring with her. Lily set down the towels and approached the tub, bringing the box.

'This is for you, miss.' Her eyes were wide with excitement. A package was something out of the ordinary when it came by post, wrapped in brown paper. When it came in a clean, stiff white box, the kind dressmakers used, and tied prettily with yards of pink silk ribbon, the package was immediately elevated to the extraordinary. 'I think it's from London.' Lily was nearly breathless with excitement.

'For me?' Annorah couldn't recall having ordered anything from the village, let alone London, since her last glorious splurge. The prospect of a present was far too exciting to pretend it wasn't. She could no more feign indifference over the arrival than Lily could. She let Lily wrap her in a towel and they set about studying the box together.

The lid was embossed in large, swirly, gold lettering that read: Madame La Tour's Salon for Women. Then in smaller gold lettering the address was given: 619 Bond Street, London. Lily gave a little squeal as Annorah read the lid out loud. 'The box is too pretty to open.' Lily sighed.

Annorah had to agree, but curiosity wouldn't let her stare too much longer. She untied the enormous length of pink-satin ribbon and made a gift of it to Lily, who couldn't believe her good fortune. Inside the box was a layer of crisp tissue paper, there to protect the delicate item beneath. Carefully, Annorah folded back the tissue to reveal the garment inside.

'Oh, miss!' Lily gasped as Annorah lifted it out of the box. It was two garments really. The more substantial garment, although that wasn't saying much—both were delicately made—was a white-silk nightgown unlike anything she'd ever seen. There were no sleeves, just two white straps. The heart-shaped bodice was covered in a beautiful overlay of Venetian lace before the gown fell away in gentle folds of silk. Nipped at the waist, the fabric would flare out again to fall gently over the curve of the hips. It would fit exquisitely. The other garment was a sheer robe meant to be worn over the gown with lace-trimmed short sleeves.

The woman who wore this would be riveting— a most prurient thought, which was quickly followed by another: to be riveting, one had to be seen by another. Then it struck her, that woman would be her and the man who would see her would be Nicholas.

'There's a card, miss.' The awe in Lily's voice was unmistakable.

Annorah's fingers trembled as she opened the small card, although by now she knew who it was from. Only one man she knew would dare such a gift. He was quite possibly the only man who could pull it off without the gift seeming lewd.

The note read simply, 'For tonight. Yours, Nicholas.'

Hers. The very thing she'd just wished for.

'It's from Mr D'Arcy,' Annorah said quietly. There'd be no way around *not* confessing that to Lily at this point.

'It's the prettiest thing I've ever seen.' Lily touched the fabric reverently. 'That's fine silk. What a pity it's just for sleeping. I'd want to wear it everywhere so everyone could see me.' Lily paused, her thoughts catching up to her words. 'He's not really a librarian is he, miss?'

'No. He's not.'

Lily had the good sense to not ask anything more. But her idea was tempting. Maybe, Annorah thought, she should wear the peignoir set to dinner. Perhaps that was even what Nicholas intended. But this gown was not for eating, it was for other things. It would be a tragedy to spill anything on it. Annorah gave the gown a final caress and set it aside, laying it out on the bed for later.

Later. The very prospect of later sent a rush of warm heat through her. If later was anything like this afternoon, it bore repeating.

'Would you like the oyster gown?' Lily held up the dress she usually wore for dinners. It was pretty enough, but it was plain and that would not do. Annorah smiled to herself. She knew exactly what she wanted; a dress that would appeal to the whimsy of a summer evening, something softly feminine, yet with a hint of allure and the provocative. 'I want one of the new dresses. The peach chiffon, I think, Lily.'

When she'd bought it, she'd been unable to come up with a single occasion in the country it would be appropriate for, mostly because there was no call for such a gown at Hartshaven. The neckline was cut low and tight and trimmed in tiny seed pearls that made it far too sophisticated for the village assemblies or the occasional dinner at the squire's. Yet with that sophistication there was the whimsy she sought in the fullness of the skirts that made her feel like a fairy princess. Such a feeling would not go amiss tonight.

Annorah fastened a thin strand of pearls about her neck and sat still while she let Lily put her hair up. 'It's a new fashion I found in one the magazines.' Lily stuck in the final pin and stepped back. 'Do you like it?'

Annorah turned her head left, then right, to catch all the angles. She did like it. Two soft braids were drawn over her ears into a bun that rode low at the back of her neck. She looked younger—not that thirty-two was old. But perhaps looking older had been a casualty of her exile, too. Maybe she'd inadvertently let her appearance falter just a bit. It would have been easy to do with no one to see her except the servants and the villagers. It would have been a simple armour to don to keep potential suitors at bay.

Annorah dabbed perfume at her pulse points, a

light floral scent that complimented the mood of her gown. The woman in the mirror was ready.

So was dinner. So ready in fact that Nicholas was not waiting for her in the drawing room when she arrived. It took a moment to pick up his trail. Candlelight glimmered from the next room and another flame flickered just beyond it. Ah, she had it now. A little trill of excitement fluttered through her as she followed the candlelit path leading through the informal dining room they'd used last night to the terrace, which was now strangely empty *sans* table. The French doors were open and past them Nicholas stood beside the newly relocated table.

Like her, he had dressed for the evening with the utmost care in dark evening clothes. Not much of the fisherman remained in the gentleman who stood before her, but it was hard to mourn the loss for long when she was faced with this debonair male in his place.

'I thought we could continue the tradition of serving ourselves.' Nicholas held out her chair.

Privacy. More time to be with this intriguing man who could cast a line as well as she, who'd swum in the swimming hole and given her so much more than just a set of experiences today.

Nicholas reached for the champagne and she thought, *This is heaven.* Why hadn't she eaten like this before: outside, under the stars, a single candle on the table covered with a glass chimney? It was a simple matter to move the table. But she knew why. Meals had ceased to be an occasion. She raised her glass to sip, feeling Nicholas's eyes on her, hot and piercing over the rim of his own flute.

'What is it?' She touched a self-conscious hand to her hair. Perhaps a pin had come loose.

'Nothing.' Nicholas smiled. 'I was just admiring the lovely woman across from me. The peach becomes you.'

'Country living becomes you,' she dared. Annorah gestured to the slight red cast on the bridge of his nose.

'That's not the only place that saw a bit of sun.' He winked naughtily.

Annorah laughed. 'Are you always this audacious? Do you make a habit of saying whatever comes to mind?'

Nicholas leaned forwards. 'Yes, absolutely. I

don't believe in mincing words when something needs saying.'

Annorah toyed with the stem of her glass and shot him a coy look. She felt bold tonight. Why not ask the things that were on her mind? 'You don't lie, you don't mince words. I know a lot about what you *don't* do. Why don't you tell me about something you *do*?'

'Everything, anything.' He gave her a sinful smile and a seductive stare, his eyes lingering on her lips to make his innuendo plain. She shook her head, unwilling to settle for the distraction his wordplay offered. Without thinking, she leaned forwards and covered his hands with hers, a gesture she would have not dared yesterday.

'No, really, Nicholas, I want to know.'

Dodge, deflect and repeat for as long as necessary. That was the usual recipe for handling such probes. He was normally adept at such parries. But Annorah was persistent. Of course she'd want to know. She was that sort of woman; the rare sort whose beauty wasn't limited to the outside. She was the sort who genuinely cared for others. He'd heard it in her voice last night when she spoke of her family, her cousins, her grandfather. She was a social creature, not made for isolation, which made her situation here all the more intriguing and at the same time incongruous.

'Aren't you afraid knowing will ruin the illusion?' He took her in, her features soft in the candlelight, her hair a halo of dark gold tonight. She was both ethereal and approachable, not an ice-cold winter beauty, but the warm beauty of summer. She was the sort who should have children clinging to her skirts, all of them laughing. She would be good at playing.

Something tightened in his gut: an ache, a longing. He'd once thought of himself that way, too—a man who wanted a lot of children to toss in the air. He'd not allowed himself to think of that for a long time now. It had been one of the dreams he'd set aside.

Her thumbs ran along the sides of his hands, a smile curving on her oh-so-kissable lips. 'Absolutely not. Why would it? Why would a man who tells no lies be worried about illusion?' This last was said quietly and with a hint of challenge.

Nicholas knew an uncharacteristic moment of vulnerability. He knew what *not* to tell her:

that he'd only come to the country because he'd been escaping the wrath of an angry husband, who might or might not know he'd slept with the man's wife; that he was notorious in certain circles for his ability to make a woman scream with pleasure.

But Annorah had already made it plain she wasn't interested in nots. She was hunting for truths and that's where the fantasy became tricky, as he'd known it would. How did one build the intimacy without exposing oneself? Perhaps he would let her lead.

'What do you want to know?' He gave her a sincere smile. She did not want flirting and innuendo. Women tended to ask the same questions, have the same intrigues about him, after all. It should be fairly safe. He could almost predict what she would ask.

Annorah leaned back, releasing his hands, and he most unusually felt the loss of her touch. He reached for his glass and drank. 'All right, then.' She smiled mischievously, getting into the spirit of the conversation. 'I can ask you anything I want?' The smile lit her eyes and transformed her face into a livelier version of its softer, gentler self. 'How is it that you're such a good fly fisher?'

The champagne nearly came out his mouth. He swallowed and coughed, literally choking on his surprise. He'd not been expecting that. He'd been expecting: How did you get into this line of work? But her question had nothing to do with sex.

Annorah swiftly came over and pounded him on the back, concerned. 'Are you well?'

Nicholas wiped his mouth with his napkin. 'I'm fine. I just took too big of a sip.'

'Gulp,' she corrected. 'You took a gulp. People don't choke on sips.'

He laughed. 'All right, gulp.'

Annorah settled back in her chair. She leaned forwards in expectation, waiting for his fly-fishing answer, the low cut of her en coeur bodice putting her bosom on enviable display. Did she know? Nicholas felt desire quicken. She had beautiful shoulders and the peach chiffon showcased them as well as it did the gentle thrust and slope of her breasts.

'Fly fishing?' she prompted when he'd hesitated too long, thinking of a lure of a different sort.

'Well, I was born in Mere. I grew up fishing on the Stour River. It came naturally.'

'You must have liked growing up there a great deal. You're smiling.'

'Oh, I did,' he answered without faltering. 'My brother and I would fish every afternoon after lessons in the summer. Sometimes my father would have to send one of the servants to bring us home. On very rare occasions, we'd be allowed to camp overnight, though.' It was his turn tonight, to spin stories of his youth. He had not meant to, but she drew them out of him one by one: the trees they'd climbed, the trails they'd hiked, the ponies they'd ridden as young boys and the horses they'd graduated to.

'My pony was Alfy and he was a stubborn Welsh.' Nicholas laughed, dividing the last of the champagne between them. 'One day, we were up in the hills, looking for treasure.'

'Treasure?' He loved the way her eyes lit up. 'Your home sounds very exciting.'

'Oh, it was, we were surrounded by legends. There was gold in the hills, left there by supporters of a would-be king. Stefan and I were always hunting it when the fish weren't biting.

One day, we were up in the hills and we went to cross a stream. My stubborn pony, who, I might add, had no trouble fording streams in his entire life, decides he won't cross. Stefan is on the other side already. Alfy races up to the stream and just stops.' Nicholas snapped his fingers. 'Just like that. He stops and I go sailing over his head straight into the water.'

Annorah laughed. 'I hope you were more wet than hurt.'

'I was. It takes a lot to hurt a boy. Boys are tough. But so was Alfy. It took us a half-hour to get him over the stream. We didn't find any gold that day.'

'Did you ever?' Annorah's voice had dropped to a near-whisper and the moment changed to something more potent, more dangerous.

'My answer might surprise you.' He held her eyes, his own voice quiet, too. 'We found a few coins over the years, old Spanish doubloons. To this day, I think there's treasure up there, some-where.' The magnitude of what he'd done was starting to settle on him. He'd talked of his child-hood, he'd talked of Stefan *and* it had felt good, devoid of the usual rush of guilt. Even now the guilt would not come. There was only the glow of happiness inside him as he recalled those summers.

'You should go back and claim it.' Annorah said. He knew she meant nothing by it, *couldn't* mean anything by it. She was talking about the gold. He was the only one thinking of claiming a time long past. He needed to end this.

'It's a child's wish born of bedtime stories, Annorah, nothing more, but I like to hold on to it anyway.' He rose and took her hand, drawing her to him. 'I have other bed times, and other wishes on my mind tonight.' He kissed her, tasting the champagne on her lips, feeling her passion rising stoked by memories of the afternoon and the intimacy of their conversation. Her want for him was sincere and for once, he thought, his might be, too. 'Annorah, my love, it's time for bed.'

Chapter Eight

Annorah lit the last candle and stood back to see the effect: just enough light, just enough shadow. They wouldn't be entirely in the dark. It was a purely calculated guess on her part. What did she know about seductions? Should she already be in bed? Should she sit in the chair by the window? She really ought to stop thinking. She did better when she didn't.

Annorah nervously smoothed the silken folds of the nightgown. It had fit perfectly. She'd known a moment's worry when she'd changed. What if it didn't fit? It would be a small tragedy if the beautiful gown hadn't, but it had. She slipped on the filmy outer garment and glanced at the little clock on her bedside table. Nicholas had said he'd come in twenty minutes when he'd left her at the stairs. She had five minutes remaining for any preparations she wanted to make. She'd brushed her hair, lit the candles, put on the nightgown. She couldn't think of anything else. Maybe she should... *No*, she told herself, *don't overthink this. Go sit in the chair and read a book until he comes or at least pretend to read one.*

She didn't have to wait long. Nicholas was prompt. He looked enviously at ease in her candlelit bower. His dark hair was loose on his shoulders and he was dressed simply in a silky paisley banyan trimmed and belted in black. The vee of the neckline gaped slightly, leaving no question that he was naked underneath—no fussy nightcaps or bulky nightshirts for this one.

He smiled at her as he stopped briefly at the bedside table and put a few small objects on it, his smile chasing away her nerves and replacing them with a trill of excitement. This was going to happen and it was going to happen with him, with Nicholas D'Arcy, who had managed in a short space of time to rivet her with his grace and command of both the indoors and outdoors, with his stories, with his touch, with his interest in her. It was quite an intoxicating combination, never more so than now when he stood before her, his hands in the empty pockets of his banyan, looking down at her with fond eyes and a smile.

'A pound for your thoughts, Annorah.'

She laughed. 'I thought it was a penny?'

He gave an easy shrug and took the chair opposite her. 'It is, but your thoughts are worth more than that. Tell me.' In the candlelight, he was irresistible, but that was just an excuse. She knew he was irresistible anywhere.

'I was thinking how I feel I've known you far longer than a day. Logically, I know that is the height of silliness. I'd never set eyes on you before yesterday. It's foolish, I know.' She shook her head. Foolish, yes. True? Yes.

'There are primitive religions that believe souls meet in dreams even before they encounter one another in life,' Nicholas postulated softly. 'Perhaps we've met there.'

'Do you believe things like that?'

'I think we ought to be careful what we hastily discard simply because it seems improbable, especially when so many people believed it.'

Annorah leaned forwards, her elbows on the little table between them, intrigued. 'Truly?'

He leaned forwards, too, his earnestness drawing her in. 'Us being together is improbable and yet here we are. Something wanted this to happen.' His soft, clipped tones rolled over the words, slowly, carefully. 'So many things had to align in order for us to be here tonight. I can't believe it is purely by accident.' Nicholas gave up his seat and knelt before her, taking her hands in his. 'We are meant to be, Annorah.'

Warmth and strength flowed through his hands, his face a study in reverence as she held his gaze. 'Do you honestly believe that?' She'd never heard anyone talk this way. Her dyed-in-the-wool Church of England family would have found it as scandalous as what she'd done in inviting him here. She was aware his hands had moved to her hair, combing through the long tresses she'd left loose over her shoulders.

'I believe it, Annorah.' His voice was husky, his eyes dark with desire as he spoke, leaving no margin for doubts. He moved away from her then and stood, drawing her up as he'd done at the table. He held her arms out to her sides, giving himself full purview of her. 'White lace be-comes you,' he murmured.

His mouth was at her throat, expertly kissing a trail to the pulse at the base of her neck. Her arms twined about him of their own accord as if it were the most natural of movements, her body arched into him, her head thrown back in full abandon. She let him suckle, let him lick, let him kindle the fire that burned in her. She let the sweet heat of that fire take her and in those flames all inhi-bitions, all doubt was burned away, replaced by unrestrained want.

The transparent robe fell first. She barely felt it. His hands were at her breasts, moulding and cup-ping through the silk, his breath a ragged pant. He urged her to sit again and he knelt before her, moving down her body, hands shaping her hips, his mouth pressed to her most intimate juncture, his breath warm through the thin fabric. Then his hands were gathering up the gown, up past her calves, past her knees, until it bunched about her waist and she was bare and exposed to him, a sensation that was both delicious and decadent.

There was only a moment to contemplate the wanton in her before it was overcome by a new sensation—his mouth directly on her *down there*. Part of her, *a very small part of her*, argued she should feel some embarrassment at this boldness, but the embarrassment simply would not come. There was only a keen awareness of his breath against her damp curls, of his tongue stroking a secret place within her folds. Oh, how that place wanted to be stroked! Every nerve in her body was centred on that spot, drawn there by his touch.

An intense wave of pleasure swept her and her body slid forwards in the chair. She anchored her hands in the thick depths of his dark hair for balance, searching for purchase against pleasure's return. This was the pleasure of the afternoon repeated, but yet there was an entirely new level of anticipation. This time she knew what awaited, eagerly sought it and the knowing provided an exquisite torture of its own. She arched into him one last time, the wave finally cresting and she rode it to completion.

Her senses returned one by one and in no great hurry. The world settled into its ordinary pattern except for the fact that Nicholas still knelt before her, his eyes intense blue coals, his hand resting lightly on her thigh. Slightly self-conscious now that the initial wave of passion had passed, Annorah tugged her gown down.

'I'll allow that for now, Annorah. But not for long.' He smiled and rose, stepping away from her. 'Now it's your turn to watch.' His hand went to the wide black-satin belt of his banyan and slowly drew out the knot. The banyan came off and he stood before her, gloriously nude. 'Look at me.'

Look at me, watch me. Yes, she would look, she would watch. The temptation was too great to resist. Her voice came out in a hoarse whisper. 'Yes.' Every inch of him was perfectly sculpted male. The map of his musculature was an atlas of ridges and planes all carved to lead the way down the smooth bronze expanse of his chest to the most male part of him, to where the peninsula of his phallus jutted proudly from his body.

Nicholas reached out a hand and pulled her to him. 'Now, you.' His hands capped her shoulders, his eyes holding hers as his thumbs slid beneath the straps of her gown and guided them down her arms until the gown was able to slip off of its own accord. His hands framed her, warm on her bare skin where they palmed her breasts, thumbs rubbing across her nipples in a delicious friction.

'You're so beautiful, so perfectly made for me,' Nicholas whispered. He danced her backwards until she hit the bed. He followed her down, his body above her, his dark hair falling forwards on his face. He looked like a warrior prince of old come to claim his prize. Her body thrilled at the savage imagery of it.

His phallus nudged her thigh, looking for invitation and she gave it. She wanted to be the prize, wanted to be claimed. She was weeping with it. Nicholas bracketed her with his arms, muscles locking as he rose over with unerring position. Then he sheathed himself, sure and slow. This, too, was an exquisite torture, both pleasure and pain. She felt her body stretch around him, accommodating, learning this new invader and with a final thrust, he was home, the invader no more.

Annorah moved instinctively beneath him, the pain of his entrance giving away to the pleasure of his full arrival. The rhythm began; the rocking, the little withdrawal and forwards surge of him within her over and over until she was mad with it as she had been at the river. But this time, as powerful as the pleasure was, it wasn't enough.

She was alone in the pleasure when it took her. In those raw moments of discovery she knew she shouldn't be alone. Nicholas should be there with her and he wasn't. Nicholas had withdrawn mentally long before he'd withdrawn physically. The realisation stabbed at her like a jagged edge of otherwise smooth glass and, like any jagged edge, it cut, slicing through the fragile fabric of her fantasy.

Nick was in a wonderful place. Sunlight lay just beyond his eyelids and there was a beautiful woman within arm's reach. There was nothing like lazy sex in the morning to start the day off right. He reached for Annorah, his body remembering her ardent responses in the night, only to find the bed cold where her warm body should have been. His eyes flew open, all senses alert. Something was wrong.

A quick scan of the room revealed she was not in it. She had not only left him in her bed, she'd left the room. He'd not anticipated this. Nicholas threw back the covers and grabbed up his robe.

He made his way back to his room and dressed quickly. She would not get away so easily.

Nicholas caught her on the steps, moments from a clean getaway. 'Annorah, you're up early.' At least she was for someone who'd spent the night in his arms. Half past ten was early indeed. He kept his tone casual, but the signs were damning. Annorah was dressed for going out in a striking blue driving ensemble. She'd meant to leave him. He'd startled her and when she'd looked up at him coming down the staircase, there'd been a moment of guilt in her eyes.

'I have an appointment in the village. It slipped my mind.' She smiled to dispel any doubt about the authenticity of her claim.

'I'll go with you,' Nicholas offered, his mind racing. What had happened in the night? The way she was twisting her driving gloves was a sure sign of nerves and awkwardness. He'd thought last night had gone well. She'd shown only the slightest of discomforts from the initial pain and there'd been pleasure for her. He wasn't sure what had gone wrong. What had he missed? He'd given her a near-perfect experience. In fact, he'd nearly given himself one as well. It had taken all of his discipline not to get caught up in it, too. He'd not felt genuine pleasure in the act for quite some time and it had crept up on him in complete surprise last night. Fortunately he'd caught it in time. There was only trouble down that road.

'That's not necessary, it would just bore you. I'm helping children in the village with reading lessons.' Annorah politely dismissed his offer, but he would have none of it, even if he had to insist.

Nicholas strode down the stairs and took her arm. 'As it happens, I'm very good at reading. Most librarians are. It's an occupational hazard, or so I'm told.' He gave her a charming smile and marched the two of them out the door to the waiting gig.

Once they were underway, Nicholas took a more serious tone. 'Now, tell me what's really going on.'

'*Nothing* is going on, I'm sure I don't understand what you mean.' Annorah kept her gaze fixed straight ahead on the empty road.

'Then I can only deduce from the empty bed and your attempt to leave me alone for the better part of the day that this is about last night.'

'Oh, no!' she assured him a bit too hastily to be

convincing, but at least he'd stirred up a measure of guilt for her covert attempt at abandoning him.

'Good, because I thought last night was practically perfect,' Nicholas put in. That got a response. Her head turned to look at him, her eyes narrowed in consideration.

'It was perfect,' Annorah said with a hint of cold aloofness to her tone.

'And that's a problem?' He understood women better than most and they were still a mystery to him at times. What could possibly be wrong with perfection?

'It was *too* perfect, Nick. It was an exquisite performance. I have nothing to compare it against, but I am certain your technique was flawless as I am sure it always is. I had not expected it to be like that. I had not expected to be alone at the end when it mattered the most.'

She was disappointed. The words she'd used that first evening came back to him: a mistake. She thought last night had been a mistake. His professional pride was pricked at the notion he'd finally failed a woman in bed. Nick set his mouth in a grim line and concentrated on the horse. Her own pleasure was supposed to blind her from

that small absence. Apparently it hadn't. She'd
wanted him there with her, finding release together. Didn't she know the one thing he couldn't
give her was a piece of his heart? In his line of
work, emotional exposure was a true hazard. He
couldn't even begin to imagine what would happen if he tried it. Librarians had an easier time
of it.

Chapter Nine

It was not going to be easy to face the children at the weekly reading lessons. Annorah swallowed hard, trying to subdue the lump in her throat as the village came into view. It might be the last time she saw them. If she did not marry, all this would be lost to her. The small home that had been allocated to her, should she choose to remain unwed, was up in the north.

She had not planned on facing this day with Nicholas as a witness. Nor had she planned on facing it with her aunt's latest letter fresh in her mind. She'd planned on facing it alone as she had faced so much else in her adult life. But Nicholas had risen before she could leave the house, and her aunt's latest missive had been in the mail reminding her of all that stood to be lost if she didn't come to the house party and make an agreement with the suitor her aunt had waiting.

Her aunt was more desperate to keep the money in the family than she was to keep Annorah. Annorah could only wonder at what kind of suitor she'd managed to find this time. Over the years, there'd been plenty. Her aunt hadn't given up even after Annorah had. Two broken hearts and several lukewarm ones had been too much for Annorah to bear. She'd retreated from the field, never believing it would really come to this. She'd always believed the lawyers would find a way out.

Nicholas parked the gig at the side of the vicarage and came over to help her down. He'd not said much since she'd essentially called his lovemaking an empty performance. That was fine. She had too much on her mind at the moment to be much of a conversationalist.

'Are you all right, Annorah?' Nick asked. 'You're pale. Are you tired?'

His tone was so solicitous she felt badly for how she'd treated him this morning. She forced a smile and took his arm. 'Perhaps just a little.' She was tired. Tired of feeling dead inside, tired of battling a foe she couldn't defeat. It was hardly fair to take her frustrations out on Nicholas, who, like the villagers, knew nothing of her true situation. Last night he'd just been doing his job. No doubt, his sophisticated clientele in London handled the arrangement with more discernment than she.

'Miss Norah, Miss Norah!' A dark-haired boy ran up to them and grabbed her hand, swinging hard. 'I learned the passage you gave us last week. Can I read first?' He noticed Nicholas. 'You brought a friend!'

Annorah widened her smile. She would get through this. She would let herself enjoy this and not think of all the 'lasts'. 'Thomas, this is Nicholas.'

Nicholas offered the boy a hand to shake. 'I'm here to help Miss Annorah with her books.' That was a very clever way to put it without telling the child an actual lie, Annorah thought.

Thomas was their personal welcoming committee. He ran ahead of them to the tree where the children were assembled, shouting the news that Miss Norah had brought a friend. There was the initial chaos of introductions as Annorah tried to introduce all the children by name and Nicholas at the same time.

Vicar Norton was thrilled to meet Nicholas, declaring having three adults would make the reading circles so much better. 'I've always found smaller groups are more conducive for learning. One can't rely on others as much. It encourages responsibility for what one knows and sometimes for what one doesn't know,' he confided as he broke the children into their sections.

Annorah shot Nicholas a covert glance to see how he was taking it all. Surely he hadn't got up this morning, thinking to spend the day under a tree reading with children. Regardless of what he thought he'd be doing, he didn't seem to mind this change of plan. He was smiling and nodding at whatever the vicar was saying and two children, Danny and Esme, had already attached themselves to each of his hands.

Before long, all three groups were settled in the shade. Little Annie was in Annorah's lap and all was as usual, except that her eyes kept straying to the spot where Nicholas sat, looking entirely at ease. Every once in a while she'd catch his voice saying things like, 'Try that sentence again, you've almost got it. Remember, the A will say its name because the word ends in an E. There, that's very good.' Or, sometimes sternly, but never meanly, 'Jack, you have to sit still. We're not done yet.'

The sight and sound of him working with the children did odd things to her stomach that had nothing to do with her impending dilemma. He would have made a fine headmaster; strict but kind.

When lessons were done, he played tag with some while Annorah made daisy wreaths with others. He was 'it' and he was sweeping the children up and swinging them around in wide circles when he caught them, much to their screams of delight.

Annorah nearly lost her composure then. Watching him like this was as potent as the fantasy he'd woven last night. His hair had come loose from all the rough-housing, his jacket was off, his sleeves rolled up, a huge smile on his face as he played with the children. He looked like he was having fun, *genuine* fun, like he'd looked yesterday at the river. There'd been moments—tugging in the fish, swimming—when he'd looked like this, like Nicholas, a person.

Of course, that was a ridiculous conclusion. He was Nicholas, he always looked like Nicholas. But this Nicholas was different in some subtle way. This Nicholas was real. Her heart constricted with the power of this revelation. The Nicholas who sat at her dinner table, who had strolled in her garden and made clever innuendo and sent her silk nightgowns was likeable, too, *very* likeable. But there was a slickness to that man that put him beyond reality. He was a fantasy come to life, in some ways a product of her imagination. That was not the case with the man who cavorted on the grass with the children. This Nicholas was so very real it nearly brought tears to her eyes to watch the simple pleasure of them playing. This Nicholas would be a magnificent father, with love and time to give aplenty. The other Nicholas was easy to like. This Nicholas would be far too easy to love. This was a man she could want.

At last, Nicholas led his troops over to her and plopped down beside her. 'Did you make me one?' He was sweaty and messy and his blue eyes were laughing as she slipped a daisy wreath over his head.

'You're fun, Mr Nick.' Thomas scooted on to his lap. He hadn't left Nicholas's side since they'd arrived. 'Will you come again? Please?' Thomas looked beseechingly at Annorah, his earnest little face breaking her heart. 'Please say you'll bring him back.'

Annorah bit her lip and cast a silent plea Nicholas's direction. What to say? The truth? Would it be better to tell a half-truth and raise false hope?

'Thomas, I'm not sure I'll be back,' Nicholas began, jiggling Thomas on to his lap. 'I'm only here for a short while to help Miss Annorah with her books. Then I have to go back to London. I'd like to come again, but I don't know if I will be able to.' Before Thomas could protest, Nicholas leapt to his feet. 'Who wants to come with me? I have an errand to run before Miss Annorah and I go.' Within moments, he was off, a gaggle of children surrounding him like a noisy cloud, leaving Annorah to pick up the books and chat with the vicar.

'Your friend is good with them.' Vicar Norton helped collect the books and slates. He was a likeable man in his early fifties. He and his wife had been here five years now, ever since the last vicar had died. 'He's a good influence on them. Too often men don't have time to spend with their families.'

Annorah smiled. It was one of Norton's favourite topics from the pulpit; the importance of fathers being more than breadwinners for their families. 'I think he enjoyed himself today, too.' She wondered what Vicar Norton might say if he knew what Nicholas really was, which was not exactly 'family man' material. How was it that a man so good with children would opt for the life Nicholas had chosen?

Nicholas and the children were back. Nicholas carried something and he stopped by the gig to strap it to the back. Annorah felt a butterfly of excitement flutter in her stomach. Did he have something planned for them? Is that what she wanted after last night? Could she settle for the return of Slick Nick? An idea came to her— maybe she could keep Real Nick a while longer if she tried hard enough.

They said goodbye to the children and set off, but not towards home. The day was sunny and warm and going home would only have meant facing uncomfortable truths. 'Where are we going?' Annorah asked.

Nicholas winked playfully. 'To the fairy fort. I have it on best authority from the children that nothing is better than a picnic there. I trust you'll know where it is if I get lost? I have to say their directions were a bit jumbled.'

Annorah laughed as he began describing the children's directions. 'Don't worry, I know where it is. I hate to mention this, but we don't have a picnic.'

'Yes, we do. The children helped me find the inn and talk Mr Witherby into providing us with a lovely lunch.'

Annorah felt her cares recede. She leaned back against the seat, closed her eyes and let the sun bathe her face. There was nothing better than this, a warm day, a drive in the country and an impending picnic at the old ring fort. 'You couldn't have known, but the fairy fort is one of my favourite places.'

'Then I'm glad the children suggested it.' There was a touching softness in his tone that made her open her eyes. He was looking at her, a quiet smile on his lips.

She paused before she ventured the next question. 'Did you mind?'

Nicholas shook his head, understanding her reference immediately. 'Not at all. I like children.'

A gentleman escort who liked children. That was a wondrous thing indeed. She would have to ponder what that meant. Nicholas D'Arcy was a man full of surprises and she had all afternoon to probe them. What a delightful pastime that would be and an important one if she wanted to keep Real Nick with her.

This must be what a honeymoon feels like, Annorah thought as she settled on the blanket and soaked in the warm sun while she watched Nicholas race up and down a length of grass with a kite outside the fort ruins, trying to catch the breeze. So far they weren't having much luck with the kite, but she didn't mind. She was having too much fun watching Nicholas run, barefooted. His boots had been the first to go when they arrived. He wore only his shirt and breeches and looked utterly boyish with his dark hair tied loosely behind him.

She offered a few suggestions as he passed. 'Let out the string, no, not too much.' The kite caught on a breeze and for a moment it was aloft. Nicholas shot her an exultant look and she smiled back, trying to ignore how the simplest glance from him could make her pulse race.

The kite swerved and crashed to the ground. Nicholas retrieved it and tried one more time to launch it. On his second attempt he gave up and fell on to the blanket beside her in a dramatic collapse. 'I give up! There's not enough wind.'

Sweat shone on his brow, a product of the warm day and his efforts. She wanted to remember him just like this: hair loose, casually clothed, lying on his side, one bare leg propped up. She closed her eyes, trying to capture the image of Real Nick.

'What are you doing?'

She opened her eyes to find him smiling gamely at her. 'I'm trying to make a picture of you,' Annorah confessed some of it. She wanted to remember everything about today: the last reading lesson, the children all gathered around them, how it might have felt to have a family, *to be* a family. It would seem a rather odd fantasy to fulfil for someone in Nicholas's profession. He probably didn't get many requests to play a family. 'I just wanted to remember—'

He didn't let her finish. Nicholas pressed a finger to her lips. 'There will be no talk of that.' He moved into her, kissing her softly. Would she ever get used to the way he touched her? The way he could make her feel with a simple kiss? *Don't you dare get used to it*, part of her railed. It's not real and he'll be gone anyway. But not yet. There was still time to fall: into his kisses, into his arms, into love. Those were dangerous words.

No, not love. She didn't dare. Annorah looked up into his eyes. This only *felt* like a honeymoon. It wasn't a real one. This wasn't the beginning of a life together. It was the end of the life she knew. But it was a good end. Here in the sun, she was glad she'd done it even if last night had shown her the limits of what a fantasy could do. 'I'm sorry for what I said this morning, about last night.' She would not apologise for wanting more, only for expecting it.

Her words seemed to catch him off guard. 'Are

you?' His eyes were darkening, turning to midnight in the middle of the day.

'Yes, I'm glad you're here.' Here at the end of all she knew. Of course, he'd be gone when the real end came, when her aunt sent the carriage that would take her to Badger Place and the dreaded house party and the odious suitor who waited for her final decision: the wilds of the North or her freedom in exchange for Hartshaven.

'I'm glad I'm here, too.' Nicholas smiled warmly and reached for her, drawing her close to him on the blanket. A shadow had fallen across her face, reminding him that for all the apparent perfection of her life, there was darkness in her. He'd seen it assert itself with the children. It had seemed an odd place for it to show itself. The children clearly made her happy and she was just as good with them as he'd imagined. But the darkness had been there, none the less.

He found himself eager to dispel that darkness. Annorah was a summer woman, with her mossy eyes and wild honey hair. She shouldn't be beset with darkness. He didn't think anyone else saw it. She masked it admirably and people weren't used to seeing a difference in those they saw every day. People also didn't see what they weren't looking for. No one had any reason to seek out the darkness in Annorah Price-Ellis, a woman who looked as if she were living a charmed life. But a man like him knew there was no such thing as a charmed life—perhaps that's why he saw it and others did not.

He felt his body begin to stir. He knew one way to dispel dark thoughts. Perhaps if he tried again, he could find a way to be more engaged for her. Perhaps he could give her a little piece of him. If she wanted to touch his core, so be it. She was an extraordinary woman, she would want extraordinary things. He could pull himself back any time he wanted to.

At least that's what Nick told himself on the picnic blanket in the middle of Nowhere, west Sussex. 'I'm having a grand time, Annorah.' Nicholas laughed. 'You've awakened the country boy in me. My city friends would be amazed. Do you know what else is fun to do on a picnic?' Nicholas whispered at her ear.

It was a rhetorical question. He undressed them

both, then moved over her, slow and sure, his mouth on hers as he entered her. This was languorous coupling at its best. He knew of no finer way to make love than on a picnic blanket, outdoors in a warm afternoon; there was nothing like feeling summer air on bare skin to release one's inhibitions, to feel at one with nature. With the slowness, the tenderness, he was promising her he'd be there at the end of it, that she would not make the journey to pleasure alone today.

Annorah moaned as she stretched into him and Nicholas let the joy of honest lovemaking take him. In the midst of the enchanted summer afternoon, he let his carefully curbed restraint slip its leash, finding true release at last—a slow, cresting wave that rolled endlessly over both of them before depositing them on its far shore. Whether Annorah knew it or not, he'd just given her all he could, all he'd not given anyone in quite some time, certainly not since he'd come to London. It was one of an escort's many secrets: avoid emotional attachment at all costs. As with any business, there was no room for sentiment *and* money.

In the aftermath of their lovemaking, he wasn't

sure why he'd done it. He wasn't sure he'd even planned to do it when he'd started. In the heat of coupling he'd simply been overcome.

'I think it might be true that this place is enchanted,' Annorah murmured, curled against his side, his arm wrapped about her. She traced a circle around the flat of his nipple with her finger. He revelled in her touch and what it signified. She was becoming comfortable with him. He could nudge them towards more sensual play if she was willing.

'Is it?' Nicholas was drowsy beside her. He'd be happy to chalk his choice today up to the work of fairies. It was better than the alternative.

'All the Iron Age forts are enchanted around here. They're considered the natural abode of fairies.' Annorah gave a soft laugh. 'We don't have pirate gold like your home, but we have fairies, especially in west Sussex.'

'I never said it was pirate gold,' Nicholas corrected playfully. 'So, what kind of fairies are here?'

'Oh, all sorts.' Annorah propped herself up, warming to the subject. 'There's sweat fairies that help you with work, there's pucks or goblin fairies. Really, there's a fairy for everything. If you know the chants, you can call the fairies to you. There's one my nurse taught me: come in the stillness, come in the night, come soon and bring delight.' She blushed a little, perhaps seeing the words differently after last night.

'It sounds very promising.' Nicholas chuckled. 'We'll have to see if it works.'

They spent the rest of the afternoon staring at clouds and searching for shapes. She sang fairy chants to him and wove crowns from wild flowers, but even as the idyllic day passed Nick was aware of a creeping tension beneath it all. He was starting to worry. He had not bargained on this: on feeling a closeness with her, on wanting to ask her what the darkness was that she held inside. There was danger in that. If he asked, then he'd know and he'd want to help. Where had this rush of sentiment come from? He'd navigated women and their needs for four years without such a reaction. Perhaps it was the product of having let himself foolishly step over the line with the love-making. Maybe it was only the weather.

By the time they climbed back into the gig to go home, the blue sky had become overcast. Grey clouds had overtaken the fluffy white ones and a breeze had come up. 'We could fly that kite now,' Annorah joked, raising a hand to steady her hat.

Nicholas cast a grim eye to the sky. 'It will be a summer storm by tonight.'

'Rain perhaps,' Annorah contradicted, laughing at his seriousness. 'Hardly a storm. But it's a good thing we went fishing yesterday. The river will be too deep for it tomorrow.'

Rain, storm, call it what you will. That would create a complication for him. He never slept well during storms—too many nightmares, too many memories that stirred to life.

Chapter Ten

By evening, he thought they both might be wrong. The sky had stayed gloomy, but the rain had held off. They stayed inside for dinner and afterwards they walked the second-floor gallery, where all the Price-Ellises past were on display. Nicholas had brought a second champagne bottle, pouring them brimming, bubbly glasses as they strolled.

They were laughing again, heads together as she spun tale after tale of her family. There was Great-Uncle August, who'd wisely invested in canals, Aunt Flora, who married the shipping magnate and inherited all his millions when he drowned in a sailing accident. There was Grandfather George, the one who taught her to fish and who'd played ceaselessly with the grandchildren.

'Who are these?' Nicholas pointed to a set of portraits at the end of the line when her dissertation trailed off.

She hesitated and Nicholas wondered if maybe she'd meant to stop the tour before she'd got that far. 'Those are my parents.' She didn't want to say more. He could hear the finality in her tone, but he couldn't let it be. Instinct told him he was close, close to the mystery and close perhaps even to the darkness she kept deep inside.

Curiosity pushed him to ask, 'What happened to them?' His voice was soft in the darkness, coaxing an answer.

'There was a fever here fifteen years ago. It hit a lot of families in the village, rich and poor alike.'

Ah, Nick understood the underlying message. Even the Price-Ellises had succumbed; their enormous fortune could not save them from death.

'Grandfather had already passed away by then, as had Flora and Augustus. They'd had good long lives, but my parents had been young. My mother went first, exposed most likely to the illness by caring for those suffering in the village. My father died two days later ostensibly from fever, but I've always thought he simply hadn't the will to live without her. My aunt Georgina left after that. She packed up my cousins and me and we went to live with her husband's family.'

'You lived away from here?' Nicholas asked as they moved down the row to the final pictures.

'For a few years.' Annorah blew out a breath. 'My aunt tried. She saw to it that I had a nice coming out, that I met eligible men, but I was a disappointment to her and after a while I just came back home.'

There was more to it than that. Nick would wager his diamond stick pin. No one just came home to live alone when one's family was able to provide for them.

'I see,' Nicholas said thoughtfully, pouring more champagne. There was more to know, but she was done with those stories for tonight. 'Well, I, for one, am very glad you did. Otherwise, I would not have been able to learn about fairy chants. I liked that one you did today.'

He took the glass from her and set it aside. Annorah protested. 'What's the point of filling the glass if you won't let me drink it?'

'Tut-tut, Annorah,' he scolded with a grin. 'I

didn't think your imagination was that limited. Champagne is good for other things besides drinking.' It was time to test her willingness to venture further into the sensuality that lay between them. He'd been eyeing the upholstered velvet viewing-benches in the middle of the gallery since they'd come up. Those benches offered infinite possibilities and positions.

'Come, Annorah,' Nicholas beckoned from the benches, his hands resting on the waistband of his trousers, a tried-and-true technique for drawing her eye to that place where no decent woman looked at a man. He watched her eyes widen first with surprise and then delight as she realised exactly what else champagne could be used for.

He held out his hand and drew her into his arms, whispering the fairy spell in her ear. 'In the darkness, in the night, we two will find our delight.'

He favoured her with the long slow kisses she loved, her excitement and arousal growing apace beneath his lips. He danced her back to the edge of the wide bench, but Annorah had other ideas, ideas sparked by the champagne bottle.

'I've learned my pleasure well,' she whispered huskily. 'Now it's time to learn yours.'

His pleasure. He was already hard, the very words a potent aphrodisiac. Nicholas could not recall a time when his pleasure had been important to a partner. This was new territory indeed and most unexpected. He'd driven her to impossible lengths of pleasure over the last two days. What could she do to him? Was it possible she might bring him to that same brink? This afternoon, he'd brought his own pleasure. It was the only excuse he had for what had happened. What would he have left if *she* could do that to him?

Annorah tugged at his cravat, drawing it free in a fluid movement. His shirt came next, pulled from his waistband by eager hands. She unbuttoned it, running her hands up the contoured atlas of his chest, her fingers tracing each sculpted ridge and plane as they explored upwards, thumbs rubbing over the nub of his nipples. He felt them pebble in response to her soft strokes. He took a ragged breath. 'That feels good.' And it did. He was not playacting.

Her touch on his bare skin created the most delightful of fevers in his blood. His body ran hot for her, his phallus rigid and straining. How far did she mean to take this? Nicholas tested the waters with a kiss. If she was ready for him to take over, he'd know. She returned his kiss only briefly with a scold. 'I'm not done with you yet. Why don't you sit?'

Nicholas did as he was told, his blood surging in anticipation. She knelt before him, working the fastenings of his trousers, her intentions becoming clear. She meant to pleasure him as he had her at the river. Nicholas leaned back on his arms, affording her better access. She gave him a wicked smile, her hand finding his length. Nicholas gave a groan at her first stroke. His honey-haired Annorah had become a temptress, but there was awe in her eyes, too. She was exploring him, literally learning him as much as she was seducing him and the combination was intoxicating.

Her thumb rubbed over the tender head, almost reverently, spreading the bead of moisture down his length until he was slick with her ministrations, the pressure of the pleasure she brought building slowly, unmistakably inside him. Then she upped the ante.

Annorah's other hand sought the tight sac of his balls and squeezed. He gave a primal moan. 'Oh, God.' He wouldn't last long at this rate. 'Use your nails,' Nicholas ground out. She did, a light, tantalising stroke of fingernails across the tender skin of his balls. He clenched his buttocks against an uncontrolled climax, wanting to make this last. He wasn't ready to let go of this now, or ever if it were possible. But Annorah wasn't done yet. She held his eyes, her own green gaze dark with desire and the thrill of having discovered a woman's power. Her hand reached for the champagne bottle. Just the thought of what she meant to do nearly drove him to orgasm, clenched buttocks or not.

She dribbled the bubbly on the tip of his phallus and gave him the naughtiest, most enticing of looks. 'And you thought I had a limited imagination.'

'I thought wrong.' Nicholas managed to get the words out as her warm mouth closed over the most male part of him. He thought very little, right or wrong, after that. When climax took him it was all-encompassing, robbing him of any complicity, any control in the act. He'd bucked hard against her, giving her the merest of warnings before his release surged. She'd been ready for him, rocking back on her heels and taking him in her hand as he pulsed and spent, for her, because of her.

Had he ever been so thoroughly worshipped? It was his first thought in the utter clarity that followed climax, that perfect moment when the world made sense. His pleasure had been entirely at her behest. His release, when it had come, had not been under his own volition, but hers, a most extraordinary feat for a man who prided himself on being in charge of every aspect of the sexual act from beginning to end. There were no surprises that way.

He pulled Annorah to him. Her face was flushed, her hair falling down from the elegant pile she'd worn to dinner. She smelled faintly of the scents of sex. He thought her beautiful in the moments of his afterglow. That was not new. He'd thought her beautiful from the start in an understated way, but tonight her beauty radiated from somewhere deep inside her. This was a beauty that could not be duplicated with gowns and coiffures and expensive jewels. These intimate moments had completed her as much as they'd completed him. He told himself he'd seen women look that way before when he'd pleasured them. It needn't be a concern.

He would make love to her, give her reciprocity the best way he knew how later. For now, he simply wanted to lay on the wide velvet viewing-benches, half-clothed, and hold her until his strength returned. He was boneless. He couldn't summon the energy to even do up his trousers but he was in no hurry. When strength and consciousness returned, they would claim the serenity currently enfolding him.

Eventually, however, they did return. Annorah stirred against him, where she'd fallen into a drowsy nap, a hand on his chest where his heart beat. Nicholas gathered her to him and carried her to bed, his mind and body busy contemplating all the ways to wake her. When the first clap of thunder shook the skies, he didn't hear it.

Nick stood at the open bay of windows in Annorah's room, taking in the morning.

Outside the sun shone. Summer had returned to Sussex, but its brief hiatus was evident outside on the wet bricking of the veranda and he'd slept through it. He never slept well during storms. Champagne and sex had saved him last night. Fairy magic, too. He couldn't forget that. His list of explanations was getting ludicrous. He was going to have to face facts, but not just yet.

In the bed, Annorah stirred and raised up a bit. He turned to look at her. She was glorious in dishabille, her hair falling over one shoulder, her eyes dancing as she took in his naked self. 'I see it did rain, after all.' Nicholas nodded towards the outdoors.

'It did, and a little thunder, too, around one this morning.' Annorah flashed him a teasing smile. 'Not that you noticed. You were absolutely dead to the world.' Of course he was, he'd been pleasured within an inch of his life.

'You should have woken me if you couldn't sleep.' Nick walked back to the bed and slid beneath the sheets beside her. It was still almost impossible to digest. He'd slept through a storm? He could tell from Annorah's tone the weather barely qualified as a storm in her opinion. Still, there'd been thunder. Sleeping through a storm, even a light one, was something he hadn't been able to do for years.

Those were the evenings when the nightmares came. The only way to avoid them was to stay awake, but that was often just as tortuous, his mind plagued by real and waking 'what ifs'. What if he'd guessed sooner? What if he'd run faster? What if he hadn't stopped to put his boots on? Would those precious seconds have been enough? What if he hadn't been doing what he was doing in the first place? Maybe none of it would have happened.

'I wasn't awake for long.' Annorah snuggled against him, fitting her bottom against his groin. 'What shall we do today? Shall we search for treasure?'

Nicholas laughed, glad she couldn't see his face as he pushed aside his thoughts. 'Everything, anything.' Very soon he'd have to bring his end of the fantasy into line. Today was day four. The time had flown. He'd be leaving soon, perhaps that was for the best. She'd had her pleasure. He'd done his job and more.

Things had got out of control. He'd let himself wander too far from the usual path he trod. Last night he'd given himself over entirely to the fantasy as a gift to himself, but now he had to get back to business. It was time to start the gentle severing by putting some distance between them bit by bit today, so that tomorrow she'd be able to let him go. But first, a morning love game wouldn't go amiss. There would be time to say goodbye later. He dropped a kiss on to her hair and pushed up from the bed. 'Wait here, I'll be right back.'

There was something to be said for watching Nicholas walk away naked. In the light of day without a stitch on him, she could appreciate just how marvellously made he was and what fabulous shape he kept himself in: the well-muscled back, the lean waist, the smooth, taut perfection of his buttocks, bracketed as they were by the sexy indentations of his love handles. The only thing better was watching her man return.

Her man. He was truly that for a short while longer at least. Yesterday's lovemaking at the faerie ring had been more satisfying than the previous night. Something had changed for the better. It had not just fulfilled her physically, it had moved her. She had dared much with this last adventure and it had been worth it. It would be enough to sustain her, whatever choice she made and there was some comfort in that knowledge. 'What's in your hand?' Annorah nodded towards the satin bag he carried.

Nicholas gave a wicked grin and sat on the bed. 'Everything we need for a treasure hunt without leaving the room.' He opened it and pulled a roll of white silk that looked like lengths of bandages. 'You get to be the guide. For that, I need you to raise your arms above your head.'

She did as she was told, a bit surprised, however, when he began to tie her wrists to the bedposts. 'What are you doing?'

Nicholas smiled and kept working the lengths. 'The guide knows where the treasure is, but can't get the treasure herself. But she can tell the hunter where to look. We have to make sure you play by the rules. After all, you are something of a rebel.' He winked and she relaxed. It was only a game and the bonds were loose, tied more for effect than purpose.

He drew out two more lengths. 'Will you let me tie your legs?'

Annorah's mouth went dry, a wicked warmth pooling at her core at the suggestion and how that would be accomplished. In order for the lengths to reach the bedposts, her legs would not be tied together, but apart. She would be spreadeagled and exposed most intimately. The old Annorah, the one who had closeted herself away at Hartshaven, would have refused. Hands were adventure enough. But the new Annorah, or perhaps better termed the once and future Annorah, who took risks, said breathlessly, 'Yes. You may tie my legs.' She even bent them just so as her lover slid the bonds about her ankles. When he offered her the blindfold, she didn't hesitate.

'It's better for your senses if your eyes are shut,' Nicholas murmured in his seductive tones as he fastened it. 'There's no distractions, no visual interruptions to your pleasure.' She breathed deeply. The blind smelled faintly of him, as if it had been tucked in a drawer next to his clothing.

'If I'm the guide, who are you?' she whispered, surprised by the huskiness of her voice.

'I am the seeker, the hunter. But I can only go where you tell me to go.' Nicholas shifted his weight and she felt the bed move. He took up a straddle position at her hips, his buttocks resting on her thighs, the brush of his sac against her leg. Nicholas was right. She could feel everything much better and without being self-conscious. With her eyes shut, she was in a world of her own construction. There was the soft slide of fabric and she could hear him rummage in the bag again.

'Every treasure hunt needs a map,' Nicholas said softly. There was a quiet pop of a cork or bottle stopper being removed. The scent of lavender mixed with something else pleasant filled the room. She heard him blow out a breath. 'I have the lotion made especially for me in London. I'm warming the lotion in my hands before I put it on your body.' His words sent a shot of heat through her. There was another breath. 'It's ready for you now.'

Nicholas's fingers touched her chin, letting the lotion's scent fill her nostrils with its nearness, setting the tone for their play. He drew his finger down the column of her neck. 'The treasure can be anywhere. Here at the river waterfall, or in the valley.' His hand rested between her breasts. 'Maybe it's in the mountains.' Both his hands traced simultaneous paths of circles up to the peaks of her breasts. 'Perhaps the treasure is at the summit.'

She felt her nipples tighten as his thumbs ran over their tips. Even the lightest of touches teased them mercilessly. His warm hands moved down her midriff, massaging with the lotion. Annorah wished her legs were free. She wanted more than anything to rub her legs together, to offer herself some measure of relief against the need rising in her. She felt deliciously aroused and yet raw with desire, every nerve on edge. She arched, straining against the bonds in a futile effort.

'Tut-tut,' Nicholas scolded playfully. 'None of that yet.' His hands drifted to her thighs, his thumbs teasing the slick folds that lay between. 'You may only cry out once we've found the treasure.'

She understood the game completely now— how long could she last?—and of course the underlying assumption that the longer she did last, the greater the arousal she'd achieve and subsequently the greater the release.

His hands caressed down her legs even to her feet. 'The map is complete.' He placed a tantalising kiss behind each knee as he journeyed back up. The mapping had aroused him, too. She could feel the firm length of his erection against her leg. 'Tell me where to look, Annorah.'

He was over her, his breath soft on her lips. 'Is it here in this cave of wonders?' He kissed her. She opened her mouth to him, letting his tongue tease the tip of hers, letting him taste her.

'Try the mountains,' she offered after a while and he journeyed south. His tongue could do marvellous things, she reasoned. Perhaps it could even cool the fire in her skin. Her 'mountains' were more like volcanoes, her flesh heated and sensitive to his touch. The heat was not unpleasant, but the constant burn of pleasure was fast driving her towards the madness of wanting to claim the ecstasy she knew awaited.

Nicholas sucked and laved each peak until she thought she would snap. Only the wanting of his mouth at one final destination delayed her cry. 'The forbidden springs,' she gasped the command in a near fever pitch.

He was there at last, his mouth at her core, his tongue flicking over her pearl, the treasure within the folds. Annorah cried out at last. Nicholas moved between her legs, his mouth replaced by the hot length of his phallus, not at her nub but at her entrance. He thrust home. Climax was swift and powerful as it came. She felt as if the great pressure that had built within her had been released in one enormous burst, the force of it explosive and welcome. Nicholas collapsed against her, spent, his heart pounding, and he held her to him. What an extraordinary way to start a morning. She felt as if she could live on this moment for ever. She might have to.

Chapter Eleven

Over their now very tardy breakfast, Nicholas tried out the farewell in his mind. Tomorrow, they'd make love one last time when they woke, and they'd have a lingering meal. He didn't want to create the impression he was in a hurry to leave. He would depart, probably in the late morning for the sake of not dragging his goodbye out. He needed to be gone by eleven if he was to make the opera with Lady Burnham, who was expecting him. She'd booked him for the evening weeks in advance.

Annorah sat across from him, looking fresh and radiant after their treasure hunt in a pink muslin dress sprigged with white flowers, her hair put up simply. She looked happy and content, relaxed even. Would she look that way tomorrow? He was met with a twinge of sadness at the thought. After tomorrow, he would not see Annorah Price-Ellis again. This was not a sentiment he was used to when an assignment ended. But this short week had been utterly different.

He'd had perfection for a short time. He was not foolish. He understood the importance of the word 'short' in that sentence. Perfection was an expensive fire to fuel and could not be sustained for long. Eventually, this, too, would pale. Better to leave while the bubble was still in the wine. But the thought nagged at him over his eggs: to never see her again?

Unless she came up to London and sought him out. He hoped not. That was an idea he rapidly pushed away. He wanted Annorah to remember him as he'd been here, not as the man she'd see in London: the paid escort, the man who made husbands jealous by paying indecent attention to their neglected wives.

Nor did he want Annorah to know him beyond this context. He was riddled with imperfections. To know him much better would only sully him in her eyes and that would bring all nature of implications, not least of which would be—how could she have associated with such a man? He'd found it was much easier for women to love the fantasy than the reality of him.

'What's on your mind? You are a thousand miles from here.' Annorah glanced at him over the rim of her tea cup. Was she thinking: *he's already left?* She'd be wrong, though. He was in no hurry, and in many ways he was reluctant to go. Lady Burnham's opera box had lost much of its appeal.

'I'm sorry, I didn't mean to drift.' He was about to ask her what they should do today, but Plumsby entered, carrying a silver tray with the mail.

'Miss, there are letters.' Plumsby offered the salver to Annorah and then turned to him. 'There is a letter for you, too, sir.'

Nicholas took it with no small amount of worry. It would be from Channing. No one else knew where he was. But what would Channing have to say that could not hold another twenty-four hours? He tucked the letter into his coat pocket. He would wait and read it privately. Instead, he picked up the newspaper that lay carefully pressed beside his plate and rose. 'I'll give you some time with your letters. I'll be outside read-ing and enjoying the morning sun.'

'You don't have to go,' Annorah protested quickly, too quickly. Ah, so she was feeling it, too; the desperation of the last day, a desire to make every moment of their waning time to-gether count. He didn't want that, didn't want her thinking she'd fallen in love with him. He no more wanted it for her than he wanted it for himself.

'You'll only be a few minutes.' Nick gave her a reassuring smile, but did not relent on his de-cision. Like it or not, it was time to start plant-ing some of that distance between them. There were little ways to do it, he'd learned over the years, yet another of his escort secrets. It could be done in the slight stiffness of his posture and the slight condescension of his tight smile, let-ting his body say what words would make too cruel to hear: *it's time to start remembering this is business. You and I have ties to sever.*

When he got back to London he'd tell Chan-ning he'd never take another long assignment. This one had got too deep under his skin; it had him sleeping through stormy nights and finding genuine release in the act of coupling. Last night had been startling in so many ways. If he was smart, he'd leave it at that and not dissect those ways. No good could come from it.

Outside on the veranda, he opened Channing's letter and scanned the brief contents. Channing must have been in a hurry to make the post. There were only a few lines and the message was clear: he was not to come back. Burroughs was still on the warpath. Although fewer people were listening to his accusations, Burroughs had become more convinced of his suspicions that the man in the house had been Nicholas. Lady Burroughs had likely fed that fire, Nicholas thought uncharitably. Her sense of fortitude and perseverance had never really impressed him as being in great supply. The other lines of the note offered assurance that the agency wouldn't suffer in his absence. Amery would take Lady Burnham to the opera and see to his other appointments.

Nicholas stared at the note. He was not to go back. Just a few more days, Channing had written. Nicholas understood the double jeopardy. There was danger not only to himself, but to the agency, the League of Discreet Gentlemen. If one of them were exposed, so might they all be.

Not all of them could afford the exposure; Channing Deveril most certainly could not. He was the son of an earl. Jocelyn Eisley was an earl's *heir.* While Nicholas did this for the money, Jocelyn did it for the thrill and the adventure. Jocelyn had no need of funds. Jocelyn and Channing would certainly suffer for a bit, but they'd eventually recover. Nick wasn't so sure about himself and Grahame Westmore. As a former officer who'd worked his way up in the ranks to attain the commendation, Westmore had desperate need of the social connections Channing's agency provided him. Without the agency, Westmore would be destitute and, what's more, he'd be cast out. As would Nicholas himself. His situation was much more akin to Westmore's these days.

There was a rustle of skirts behind him. Annorah had finished reading her correspondence. Nicholas tucked the note back into his pocket and pasted on a polite smile before he turned to face her. 'How were your letters?'

The look on her face answered before words could. Something had upset her. Nicholas's gut clenched and all pretence of distance was set aside. Her face was pale and her hands gripped one another at her waist. 'We have to talk.'

Usually, when a woman said that, it meant one of two things: she wanted to declare undying love for him or it meant she thought she was pregnant. The latter was impossible. He'd been careful with his French letters, besides the fact that it was far too soon to know such a thing. As for the former, he was prepared for that, an occupational hazard. He'd handled it several times before. He knew how to let them down easy. He wondered who would let him down this time. He'd become far too caught up in this for his peace of mind.

'Annorah, what is it?' He stepped towards her, taking those tightly clenched hands in his grip.

'I have a business proposal for you. I know we aren't supposed to talk about such things, but this can't wait. My aunt Georgina has invited me to her house party.' She held up the invitation in her hand. 'Actually, she's been inviting me for weeks. Will you come with me?' She rushed to add, 'I will pay you.'

The offer would have been a miracle from the gods if not for that last part, given Channing's news. Nicholas pushed a hand through his hair. She looked so desperate but he didn't want her to beg any more than he wanted to feel cheapened by the money she'd attached to the request. He'd at least like to pretend money had nothing to do with his acceptance as he'd done with Channing.

It sat poorly with him that she might think he would allow himself to be bought. Although that was foolish in the extreme. She already knew he *could* be bought. He'd been paid to come here, after all. The idea that he'd go anywhere, do anything as long as he was paid suggested he had absolutely no moral code. That was not the man he wanted to be in her eyes.

You shouldn't care what she thinks, came the firm voice in his head, the one that helped him keep a practical equilibrium when his emotional balance was threatened. It seldom happened these days, but it was rearing its head now as she faced him on the veranda, anxiety written on her features. Not all of the anxiety was focused on his acceptance. The event that had prompted the offer had no doubt contributed, too. The need to defend her stirred deep inside him, primal and protective as it awoke. Nothing would invade her sanctuary if he could help it and the rules of the game be damned. 'Who do you need me to be?'

Annorah held his gaze as she said words that nearly floored him in the most literal sense. 'I need you to be my husband.'

'It's not that simple,' Nick began, trying to gather his thoughts but there were so many of them at the moment it was like herding cats— why did she need a husband so suddenly? What was it about this house party that had her anxious to the point of paleness? What was he to say to her? A husband was the one thing he couldn't be, temporary or otherwise.

'Yes, it is that simple.' Annorah's response was quick and fierce. Her hands gripped the invitation, leaving indents in the white paper. 'London is a half-day's ride. You can ride out this morning, get a special licence and be back tomorrow. We can marry the next day before we leave for the party.'

Two thoughts emerged from the pack roiling in his head. One, she'd thought all this out in the short time he'd left her, and, two, she meant for this to be a legal marriage. She wasn't asking him to play her husband. She was asking him to be her husband, as in for ever and ever until death did them part.

'Please, Nicholas. I'm running out of time. You are my last hope. I know it's sudden and I know it's crazy—please consider it. I swear I'll pay you handsomely. You'll never want for anything.'

'Except perhaps my freedom and my pride. Two things, I assure you, a man holds dear.' His words were sharp and they cut; he could see the hurt in her eyes. This was getting worse by the minute. He should pack his bags and walk away right now. There was nothing but trouble behind this offer. Besides, he shouldn't even consider it. He couldn't be her husband. He'd already betrayed his family. He wouldn't betray hers, too, by aligning them with his dirty past. This was absolutely as far as his association with her could go. Yet his boots couldn't seem to find their way off the veranda.

Oh, Lord, he was going to refuse and why shouldn't he? She'd just offered him the same arrangement that had been offered her: money for her freedom. She had resisted such a situation for years. Why should Nicholas D'Arcy be any different? She would let him out of it eventually, if she could. But for now, she wasn't sure that was something she could legally promise.

Annorah hoped she didn't look as desperate as she felt. She didn't want his pity, but she would tolerate it if that's what it took. If anyone was going to help her face this, it would be him. Her aunt had sent a 'gentle reminder' that the coach would come for her the day after next and that she should pack all she would need. Mr Bartholomew Redding was looking forward to becoming reacquainted and there were high hopes all around for a match this time. She did remember Mr Redding, didn't she? He'd courted her once and still held her in high esteem.

That had put her into a high panic. Redding was the stuff of nightmares, the very man who had nearly forced her into marriage years ago. It had all come down to marry or surrender and this morning, those options weren't good enough. There had to be some middle ground.

That's when she'd thought of Nicholas. He could be her middle ground, the husband who saved Hartshaven. He would certainly be a far more tolerable husband than Redding, who'd suspiciously buried two wealthy wives already and who had attempted to force his attentions on her once before.

'Annorah, what is going on?' Nicholas took the card from her. At least he was still standing there. That had to be a good sign.

Now she had to give him an honest answer. 'My aunt Georgina is hosting her annual house party and she has someone she wants me to meet. I'd prefer not to meet him.' There, that was succinct and to the point.

Nicholas crossed his arms and leaned back against the brick planter. 'You could simply stay home.'

Annorah shook her head. 'I know it looks like an invitation, but it's really a summons in disguise. She holds a house party every year in the hopes of matching me up with someone.' It was a party designed to drill Annorah with guilt for having failed the family. She knew very well her aunt held the party near or on her birthday to serve as a reminder time was passing. Every year she remained unmarried was a year closer to the family's demise, in her aunt's eyes.

'This year, she's been particularly determined.

She's been writing since April.' There was too much history she didn't want to unearth.

Nicholas handed the invitation back to her. 'I'd make her come here.' Mischief was starting spark in his eyes.

'And risk being unable to dislodge her?' Annorah had an answer ready for that. 'I think not. I'd much rather be able to leave and be rid of her when I choose.' But that was merely the surface. She knew better than Nicholas that this was not a minor female power struggle over who could make whom do what. Or maybe not. Nicholas seemed to sense the incompleteness of her answers.

He held out his arm. 'Come walk with me, Annorah, and tell me what's really going on.'

'What makes you think anything is going on?' Annorah said crossly.

'Well, for starters, you want to make your secret librarian-consort of four days into your husband. Forgive me for thinking a game is afoot.' It was not said unkindly and they both laughed a little, the sun returning to their morning. Nicholas covered her hand with his where it lay on his arm and said more seriously, 'I've known from the start that a woman like you doesn't hire a man like me unless she is desperate. Tell me everything, Annorah. What has caused a beautiful, wealthy woman to think she has no way out except marriage to me?'

Annorah turned her face to catch his gaze, moved by his words, the soft tenor of his voice filled with genuine concern. She felt her throat tighten as the words spilled out. 'I'm only wealthy if I marry by my thirty-third birthday. If I don't, by next week, I lose all of this.'

Chapter Twelve

'What?' Nicholas's head shot up, his brow knit. Surely, he had misheard or maybe he'd misunderstood. But he hadn't. He knew the truth of it in his gut. This was the answer to the darkness and it shattered the perfection of Hartshaven.

'If I remain unwed by the age of thirty-three, the Price-Ellis fortune reverts to charity and the church,' Annorah said plainly.

The answer might be simple enough, but its implications were not. Questions rioted in his head as Nicholas tried to grasp all the tendrils spiralling from the premise. Why hadn't she married? Surely there had been suitors? Any one of them could have stopped this from happening, from getting this far. But that was the mystery. *Why* had it got this far?

'Have you challenged the will?' It was the question he was least interested in having answered, but it was the most harmless of the questions swirling in his mind.

'Of course I've had it looked at.' Annorah gave him a withering look. 'I've had every lawyer of merit in England take it apart piece by piece. Not one of them found anything wrong with my father's request. In the eyes of legal England, there's nothing unusual about a father setting conditions on how and when a fortune is handed over to his only surviving child.' She shrugged. 'When put that way, I am hard pressed to quibble with the letter of the law. People set similar conditions like that all the time when it comes to inheritance.'

'But the spirit of the law?' Nicholas prompted.

She gave a wan smile. 'I find little to dispute over the spirit either. My father didn't want me to be alone. He believed the inheritance being contingent upon my marriage would ensure I *would* marry. When, in fact, it has ensured just the opposite. Fortunes attract the most unattractive of men.'

Nicholas could imagine a drawing room full

of questionable gentlemen: sharps and shades, gamblers and roués. 'But surely a fortune would have drawn a nobleman or two?' he pointed out. He knew several barons and even viscounts who wouldn't mind seeing their second sons married to such wealth, even if it came without a title.

Annorah's answer was tart. 'Having a title doesn't preclude a man from being an inveterate fortune hunter. There were plenty of titles looking for money. I just didn't want to be married for the sake of being married. Nor did I want to be bartered away for my money.' She looked up at him. 'I thought to wait it out. I thought something better, something honest, would come along. When you're eighteen, fifteen years seems like for ever.'

There was hurt in her tone. Her green eyes held sadness. Nicholas pieced a little more of the picture together. He could see how a woman like Annorah, who'd come from parents who had loved one another intensely, would be ruined by the idea of marrying simply to protect her money. Jaded and disillusioned, perhaps even broken-hearted. No, definitely broken-hearted, Nicholas decided. Young and impressionable, she would have thrown herself into love, believing that any-one she courted would feel the same. It was why she'd demanded his lovemaking be more than a performance. She would not settle for half-mea-sures from anyone, even herself.

'And now you are desperate for a husband at the eleventh hour?' Nicholas said softly. Her prin-ciples had betrayed her here at the last. There'd been no knight in shining armour.

'Yes, or else I must pluck up the courage to face a new life in the north.' She played with her fingers, lacing and unlacing them. 'I've had all this time to decide what my choice will be and I still haven't made up my mind. If I don't decide, it will be made up for me.'

Exile. That was what the new life in the north was. She'd be cut off from life as she knew it both in terms of family and finances. Nicholas had no doubts the family that remained would not tolerate that choice and remain on friendly terms. 'Didn't your aunt say she had someone for you to meet? She has a suitor for you.' He meant for the words to be encouraging. There was an eleventh-hour husband waiting in the wings, although it galled him to think so. He had to think about what was best for her.

Annorah stopped him with a swift glare. 'Bartholomew Redding is the man my aunt has chosen. I know who he is and I'd rather the choice of a husband be mine. He is not a man I would willingly tie myself to.'

But she would bind herself to him, a man she barely knew, Nicholas mused, even when she knew nothing about him, which spoke volumes as to Bartholomew Redding's character. Of course, if she really knew him, she'd be less inclined to throw herself away. The north might start looking a whole lot better.

'I'm not husband material, Annorah,' Nicholas began apologetically.

'I'm not asking you to be a husband in the traditional sense. I'll make it worth your while. I'll set up a fund for you and, after a decent period of time, I'll let you go your own way. I fear I may not be able to give you a divorce, but I can give you some freedom. I won't demand much.' She was begging. It soured his stomach to see her so desperate and he so powerless to help.

Nick shook his head. If she couldn't give him

a divorce, she would be tied to him for ever with no hope of escaping his sins. 'Think what you're asking, Annorah. You would bind yourself in marriage to a man you know nothing about, who you've known for four days, and what you do know of him is that he's a paid escort. In case you didn't know, I'm scandalous.'

'Your worst secret is better than a life sentence with Redding.'

'You don't know that.'

'I do. I saw you with the children, I saw you fishing and flying a kite and when I asked you for the one thing I wanted, you gave it to me.'

She was talking about how he had found fulfilment in the sex they had shared. It touched him that she had indeed recognised what that had cost him.

'You are a good man, Nicholas. I understand you may not love me, but you will not hurt me. Nor do I think you would disappoint those children by letting Hartshaven go when you could save it.'

Oh, she did not play fair! He could see little Thomas and the others in his mind's eye, tugging on his hand, wanting to play. Truly, she did overestimate him. He was not good at all. But he was starting to crack all the same. Channing would take him to task for this. He was about to forsake all the rules of emotional detachment Channing had ever invoked. 'Would a fiancé do, Annorah?'

A little spark of hope flared in her eyes as she hesitantly laid out the conditions. 'You will have to sign papers and negotiate a settlement with my uncle. The will is specific that if there is only an engagement by my thirty-third birthday, it must be official and a wedding must take place within a year.'

Nicholas smiled. 'I will place an announcement in the papers right away.' It was a half-measure at best, but at least he could buy her time. A year was a long while—who knew what could happen? If it saved her from the likes of Redding, it would be worth it.

'You'll do it?' Annorah let out a breath. 'I know it's no small thing I ask.'

'I'll do it.' Channing was going to kill him. It would mean he couldn't work. Engaged escorts undoubtedly lost some of their appeal. Nicholas held out his arm. 'Why don't you walk with me and we'll design a story for this fabulous fiancé of yours and talk about your birthday.'

She took his arm and it seemed that the sun had returned to the morning. He tried to tell himself as they walked that his decision was about the money. This latest ruse would make him rich, perhaps rich enough to stop working and worrying. He told himself he was doing this for his family. He even told himself he was doing it for her because she touched him in some novel way. And why not do it? It wasn't permanent, merely longer term than he'd anticipated. But deep down, he really knew he was doing it for him because he wasn't ready to let her go, especially if it meant turning her over to another man, another fate.

'You shall be a gentleman's son with comfortable prospects.' Annorah began spinning their tale.

'Not too wealthy to draw their attentions, but not poor enough to draw their suspicions,' Nicholas put in, playing along. 'A comfortably situated gentleman's son,' he said slowly, trying out the words as if they represented some novel concept. 'Do I raise sheep or make my money on the exchange?'

'Definitely sheep. The exchange is too risky for my family's tastes.' Annorah laughed up at him.

Nicholas paused and plucked a daisy from the pathway. He tucked it behind her ear with a smile. 'Sheep it is. I think this is turning out to be a most pleasant fiction.'

They laughed away the afternoon, rambling the gardens and embellishing that fiction, but the question in the back of Annorah's mind grew larger with each new plot. How far from the truth was this little ruse? Who was Nicholas D'Arcy or, more to the point, who had he been before this? Was Nicholas even his real name? She supposed it didn't have to be. But *what* his name was mattered less to her than *who* he was, who he had been.

She had clues of course. His bearing was that of a well-bred man. There was a smoothness to his manners that could not be taught, all of which suggested playing a gentleman's son wouldn't be a stretch. He'd referred to roaming the land, the way one referred to an estate. He'd inadvertently indicated servants were a part of his early life when he'd talked of long summer days spent fishing until dark. But how did a gentleman's son end up escorting ladies, eating lutefisk with Norwegian immigrants in London's East End, while also fraternising with the likes of Burlington? These were the pieces that didn't quite fit the puzzle of Nicholas D'Arcy.

They stopped beneath a tree and she risked the question with a teasing smile. 'We've made a quite background for you. How close is it to the reality?'

Nicholas was not fooled by the light-hearted manner in which the question was asked. He picked up a stick from the ground and began fiddling with it. 'Does it matter?'

'I suppose not.' Annorah hesitated. She should not have given in to the curiosity. She should have let it be. It was enough that he was willing to do this for her.

'Then why did you ask?' Nicholas's blue eyes were hard. 'Are you afraid someone will recognise me?'

That had not been her direction, but it was better than confessing her real reason in asking: she liked him. She wanted to know everything about him. It had become an obsession. 'Will some-one?' There was a moment's fear. She should have thought of that and she hadn't. It wouldn't serve her purposes at all if someone knew him. In fact, it would be mortifying if her aunt knew she'd hired an escort.

'I doubt it, unless your family frequents the circles of the *ton*,' Nicholas said derisively. 'You needn't worry that I'll embarrass you.' It took her a moment to refocus her thoughts and realise the derision she heard was for himself, not for her.

Annorah reached for his hand. 'You would never embarrass me. I'll always be proud to stand beside you in any drawing room.'

The tightness of his features eased and he gave her a half-smile. 'It's a worthy sentiment, at least, but perhaps you should reserve judge-ment.' Nicholas threw the stick as far as he could. They watched it sail out into the meadow.

'You're the one I'm worried about. You haven't met my family yet.' She tried to restore levity.

'Why is that? Are they all like you?' He gave a mock look of horror at the possibility. But he had met them already through the portraits, through the stories Annorah had shared. They'd been likeable once. But no more; whatever sympathies he'd had for her father, pining away for her mother and leaving Annorah to fend for herself, were gone when weighed against the pressures he'd created for his only child in his rather idiotic will. Annorah's aunt was no better with her greed-based motivations for thrusting Annorah into a marriage, any marriage, to save her own portion of the estate's wealth.

'No!' Annorah gave him a playful punch in the arm, glad her tactic had succeeded.

He grabbed her about the waist and spun her around, she gave a yelp at the suddenness of the movement. The oak tree was at her back when he set her down. His arm rested over her head against the tree trunk, his body angled close to hers. She could smell the scent of him, all man and summer as he smiled down at her. 'Good. There should only be one of you.'

He kissed her and the fiction was back in place. Perhaps for them both. Annorah wanted to believe he could keep her safe and he wanted to believe it, too, even if it meant simply keeping her safe from him. She might look at him as if he were indeed her knight. Only he knew just how tarnished the armour was and he wanted to keep it that way. He was selfish. There were things about him he never wanted Annorah to know.

Chapter Thirteen

Financial security was a damnable thing, Nicholas thought once he'd had twenty-four–hours' distance to assess what he'd committed to. The enormity of it was beginning to swamp him. Annorah had left for the village with some last-minute errands. He had Hartshaven and all his thoughts to himself for the afternoon. He'd rather not have. Those thoughts were daunting.

For the first time in years, he could afford to contemplate the future, only to find that financial security had opened up other insecurities. Annorah had insisted on settling a large sum on him for his role as her fiancé and he had to take it— logistics required it. Logistics also created other consequences: he need not work again when this was done. That was the polite way of looking at it. The other way of looking at it was that he *could* never work again. His days as Nick the Prick were very likely at an end.

Nick strolled the veranda idly, letting his mind wander over the idea. Channing would be surprised. Channing had always predicted he'd go out with a bang, exiled over a hot-headed duel. No one, not even himself, had thought he'd quietly disappear into the respectability of a financially stable gentleman. On the surface that's what it would look like. He was engaged and he would be for a year. He could go back to London but he certainly couldn't pick up where he'd left off. Affianced men didn't work as paid escorts.

And London would know, too. In fact the whole city would know in another day. The engagement announcement would be printed in *The Times* for all to see. It was all part of making the engagement look legitimate. For all purposes, the engagement would be legal, it had to be in order to pass muster. Only he and Annorah would know the temporary intentions of that engagement. What they had invented in the garden paths the previous afternoon might be a fiction, but the implications would be real.

Nick supposed he could go back to work after his year was up, but he wouldn't need to. Annorah had made it possible for him to never need to work like that again. It wasn't the loss of the thrill of bedding women that bothered him. In truth, that had begun to pale before Annorah. There was no challenge in it. The nights all began with the same foregone conclusion. It was the loss of the identity that worried him. Who was he if he wasn't Nick the Prick? Who would he become? He had a chance to refashion himself and the thought was frightening.

Being a gentleman escort had always been his excuse for not going home. Now there would be none. He could go home and mend his fences and become a sheep farmer in truth if that was what he wanted. He could face his mother, his brother, his past. Would he? Or would he play the coward?

It was a lot to take in and that was only half of it. What would he do about Annorah? He'd pledged himself in a sham engagement to buy her a year. But then what? What happened when the year was up? It wasn't as if she could be courted by potential suitors during her engagement. It was unlikely there'd be another suitor waiting in the wings at the end of her year. Unless he could quietly help with that. He supposed he could ask Channing to send a few recommendations her way—nice, titled men who would treat her well.

His gut clenched at the thought. He didn't like that idea any more than he'd liked the idea of her marrying a stranger to save her estate. It wouldn't be the first time a woman had done such a thing. But he didn't want Annorah to join those ranks. Lucifer's balls! Nick sighed, dead-heading a peony. The woman had got under his skin and he was in over his head.

The future was a difficult subject to think about. Better to return to his usual method of taking each day as it came. They were leaving for Badger Place, her aunt's home, in the morning. Tonight would be their last night at Hartshaven and Nicholas knew exactly how he wanted to spend it: a private birthday evening for two, a chance perhaps to say a subtle farewell to their days in paradise.

No matter how the house party ended, everything was about to change between him and Annorah. At the very least, he'd return to London and they'd part. Engaged or not, he could not continue to live at Hartshaven and who knew what sort of arrangements they'd be required to uphold in order to protect the ruse. But those were thoughts for later.

If he meant to have a party, he'd best get started. Annorah wouldn't be gone for ever. There'd been a summerhouse he'd spied on one of their walks and an idea started to form, especially if the summerhouse was as well kept as the rest of the estate. Nick called for Plumsby and began to marshal his troops.

Three hours later, Nicholas stepped back to survey his work. The interior of the old summerhouse had been transformed into a rustic but romantic bower. The biggest job had been arranging the summerhouse furniture. He'd decorated the table with fresh flowers and an old set of dishes he'd scrounged from the kitchen. He'd moved the wicker chaise and matching chair to the front of the house where it overlooked the lake and draped the ageing furniture with quilts to disguise the wear—also perfect for cuddling under once the evening cooled and the stars came out. Best of all, set behind a dressing screen was the bed, now made with clean sheets and blankets and scented with roses for a night of pleasure. Annorah's nightgown and their personal items were neatly laid out on a makeshift bureau.

Everything was ready. Cook and a couple of footmen were bringing the supper down later. Champagne was chilling in advance. He even had a birthday cake arranged.

It was arguably his finest work. Not even the evening at the Greenwich Observatory he'd planned for Lady Carruthers came close to this. Quite possibly because this wasn't work. He didn't want to think of this as work anyway. He *wanted* to give her a birthday she'd never forget. He hadn't wanted Annorah to celebrate her special day on the road, or worse yet, to have to celebrate it at her aunt's, a place she had no desire to be. His family had always felt birthdays should be joyous occasions held in joyous places with people you loved. In the absence of anyone else, she would have to settle for him.

Easy, old boy. Nicholas reined in his thoughts. He needed some perspective. It was never a good sign when one started using adjectives like love and joy in the same sentence. Annorah had perspective. This was another level of business to her. Yes, she'd been emotional and distressed yesterday when she'd made her offer, but that didn't mean she was in love with him, or that she'd forgotten what he was. She was paying him. It was all still business to her at its core. Desperate business. She had rushed headlong into her decision, blind to the most obvious pitfalls in her effort to avoid 'the curse'. He hoped she'd forgive him for that if the worst happened. But that was all in the future. They would sort it out when and if it came.

For now, all that remained was returning to the house and inviting Annorah for an evening carriage drive. And settling on a gift. That was the one sticking point he hadn't managed yet in his plans. He knew what he'd like to give her, if he was brave enough. His friends in London, Amery and Jocelyn, would laugh at the notion he was afraid to give someone a gift so small it fit into a pocket. In their town circles, it was nothing more than a token of a gentleman's affections. It would not be so casually given tonight.

Annorah was waiting on the front steps when he returned from the summerhouse. She waved to him, making a fetching picture with one of her wide straw hats dangling from her hand. As he tooled up the drive in the little gig, he entertained the fancy that he was coming home to his house, that children would spill down the steps any moment, that his wife would call to them to stay out of the way of the prancing horse. *His wife*. Where had that notion come from? That was the danger of fantasies. They made you believe in the impossible.

Nicholas jumped down and took the steps two at a time. 'Are you ready for an evening drive?' He took her hand and tugged her towards the gig.

'What about dinner?'

Nicholas laughed and helped her up. It was just like Annorah to worry about upsetting someone else's schedule. 'Dinner has been taken care of. It's a beautiful evening and we're going to enjoy it.' He settled beside her and chirped to the horse. 'Tell me about the village. Did you get your errand taken care of?'

He let her regale him with news from the village even though he didn't know a soul beyond the children. She had encountered Thomas while she was there. Thomas had asked after him.

Nicholas smiled. The boy had made an impression on him, too, and his soul ached for all he'd never have. It was one more sign he'd fallen for his own fiction. He could never belong in a place like this or with a woman like this, so good, so decent. But it could be his for a while, if he dared. A cautious man would have left today when he was supposed to.

'What is this?' Her face was a mixture of excitement and incredulity as he swung her down. Her cheeks were flushed from the drive and her eyes sparkled as if she suspected some mischief on his part.

He grinned and put his hands over her eyes. 'You'll see. Keep your eyes shut and I'll guide you.' He led her up the shallow steps and ushered her inside. He made her wait while he lit the lamps and candles. 'All right, you can look.'

'Oh! It's beautiful!' Annorah gasped, her eyes trying to take it all in at once, but no matter where she looked, her eyes kept coming back to him. 'You did this? All this afternoon?' If he'd been uncertain or in denial of where he stood in this fantasy, there was no mistaking it now. When those eyes shone on him, with their genuine gratitude and delight, he was lost. Annorah Price-Ellis might possibly have succeeded in sweeping him off his feet when he'd least expected it.

'Happy birthday.' Nicholas dropped a kiss on her cheek. 'Dinner will arrive shortly, but perhaps I can interest you in champagne and the view?' He led her to the chairs overlooking the lake and poured their glasses. He should give her the gift now before he lost his nerve.

'I think a toast is in order.' Nicholas raised his glass. 'Happy birthday to a beautiful woman on a beautiful night. May you have many more.' It was the best he could do. The only other toast he could think of was one of Jocelyn's inappropriate rhymes: *another year lies behind, a new year lies ahead, may a lovely woman always lie in your bed.* No matter that it typified his hopes for the evening. What hopes? He wasn't some besotted swain. If he wanted her in bed, he'd have her. Good lord, had he really fallen so far into his fantasy that he'd forgotten he was Nicholas D'Arcy, seducer extraordinaire?

She tapped her glass against his. 'This is better than anything I thought I'd be doing tonight.'

Nicholas didn't need to ask what that would have been. She would have been packing, making last-minute preparations, and saying goodbye. 'You were supposed to be gone. I'm glad you're not.'

'Me, too.' Nicholas smiled softly, his gaze lingering on her mouth. He meant it. He'd had far more fun putting together this impromptu birthday celebration for Annorah than he would have had at the opera.

She raised her glass. 'I believe it's customary for the recipient of a toast to offer the next one. To you, Nicholas. This is beyond any of my imaginings.'

He was touched. Annorah's appreciation of those efforts was far more meaningful than Lady Burnham's desire to show him off to all her friends. 'If this is beyond your imagining, wait until after dinner, my dear. The night is young and so are we.'

He'd expected her to laugh at the little joke, but Annorah cocked her head and studied him, becoming serious. 'I'm turning thirty-three. How old are you?'

'Twenty-eight,' he said truthfully, although

there'd been a split second where he'd considered lying and saying thirty-three.

She looked down at her glass. 'I'm not so young any more.'

'Is thirty-three old?'

Annorah shrugged. 'Society thinks it is. My aunt thinks it is. It means I'll never have children of my own. I might manage to snare a widower and raise *his* children if I'm lucky.'

The similarity he'd felt with her that first night surfaced again. He knew what it was to give up hopes of that magnitude. Nicholas reached for her hand. 'There will be no more of that talk. We can't know what the future holds. It does us little good to worry over it.' Worry could no more change the future than it could prevent it.

Nicholas reached into his pocket, hoping to use his gift as a diversion. His fingers tightened over the little box. 'Where I come from, birthdays are often commemorated with a gift.' He put the box in her lap.

'How?' she asked with no small amount of awe. 'How could you do all this *and* come up with a gift? I wasn't gone that long.'

Nicholas smiled. 'Haven't you learned not to

ask? Let the impossible take care of itself. You don't need to know everything, it ruins all the fun. Besides, you haven't opened it yet.'

He held his breath as Annorah unfastened the lid. He watched her eyes light up and found himself smiling along with her. The cameo pendant dangled from her fingers, the filigree of the thin chain catching the light. 'It's gorgeous.' She paused, studying the detail work on the cameo engraving. 'It's too much. I can't possibly accept it.'

'Yes, you can.' Nicholas took the cameo from her and stepped behind her. He undid the clasp, surprised to find his fingers trembling a bit, and slid it about her neck, his hands resting on her shoulders. 'It's my mother's. She gave it to me when I left home and now I want you to have it, as a personal gift from me, apart from any other arrangement we have.' He kissed her neck, breathing in the lemon-citrus scent of her. He could feel her pulse quicken beneath his lips where he touched her.

Her hand covered the cameo where it lay against her throat. 'I don't know what to say.'

He could hear the catch in her voice. The gift had moved her. He was glad he'd taken the risk.

'Then say nothing. I want tonight to be for us alone, a night apart from all else. Can it be that, Annorah, or have I presumed too much?'

Her eyes were closed as she leaned into him, her lips reaching up to brush his cheek, her neck arched, her throat exposed. His mother's cameo had never looked lovelier or more right than it did around Annorah's neck.

'Yes, Nicholas,' she breathed, 'we can have tonight.' They were not out of the woods yet and they both knew it. A fiancé was a different thing than a husband. But he could not saddle her with himself permanently without telling her all that he was.

Whenever she'd imagined decadent fantasies, she'd always imagined something like this, but this was better, far better. They ate dinner, they drank champagne, he fed her strawberries and cake over candlelight with the moon coming up outside. No wonder women swooned over him. He could make even the fantasy seem brilliantly real. When he stood and said her favourite three words, 'Come with me', she didn't hesitate.

Only he didn't take her to bed as she antici-pated. He took her to the porch of the summer-house overlooking the lake. 'Have you ever swum naked? Have you ever worn moonlight and only moonlight?' His voice was a decadent caress at her ear. 'Tonight you shall do both.'

He undressed her then, until she stood naked before him, and she was not ashamed. She was proud that his eyes glittered like dark sapphires when he looked at her, that her body pleased him. What a glorious, splendid thing honest sexual-ity was. It was one of the many gifts he'd given her. Nicholas stripped out of his clothes in record time and gave her a wink. 'Last one in is a rot-ten egg.' He executed a perfect dive off the porch and she followed him.

They swam and splashed. She revelled in the play of the moonlight over his sleek muscles. He pulled her into his arms and their play took on a more seductive cast. She wrapped her legs about him, letting him carry her back to the porch and boost her up.

'Now for the second part,' Nicholas flirted. 'Time to wear the moonlight.'

'I thought we'd already done that.' Annorah heard the desire in her own voice as she flirted back.

'Not like this we haven't. Wrap your legs about me again,' he ordered, his own voice husky. He lifted her and bore her back to the wall. She was starting to have some idea of how they'd wear the moonlight and her body thrummed with the thrill of it. They'd been intimate in the outdoors before, but not like this, not with a certain rush of heat, coming hot and fast between them.

He came into her hard and fast, balancing her against the wall. She cried out and gripped him tight. This was ecstasy at its finest. The sheer power and strength of him was on display, the moonlight falling across his dark hair. 'Scream for me, Annorah,' he rasped, withdrawing and plunging again and again until she had no choice to do anything other than that. 'Howl at the moon.'

Howl she did. Release was upon her and she let loose her cries into the night, a celebration of life and perhaps even a celebration of love or something that passed very, very close to it. For tonight that was enough. Nicholas had given her exactly what she needed. She could howl at the moon and for a while the madness of her world was held at bay.

Chapter Fourteen

This was madness. Absolute madness! Irrational panic gripped Annorah as the carriage rolled to a stop on the gravel drive of her aunt's home. She was about to pass off the likes of Nicholas D'Arcy as a fiancé in the hopes of saving both the estate and her freedom. If her ruse was discovered, the consequences would be devastating. They would put paid to any future matrimonial hopes, or any chance of saving the estate. In the forty-eight hours since she'd made her rash proposal to Nicholas, she'd not allowed herself to dwell on the consequences. But now they hit her full force.

She took a deep breath to steady her nerves and silently repeated the mantra she'd formed: she was perfectly safe, she was risking nothing except her pride. She would not be caught. It was *true*. She could believe this. Nicholas knew his job. He could be trusted to execute his role flawlessly. No one would recognise him.

She'd have to find a way to explain the lack of a wedding in a year and she still had to have an answer to the dilemma that would resurface then, but that seemed a small detail to weigh in the balance of avoiding Bartholomew Redding. The past had not been kind to her when it came to intrigues of the heart, Bartholomew Redding not the least in that regard. She'd not been entirely truthful with Nicholas when it came to her situation. Bartholomew Redding was not a new suitor her aunt was throwing at her, but rather a piece of her past, an old suitor come again to stake his claim. Redding wasn't the only thing she hadn't told him. She hadn't told him about the settlements either. She hoped he wouldn't hate her once he figured out exactly how much she was worth to a husband.

'Nervous?' Nicholas asked. She could hear the coachman outside getting down and setting the steps. There were only seconds left before all this became real.

'A little. Are you?'

Nicholas smiled lazily. 'No. You shouldn't be either. People will believe what we tell them to believe and see what we tell them to see.' Annorah wished she had half of his optimism. She made a joke in her head: he only knew half of it. If he knew everything, his optimism might fade. He didn't know Redding, he didn't know about the settlements and he didn't know her aunt. Aunt Georgina would be *very* disappointed at the latest flanking movement to her plans.

The steps were set and the door opened. Nicholas gave her a wink and exited first, turning back to give her a hand down. His grip was warm and reassuring. Annorah looked up at the house and pressed a hand to her stomach. Badger Place had never inspired positive images for her. It was her aunt's husband's home and it was smaller than Hartshaven, although still large enough to impressively entertain with its tall, sharp roof lines and enormous bay windows. Her uncle had inherited it shortly before they'd left Hartshaven, but it had never felt like home to Annorah. The worst years, the worst scenes of her life, had played out in these halls.

Nicholas shot her a sly sideways glance and murmured, 'I suppose it's nice enough, if you like this sort of thing.'

She smiled back and felt the knot in her stomach ease. How it was that he could know her very thoughts was beyond her, but she was grateful for it just as she had been last night.

'Annorah, you're here!' Aunt Georgina sailed out of the door and down the shallow set of front steps to the drive, her arms open wide for an embrace, giving a good imitation of familial affection. Uncle Andrew was right behind her, his usual stiff self. One did not hug Uncle Andrew, which was fine by her. He was a gruff man who held himself apart from others, clinging to every scrap of social status he could muster from his position in the community as its squire and magistrate.

Annorah allowed the embrace and the kiss on the cheek that followed. Her aunt stood back. 'Just look at you, my dear! Has it been a year already? Oh, that reminds me, happy birthday.' Her aunt smiled. 'Speaking of birthdays, I have a birthday present for you, someone I'd like you to meet. I wrote about him in the letter, Mr Bartholomew Redding—'

Annorah cut her aunt off politely. 'I have someone I'd like you to meet, a birthday surprise of my own.' She was becoming accomplished at these vague truths. There wasn't a single word of untruth in that statement. She gestured to Nicholas, who'd had the good grace to step back while the brief reunion took place. He came forwards now, all handsome smiles, stunning her aunt into absolute silence. 'Aunt Georgina, Uncle Andrew, this is Mister Nicholas D'Arcy, my fiancé.'

A flicker of unfriendly disbelief crossed Aunt Georgina's features for the briefest of moments before it was carefully masked with a more appropriate response. 'Annorah, dear, how long have you been engaged? Why didn't you say anything? We would have thrown you an engagement ball.' *I doubt it*, Annorah thought uncharitably. *There'd be no gain in it for you.* She ought to have been thinking of an answer. It wouldn't do to falter so early in the ruse, but her mind was most inconveniently blank.

It was Nicholas who answered, putting a quietly possessive hand at her elbow. 'We decided it very recently, didn't we, Annorah?'

'Yes.' Annorah's brain was starting to work again. 'It hardly made sense to write to you, when we'd be seeing you in person so soon.' She could see her aunt's mind reeling with a million questions and a thousand schemes. This was an unexpected turn of events that cut her aunt's favourite, Redding, out of the picture.

'Well, this is news indeed.' Uncle Andrew stepped forwards at last and shook Nicholas's hand, albeit reluctantly. 'We should go inside so we don't neglect our other guests. There will be plenty of time for you to tell us everything, Annorah.' He shot a sharp, assessing eye at Nicholas. 'And to get to know you as well. Welcome to Badger Place, Mr D'Arcy.' The words were correct, all that ritual politeness required, but Annorah couldn't help feeling Badger Place was about to live up to its name.

Guests had been arriving all afternoon and were assembled in chatty little groups throughout the drawing room, sipping on tea and eating tiny frosted cakes. Done in pale shades of a limey green and finished with crisp white mouldings, the drawing room was her aunt's pride and joy. Two large, expensive carpets by Thomas Whitty adorned the hardwood floors. The one near the fireplace bore a specially woven depiction of Uncle Andrew's family coat of arms—a badger armed with a sword and an axe and the motto stitched above him: *Audemus jura nostra defendere.* 'We dare to defend our rights.' Annorah used to take a childish pleasure in covertly stepping on the badger's face when she was frustrated.

She knew some of the people assembled. Her two cousins, Eva and Matthew, were there with their spouses, their children probably tucked up in the nursery. Others were neighbours. There was Vicar Stewart and his wife, delighted to have been invited to such a gathering, and the Hadleys, who were neighbouring gentry. The rest of her nerves started to melt away by the time introductions were nearly completed. Nicholas was right. No one here would know him. This gathering of folk hardly ever ventured to London.

Her aunt had saved the 'best' for last, however. A tall, solidly built blond man with the bluff, healthy features of a country gentleman stood at the fireplace, looking carefully posed with one hand on his hip drawing back, ever so slightly, the cut of his coat in order to reveal the waistcoat and gold watch chain beneath. The sight of him was almost paralysing. She regretted not telling Nicholas about him. But she needn't have worried. Nicholas's hand move possessively to the small of her back as they approached, a sign that he, too, guessed who the man was.

'Annorah, you remember Mr Bartholomew Redding.' Remember? The word was too tame. What he'd done to her haunted her to this day. He'd changed the way she'd viewed the world. In many ways, he'd been the cause for her retreat and the reason she was in this position today.

'Annorah, it's been for ever.' Redding turned towards them, oozing charm, his hands outstretched as if he expected her take them. Annorah stopped at a distance that made touching moot. She would not tolerate his hands on her, not ever again if she could manage it.

Redding carried on as if Annorah's snub was the grandest of greetings, as if he hadn't abused her hospitality years ago.

'Your aunt has been bringing me up to date on all the details of your life.' He smiled and her skin crawled. 'I've been out of touch since my second wife passed away a year ago.'

Annorah bit back a retort. She'd heard it had been a rather suspicious death, coming so swiftly on the heels of his first wife's death and their rapid marriage. Nicholas's hand tightened at her back in covert possession. She was not alone and it gave her courage. Annorah stiffened her spine. 'May I present my fiancé, Mr Nicholas D'Arcy?'

'Fiancé?' Redding arched an eyebrow in a gesture of amused doubt. 'I was unaware of such an arrangement.' He cast a sharp look at Aunt Georgina. 'I can see that your aunt has not kept me apprised of everything going on in your life. '

'That's entirely our fault,' Nicholas put in congenially, drawing her a bit closer to him. 'It's new notice. So new, in fact, we hadn't even written ahead to tell the family since there was every chance our arrival would have preceded a letter.' He gave Aunt Georgina a dazzling smile. 'Besides, this kind of news is best shared in person with family instead of an impersonal letter. The announcement will be featured in *The Times* tomorrow.'

Oh, it was masterful and, oh, it was hard not

to gloat! Her aunt paled at the mention of *The Times*. Annorah felt a broad smile spread across her face. Nicholas had managed to answer Redding's charge and scold Aunt Georgina *while* he charmed them. Well, maybe charmed was too strong a word to use in regards to Redding, but her aunt was certainly melting.

'Have you had the banns called?' Redding asked. Apparently the mention of *The Times* provoked other tests of reality.

Nicholas gave a disgusted look at the suggestion. 'That's a poor man's avenue to the altar. We will be married by special licence.'

They would? He'd spend twenty-eight guineas to marry her? Annorah found herself blushing as if the fiction were truth. The mention of a special licence would speak volumes to those who dared to listen in about the kind of man Nicholas was. The answer was perfect for a gentleman of means. Annorah felt herself relax. It was going to be all right. Nicholas could absolutely carry this off and so could she. He had to be someone else entirely; she only had to be herself. How hard could that be, especially now that they were through the first obstacles?

Her confidence was high as she and Nicholas went upstairs to change for dinner. She'd been given her old room overlooking the garden, but Nicholas was an unexpected guest. His room was at the other end of the house. It was hard to tell whether or not that last was contrived. A room *had* been found for him while they'd gathered for tea and she *was* grateful for her aunt's industry on the matter. Still, he could have been put a bit closer if her aunt had wanted to do so. Annorah might be confident in her ruse, but she was also confident her aunt wouldn't cede the field without a fight, not when there was money on the line.

And there *was* money on the line. Upon her marriage, her fortune would become her husband's according to standard English law. A husband of her aunt's choosing would be eternally grateful for having been steered in her direction. Annorah had no doubt that her aunt fully expected privileged access to that fortune as a finder's fee. It had happened once before. She had no reason to expect it wouldn't happen again, especially if Redding was involved.

Her aunt was hungry for that money. Her youngest cousin, Mary, would come out next year. A substantial dowry would make Mary a highly attractive prize. Given the right encouragement, it could secure for Georgina and Andrew the next social rung: a baron for Mary, or perhaps the son of an earl. Not a first son, but a second or third son and their grandchildren would be known as grandchildren of an earl.

Annorah sorted through her gowns. Tonight she needed to look more like a queen than a princess, a sophisticated woman. The money awaiting her upon marriage had never mattered to her. As the sole inheritor of Hartshaven and a tidy sum to boot, she had no burning desire to claim the other portion of the fortune, which was just as well. Her parents had never intended her to marry for money.

Annorah sighed. Lily had been efficient in getting her dresses hung up and she wanted to pick just the right one. Nicholas had been devastatingly charming this afternoon. He'd drawn every eye in the room without even trying. She'd seen the looks women had cast him over their teacups and fans. A tiny part of her had surged with the knowledge that he was hers, even if that claim had been contrived. It hadn't seemed that way though. He'd delivered his part with the cheerful bonhomie of a proud bridegroom and she wanted to look his equal tonight.

That decided it. It would have to be the pale-blue flowered silk with the blond fichu. She liked how it fit with its tight corsage bodice and blond trim to match the fichu. She would be in high looks. Annorah didn't want anyone to glance across the table tonight and think: how did such a country mouse manage to snare a prize like him? That would be all her aunt needed to smell a rat.

'I smell a rat,' Redding snarled, his thin upper lip curled most unbecomingly as he paced Georgina Timmerman's personal parlour. He just wasn't sure which rat it was. Had Georgina lured him here under false pretences of another shot at Annorah, a shot he'd blown twelve years ago, or had she been genuinely surprised by Annorah's sudden engagement? If so, that meant the rat lay with the niece and the supposed fiancé.

'So do I,' Georgina said fiercely, her colour angry and high. 'I don't believe for a moment he's for real. She's trying to outmanoeuvre us and the lawyers. She thinks to keep all the money to herself, the ungrateful girl. She's been on her own too long. She needs a husband to bring her in line.'

A flicker of arousal started to stir. He enjoyed bringing a woman into line. He had a few favourite tricks he wouldn't mind trying on Annorah. A little payback wouldn't be amiss for thwarting him the first time, for making him wade through two mediocre heiresses in order to get to her.

Georgina Timmerman's response was what Redding expected. It was the only one she could give that would protect her liability. She couldn't very well confess she'd known all along her niece was promised to another suitor. That didn't mean her claim of innocence was true, though. Redding was a born cynic. He believed no one, not ever. 'What reason do we have for thinking he's a fake?'

'My niece doesn't want me to have the money. She's never liked me. She's ruined my efforts for years. I found her good offers in the past and she shunned them. Nothing is good enough for her.' Georgina gave him a sly look. 'You should know that better than anyone. You were one of those offers.'

'It seems we'll have to step up our plans. Real or not, Mr D'Arcy is definitely an obstacle. I can't very well play the doting suitor if she already has one.' He'd suspected from the start this would be rougher than it had looked on the surface. Anything that sounded too good to be true probably was. But the prize was a great one; snare Annorah and he would be set the rest of his days.

'I can compromise her.' Redding suggested. That would be delicious, having her up against a wall, skirts a-tangle when everyone walked in. He could imagine it all too well. 'I can do something that will cast doubts about her in Mr D'Arcy's mind. Perhaps I can convince him she's not the girl he thinks she is.' Dividing and conquering was always a fun game. Love, or what passed for it, was a fickle and fleeting thing, a sentiment easily trampled when tested, especially for a new couple.

Georgina's face lit up with a cruel smile. 'Meanwhile, we might consider doing the same for her. We should research this Mr D'Arcy and learn all we can just in case he's after her money. I'd hate to see my niece taken advantage of by a fortune hunter,' she said coyly. 'I'll send a note to London. It might be we can sow the same seeds of doubt for her as well.'

Redding nodded. He'd send his own enquiry to London, too. The Timmermans might be schemers, but they wouldn't know the right sort of people to ferret out the information Georgina wanted, *if* it existed. It might be that D'Arcy was simply a gentleman as he claimed. Redding doubted it. No one was simply anything. In his experience, everyone came with strings attached. Sometimes those strings belonged to a mama, other times they belonged to less savoury connections. If so, he'd be doing them all a favour in saving Annorah from discovering those connections too late. He'd learned, too, that grateful people tended to be, well, grateful. Usually with their money.

Chapter Fifteen

Her money was on Nicholas. Annorah's heart gave a dangerously emotional thump as he glanced up from his position at the bottom of stairs, waiting to take her into the drawing room before dinner. When he looked at her like that, it was easy to forget the fiction and embrace the fantasy that he was hers. He looked resplendent in black evening wear, his jaw smooth from a recent shave, his hair pulled back and sleek. Everything about him spoke of sartorial perfection. There would not be a better polished man in the dining room tonight.

'Annorah, you look lovely as always. The blue becomes you.' He bowed over her hand and favoured it with a kiss even though he didn't have to.

'Shall we go and gossip with the in-laws? His

blue eyes were merry, and full of laughter when he looked at her. This is what sells him, she thought, holding his gaze. Along with the polish he has a sense of fun. He might have more than his fair share of good looks, but he's not a snob about them. He doesn't think those looks entitle him to anything more.

'I don't see that we have a choice if we want to eat,' Annorah said, letting him slip her arm through his. 'It is truly good of you to do this for me. I do appreciate it.'

He leaned close to her ear as if imparting a secret with a smile. 'I'm happy to do it.'

That brought on a pang of guilt. It was easy to be brave when one didn't fully understand the circumstances. Nicholas thought he was merely enacting a bridegroom's official engagement introduction to the family. He had no idea that it was substantially more than that. A true bridegroom would have been apprised of the circumstances as soon as he met with the solicitor to discuss the marriage contracts. But she'd not given Nicholas full disclosure. She'd reasoned he didn't need to know in order to carry out his role.

Knowing changed nothing for him. She wondered if she'd made a mistake.

The noise of pleasant conversation drifted out into the hall. Most of the guests were already assembled. Nicholas bent to murmur something humorous and private at her ear as they stepped through the doorway to join the party, but the motion halted. Annorah felt an infinitesimal hesitation in his step, the clenching of his arm where her hand lay on his sleeve. Something had disturbed Nicholas's unflappable composure.

The disturbance was hardly noticeable. It wasn't as if he'd paled or was trembling. She wouldn't have noticed at all if she hadn't been touching him, or if she hadn't come to know him in the past week. But she *had* come to know him. She knew his moods, the way he'd withdraw if a comment struck too close to those subjects he wished to keep private.

Annorah shot a sideways glance at his profile. He was withdrawing now. Not so much with words, but with his eyes. They were like diamonds, the hardest substance nature had to offer—unscratchable, uncrackable, impenetrable blue diamonds. He was putting on his armour, although she couldn't imagine what for. She followed his sight line, searching for the foe.

The perceived threat stood in the deep bay of the window with its floor-to-ceiling glass panels. The man in question faced the doorway and was surrounded by a small group of other males, all with drinks in their hands. Even at a distance, Annorah knew this man was dangerous. Tall and broad shouldered, the proper evening clothes he wore could not disguise his disregard for convention. His hair was dark and loose, his jaw showing signs of night stubble. He possessed none of Nicholas's perfect polish, yet he was not without his own potent brand of masculinity. Annorah couldn't fathom what such a man would be doing in her aunt's drawing room of all places. He seemed far better suited to rougher environs. From the look on Nicholas's face, he was wondering the same.

The man's eyes met Nicholas's, gazes locking across the room. Nicholas swore beneath his breath. 'Bloody hell', and reality stabbed hard at Annorah's gut, her original fear over this gathering realised. Nicholas knew this man and, by logical extension, it meant this man knew Nicholas.

Her mind raced. If he knew Nicholas, he knew what Nicholas did and that gave him the power to expose her secret. The threat posed by Bartholomew Redding was nothing compared to the peril the stranger posed. No, *not* a stranger, not to Nicholas at least. Beside her, Nicholas seemed to recover himself. They'd begun to move again, working their way towards her aunt and uncle at the fireplace as if nothing were amiss.

Out of the corner of her eye, Annorah kept a covert watch on him, but he did nothing more than go back to his conversation. The dark stranger was apparently happy to let them go. He made no move to pursue them. Of course, he was the hunter. He could stalk them all night. There was no place they could hide. He could take his time, which raised the question: How long did she have before her secret was out? Horrible scenarios ran through her head. Would he do it early during the fish course? Would he wait until dessert and make her stew through the entire meal?

Nicholas was doing a credible job, chatting with her aunt and uncle about the price of sheep's wool, but he had to be worried, too. His quiet oath of 'bloody hell' indicated as much. It was all she could do not to drag him from the room and demand knowledge—who was this man, what was he doing here and how much danger did he pose? But such a move was impossible. Even if she could engineer it, it would only serve to raise the stranger's attentions.

Nicholas smiled and nodded, doing his best to give the impression of listening attentively. Talking about wool prices was demanding all of his concentration, especially when what he really wanted to do was walk over to the window bay and ask Grahame Westmore what the hell he was doing here.

He'd use those exact terms, too. Had Westmore come on purpose with news about the situation in London? Was he here on assignment? The former seemed likely, the latter seemed doubtful. Nicholas recalled from the afternoon introductions that most of the women invited had come with husbands. Such a consideration didn't stop London women from availing themselves of the agency's services, but those services were expensive. He didn't think the good country women of west Sussex had that kind of blunt, not when they'd have to pay travelling expenses on top of regular fees.

That left the option that something had happened in London. Still, the speed of mobilising Westmore was astonishing. He'd notified Channing of his direction before they'd left Hartshaven, but the letter could hardly have reached Channing in time for Westmore to be here. If it wasn't that, then what other explanation was there? With Westmore, it could be anything. He was a bit of a wild card. The only thing Nicholas knew about Westmore was that he was handy in a fight and fiercely loyal to Channing. Up until now that was all he had needed to know. It was also the only thing that kept him from racing over there and demanding private conversation.

'In Scotland, folks are favouring the block-faced wethers,' Nicholas put in. 'Of course, the sheep are grazing on highland grass. They need to be hardier.'

'Very true.' Uncle Andrew put a hand under his chin, cupping it in serious contemplation. Nicholas wanted to cringe. Lord help him, he hoped he never had to raise cattle for living. He might know about sheep, but he *could not* take them with the same seriousness as these folks did. 'I might think about buying a few ewes and breeding them with my rams this season and see what I can get.'

Nicholas hoped that would be the end of it, but Uncle Andrew was nodding. 'Yes, I like that idea the more I think about it. My merino rams would do well with them. Cross-breeding could result in finer short-hair wool.'

That was absolutely it. Nicholas had to draw the line at discussing the sex lives of sheep. 'Might I steal your lovely wife for a moment? I see a new guest has joined us since tea.' He nodded in Westmore's direction and offered Aunt Georgina his free arm. 'Annorah and I should meet him. I confess, he looks a bit familiar. Perhaps I have run into him briefly before, but his name escapes me.' This way, he wouldn't accidently expose Westmore if he was using a different name.

Aunt Georgina preened at the attention. 'I'd be glad to.' In moments, she had them across the room and insinuated into Westmore's little circle. 'Captain Westmore, you haven't had the chance to meet my niece, Annorah Price-Ellis, and her fiancé, Mr D'Arcy.'

Nicholas smiled, eyes meeting Westmore's as they exchanged a private acknowledgment. Without being aware of it, Aunt Georgina had solved numerous mysteries. He now knew Westmore was here under his own name and he was here alone. Georgina had not attached him to any of the women present. If he was here for one of them, it was in a covert capacity. Of course, this raised other mysteries. What was he doing here under his own power? Nicholas couldn't imagine Westmore electing to attend a house party in west Sussex for fun when he had ample opportunity to do it as work. Likewise, Westmore knew what Nick's own role was. He was masquerading as a fiancé.

'I thought that was you when I came in.' Nicholas was all affability. Westmore was going to let him decide how this interaction would play out. He had to use this conversation to its utmost.

'You know each other?' Georgina looked from Westmore to him.

'Mere acquaintances from London,' Nicholas said casually. 'I don't think it hardly qualifies as knowing one another, but we have some friends in common. Perhaps we'll become better acquainted this weekend.' All of it was true. He didn't know Westmore well. He knew none of the things about the very private Westmore than other men knew about their male friends. He didn't know what kind of whisky Westmore drank, where he got his boots or what clubs he frequented. Now, at least, it wouldn't seem odd if he was seen in Westmore's company.

Westmore bowed over Annorah's hand, his silver gaze sharp like a wolf as he took in Annorah, eyes lingering far too long on places best left ignored in another man's fiancée. 'Congratulations, D'Arcy. You've won yourself quite a prize.'

Nicholas wanted to wipe the smug half-smile off Westmore's face. Annorah wasn't weak, but Westmore was out of her league. He was far too coarse when he wasn't careful to wear his public face. Apparently there were plenty of London's fine ladies who preferred a bit of rough behind their boudoir doors. Westmore was always in high demand.

Dinner was announced and Nicholas took the opportunity to lead Annorah away. He'd seek out Westmore tonight once the house had settled to bed and clarify his position.

'Is he a friend?' Annorah asked under her breath as they went into dinner.

'Friend enough. You needn't worry,' Nicholas murmured, pulling out her chair. It was with some relief to note they'd been seated together at her aunt's end of the table. He was on her aunt's left, an arrangement that had obviously been cobbled together after his unexpected arrival. Annorah was on his other side and the seat beside her was filled by Bartholomew Redding.

Nicholas grimaced over the latter. By rights, Redding should have been moved since all the parties involved knew Redding had been brought to the house expressly as a suitor for Annorah. It did make him wonder what her aunt was playing at to keep pushing the man at her. He shot a quizzing look at Georgina as she sat. She knew exactly what he was asking with his eyes. 'There simply wasn't time to re-draft the seating chart.' Her shoulders rose and fell in an apologetic shrug.

It was a lie and he was tempted to challenge her on it. If there'd been time to move him next to the hostess, there was time to move Redding to the far end. He resisted. A conflict with Annorah's aunt got him nothing but a potential enemy. He would have better luck catching the proverbial fly with sugar.

The first course, a vermicelli soup, was put in front of him, signalling the opening of conversation and Aunt Georgina was an eager partner. 'Now I have you all to myself.' She took a sip of her soup and smiled. But the smile didn't quite reach her eyes, which conveyed a more assessing, more critical story. 'You must tell me everything. How did you meet my niece?'

Ah, it was to be a side of interrogation with the soup. He was ready for it. They'd planned for this part of the fiction. 'Through correspondence actually.' Again, another almost-truth. 'We had a common interest in an organisation and we finally decided to meet.' He snapped his fingers. 'The rest is history. Once we met, we knew we were well suited.'

'History takes time,' Georgina put in sagely. 'This sounds rather more like a whirlwind.' She leaned forwards, a light hand on his knee beneath the table, partly invitation, partly the gesture of one conferring private information.

Nicholas arched an eyebrow, acknowledging her presence on his leg and assuming the former. But she did not take the hint and remove it. Attractive women never did take the hint. They were too confident in their charms to really believe they'd be rebuffed. Even women who were old enough to know better. Georgina Timmerman fit both categories. In her mid-forties, she was still pretty enough. Her hair still bore a lustrous nut-brown sheen, having escaped early threads of grey, and her body had maintained its youthful firmness. But that didn't mean he wanted her.

'I must warn you, Annorah is given to high spirits. She has had whirlwind romances before that did not end well.' She shook her head sadly, but there was something of the coquette in the action. Her hand crept up his thigh. 'My niece gets swept away and forgets to think about the long-term consequences.' Apparently the acorn hadn't fallen far from the tree, then. Aunt Georgina was definitely getting swept away right here before the fish course, fishing for something else entirely.

'Has she said nothing about it? Nothing about her past?' Georgina's eyes were wide with concern. She waved a fork to dismiss the thought.

'Well, maybe it's of no consequence. It was years ago when she was first out. It probably doesn't signify and you know what's best. You're both adults. You'll know what is important to tell one another.' She emphasised the last with a squeeze close to his groin.

Praise the lord for lobster turbot. Nicholas nearly celebrated when the footmen brought in the fish. It meant he could talk with Annorah. It meant Aunt Georgina would have to find something else to do with her hand. 'How's our friend Mr Redding?'

'He's not our friend and he collects coins. He has five hundred and forty-two.'

Nicholas stifled a laugh. Clearly she'd been privy to an introduction to each one of them. 'Better coins than groins.'

Annorah choked and grabbed for her napkin just in time to avoid spitting out her wine. 'Do you want to make an excuse or something? Perhaps you have some residual carriage sickness and you need to retire?'

Nicholas laughed and covered her hand. Her excuse was completely implausible, but he loved that she'd tried. 'I can handle your aunt. It's not the first time I've had to fend off unwanted advances.'

'But you're my fiancé! It's the principle of it all,' Annorah said with a fierce protectiveness that touched him. 'She's making advances towards her niece's husband-to-be. That's despicable. And at the dinner table, too.'

'Would it be better if it happened in the summerhouse?' Nicholas teased.

'That's not the point. She shouldn't be doing it all.' Annorah was lovely in her righteous indignation. Her cheeks had coloured and her green eyes snapped. How long had it been since someone had taken his part? How long since someone had stood up for him? Channing had, of course. Channing was always running a bit of interference on his behalf, just as he had with the Burroughs affair. But that was business. When had a woman been interested in his well-being beyond the pleasure he could bring her?

The beef came, the conversation turned once more and Aunt Georgina ran a slipper up his leg. He could do nothing but tolerate it without risking an enemy. She was talkative in her little flirtation and a certain pattern was starting to emerge. She wanted him to know about her niece. The things she wanted him to know were odd. This was not the usual story telling parents and relatives were wont to do. This was not the collection of tales about skinned knees and childish pranks with the occasional embarrassing but harmless anecdote thrown in for good measure. This was something else and it was malicious in spite of the lightness she wrapped it in.

Why would an aunt slander a 'beloved' niece who'd finally found marriage late in life, according to society's standards? He would think it would be just the opposite. Aunt Georgina and Uncle Andrew should be ecstatic she was finally to be married. He understood Georgina might be put out by the suddenness of the announcement, especially after her efforts to find a suitor, but that disappointment should not have warranted such calumny, especially when a marriage would mean the money stayed in the family. Even her selfish aunt couldn't complain about that.

'But, of course, you know her,' Aunt Georgina was saying again as the last of the plates were cleared away.

Nicholas smiled and supplied the requisite answer. 'Yes, I do.' But he was beginning to wonder. Something wasn't right and it wasn't just Georgina's slipper taking a walk up his leg.

'She'll need a firm hand.' Georgina's slipper made intimate contact beneath the table.

Nicholas nearly leapt back from the table. As it was, his push backwards lacked all subtlety, earning him a humorous look from Westmore, who sat on the other side two chairs away. 'Excuse me, I thought I dropped something,' Nicholas improvised.

By the time he climbed the stairs to bed, it was clear something did not fit. He would have liked to have paid a nocturnal visit to Annorah's room and solve some of that mystery, but right now, Grahame Westmore took priority, especially if Channing had sent a message.

Chapter Sixteen

Grahame was in the library, the pre-arranged location at any gathering the league had decided on as the meeting place if there was need. 'About time you got here.' Grahame looked up from his book. 'You were surprised to see me.' He gave Nicholas a half-smile that passed for friendly.

'I was not expecting you. You have to admit, this isn't exactly the league's standard venue.' Nicholas walked to the sideboard and poured himself a drink. He held up an empty glass in enquiry. Grahame shook his head. 'Are you here for business or pleasure?'

'A bit of both.' Grahame stretched his legs out in front of him. 'I'm not working a particular assignment, if that's what you want to know.' He gave a short laugh. 'London's been very disappointing this Season. The new crop of débutantes is dismal. Milquetoast, all of them. I swear they get younger by the year.'

Nicholas took a long drink of the brandy. 'Perhaps if you smiled more, you'd find the crop less dismal.' Westmore wasn't exactly the most approachable of Channing's league. But women didn't hire him to be affable.

'I don't need advice from you.' Whatever social polish Westmore lacked, he'd certainly cornered the market on the dark, brooding officer type and there were plenty of ladies who liked that sort of thing.

Nicholas took another long, slow drink in the hopes Westmore would fill the silence with information. When none was forthcoming, he was forced to soldier on with the conversation. 'Do I assume correctly then that you have a message for me?'

Something flickered in Westmore's eyes. 'Yes, and Channing insisted I make good time reaching you. Lord Burroughs hasn't cooled down yet. He's calling for your head on a platter. He even confronted Channing at the Duke of Rothburgh's ball the other night, wanting to know where you were.' He paused. 'Channing wasn't pleased to get your note about leaving Hartshaven. He feared you might make your way to London, or that London might accidentally make its way to you. I take it Channing doesn't know about these latest details?'

'No. I didn't have time for a lengthy note and some things are best explained in person,' Nicholas said uneasily. Westmore's disapproval was evident.

'Wasn't this only supposed to be a few nights?'

'We mutually decided to extend our time together. She had need of me at this house party and I had need of a place to go.' Westmore didn't need to know he hadn't told Annorah the second part of that. That sounded utterly practical. Westmore should buy it. It was the kind of explanation that made sense to him.

'She's paying you for the extra time, of course?' Westmore put in.

'Yes.' Nicholas sighed.

'Well, then, you're making hay out of this arrangement, getting paid twice. She's rich and pretty. Good for you.'

But Nicholas didn't care for Westmore's cynical tone or his choice of words. 'What are you implying?'

Westmore leaned forwards, elbows on knees. 'What is it exactly that she needs you here for? It's clearly not sex since you're down here talking to me well past midnight.'

'That's fairly obvious, isn't it? She needed to produce a fiancé.' Nicholas scowled into his drink. Westmore's probes were hitting a bit too close to home. He'd started to wonder the same thing after her aunt's interesting conversation at dinner. Redding wasn't an unattractive man. What did Annorah have against him that she needed a fiancé for protection?

'And you took that answer at face value?' Westmore scoffed. 'What did she tell you? Or better yet, what did she do that was persuasive enough to drag you to a house party?'

'I needed a place to go. I didn't have much choice,' Nicholas reminded him, but he was already replaying the scene from the veranda. She hadn't *done* anything, at least nothing of the sort Westmore was insinuating. Annorah had simply stood there, hands clenched, face pale, holding out the invitation. He hadn't the heart to refuse her. 'She said this was an annual summons, her aunt's attempt to finally marry her off and she was tired of meeting her aunt's suitors.' But after encountering Bartholomew Redding, he couldn't understand why except that Annorah had been tense in the man's presence.

'Hmm,' was Westmore's only response.

'Are you going to explain that?' Nicholas prompted. Talking with Westmore was tedious work.

'Do I have to? The country air seems to have addled your wits.' Westmore sighed and settled into his chair. 'Very well. The way I see it, your sweet Annorah is hiding something and she's dragged you into the middle of it.'

'She's not that type,' Nicholas began, but Westmore waved the comment away.

'How do you know what type she is or isn't? You've known her for a week and that entire week has been spent in isolation, hasn't it? You've been tucked up at her estate, playing honeymooners, and the only evidence you have about who she is, is whatever she's told you.' Westmore raised his brows. 'A pretty, wealthy woman all alone in the country should ring alarms right there, D'Arcy. What did she tell you? She's tired of being alone? She's tired of fortune hunters who are after her money? Good lord, she did. I can see it in your face. What's worse, you fell for it. This is rich indeed. I think instead of you seducing her, she's seduced you. What you have to ask yourself is—for what purpose?'

Nicholas could feel his temper rising. How dared Westmore sit there and malign Annorah, who was nothing but honest and straightforward. She was goodness personified and he'd be damned if he was going to sit here and spill the 'family curse' to Westmore about her need to marry within the week. 'I don't have to justify her to you,' Nicholas ground out.

'No, but I can see you've spent plenty of time justifying her to yourself.' Westmore put up his hands in a placating gesture. 'In the end, what does it matter? You'll go your way, she'll go hers and that will be that.' Westmore pointed a judicious finger his direction. 'Never mix business with pleasure. It's not fair to her or to you. I hope you have a plan to break that engagement. It will get messy if you're not careful.'

It was hard to argue with that. It already was messy. Aunt Georgina was groping him under the table and telling him stories that didn't quite fit. It did not help matters that Westmore carried doubts, too, and his own instincts were on alert. He wasn't going to stay here and debate Annorah's intentions with Westmore, especially when he wasn't sure he had evidence to the contrary. 'I'm off to bed.'

'Yours or someone else's? Perhaps Aunt Georgina's? Her hand seemed to spend a lot of time under the table this evening.' Westmore already had his nose back in the book.

'Mine. It's been a long day.' Out in the hall, however, Nicholas was tempted to take the other corridor and head towards Annorah's room. He wanted her, wanted to wrap her up in his arms and hold her warm body against his. He wanted to lay all the questions at her feet. In the end, he went to bed alone, questions unanswered.

He wasn't coming. Annorah finally conceded defeat and blew out the lamp. She might as well get some sleep if that was the case. House parties by their nature were tiring affairs in her opinion—days full of activities and dresses to be changed. Evenings full of games and dancing, and always this pressure to be 'on'. Everyone was always looking at other people's clothes, watching their every move and mannerism, judging every word.

It had already begun. After the ladies had left the table for the drawing room, the gossip started. Everyone wanted to know about Nicholas. Some of the young women had all but sat rapt at her feet as if she were Plato at the Academy while she talked of Nicholas, her words like pearls. 'He likes the colour yellow, he enjoys champagne, he fishes...' On it went until she'd exhausted everything she knew of him. Well, almost everything. There were plenty of things she wouldn't share: *he likes woman-on-top best, his hair falls forwards like a primordial god when he rises over you, he makes you want to scream until he finally lets you shatter, he likes it when you run your nails over his balls.*

Her aunt tried once to insert the topic of Mr Redding into the conversation. 'Mr D'Arcy isn't the only one who has some nice property. Bartholomew Redding has inherited his second wife's property not far from here. His prospects are exciting.'

But no one seemed interested in Redding's prospects, farming or otherwise. They were far too interested in Nicholas. Annorah was relieved when the conversation had veered to other topics. She'd felt like she'd known quite a lot about Nicholas, but once she'd started talking, the list had been short and rapidly exhausted.

She'd been anxious to talk with him and learn more about Grahame Westmore, but there'd been no time. On those grounds alone, she'd been certain Nicholas would come to her. Even if he couldn't stay the night, he'd surely want to let her know about Westmore. But midnight had come and gone. One o'clock had come and gone. Now it was nearly two and there was no sign of him. Her questions would have to wait.

Apparently sleep would, too. She quickly discovered that blowing out the light and lying down was no guarantee sleep would follow. Her mind was too alive to go gently, and when it did, it was shortly before dawn with the realisation that she would wake up sleepy.

* * *

And grumpy. Annorah groaned against the bright daylight filtering through her window. The only bad thing about this room was its eastern exposure catching the sun. Lily was already there, pulling back the curtains and singing. 'It's going to be a beautiful day, miss. I hear talk downstairs there's to be a picnic out to the iron hill fort. I brought hot chocolate up. Your aunt had trays arranged for all the ladies' rooms.'

Hot chocolate did make her smile just a little. This ritual of morning chocolate was one of her aunt's self-proclaimed London affectations. Although to Annorah's knowledge, her aunt had only been to London twice in her entire life, hardly enough to warrant the acquisition of any affectations.

Annorah sat up and took the cup of hot chocolate. 'Any word of Mr D'Arcy this morning?' Perhaps he'd slept better than she had and was already up or had already been out on a morning ride. It struck her that she really didn't know his morning routine. The routine he'd followed at Hartshaven had been largely dictated by her: he'd slept in her bed, he'd eaten breakfast with her, they'd planned their day together. She'd missed him last night. Had he missed her? For her part, the bed had felt empty and cold. How quickly that habit had formed. She had not anticipated sleeping with another person—in this case, literally sleeping with another person—to be so comforting, so desirable.

Lily shook her head and laid out a pretty greenmuslin summer dress and matching kid boots perfect for tromping the countryside. 'He's probably downstairs with the gentlemen eating their hearty breakfasts.'

That's where she wanted to be and not just for the sake of getting answers. She wanted to be with him. It took the better part of an hour to make her ready for the day, though.

By the time Annorah descended the stairs, the hall was crowded with guests milling about, chattering excitedly as they waited for carriages and horses to be brought around.

Nicholas found her immediately before she even reached the bottom step. He was dressed for the outing, too, in buff trousers, boots and a hacking jacket. He looked immaculate and perhaps a bit tired around the eyes, although if he was, he was wearing it well, probably far better than she was. 'You've saved me from your aunt's clutches,' he whispered humorously, taking her arm, but Annorah thought she detected a bit of strain beneath his joke, a bit of reserve from his usual fun-loving self.

'Well, good morning to you, too.'

'It is now. I've been waiting for you.' Nicholas smiled and she felt warm in the rays of his charm. Perhaps she'd imagined the strain. 'I'm sorry I couldn't come to you last night. I had business to take care of.' He jerked his head to the left and she noted Grahame Westmore off to one side with a group of men. He was most definitely what one called a 'man's man'. He'd thrive in the country and was probably a crack shot, probably a crack everything when it came to the out of doors.

'I hope it was not bad business?' Annorah searched his face for any sign of worry, but found none.

'All is well. He is here for his own purposes.' Nicholas squeezed her hand where it lay on his sleeve. 'We'll talk later,' he promised.

* * *

She held on to that promise through a very long morning. She'd thought a picnic would provide plenty of opportunities to speak privately with Nicholas. She could not have been more wrong. She'd not bargained on the carriage ride out to the fort in an open-air carriage with three other girls, all clamouring for Nicholas's attention. And he gave it, charmingly, willingly to each of them in turn while reminding them in little ways that he was a pledged man. It was so neatly done, Annorah barely felt the sting of jealousy. He could smile and laugh all he liked since it was clear he had no intention of deserting her. *Of course not, you ninny, you're paying his bills.* But it wasn't the reality that convinced her. It was he. Nicholas was a loyal man. She wasn't sure how she knew that or why she even believed it, but she did. Maybe it was how he'd spoken of his brother and the tales he'd told about how they'd done everything together growing up.

At the picnic grounds, the situation did not improve. Groups were formed to walk up to the fort and they were swept along in the social tide. If she was not next to him, she was never far from him. He threw her an occasional smile as if to say all was well. He was a very good sport, she had to give him that. He fitted right in and she was having a good time talking with her cousins right up to the point where Bartholomew Redding inserted himself into their little cohort.

'D'Arcy is a popular one, isn't he?' Redding smiled in what he probably thought was a congenial manner. Annorah thought otherwise. She knew his true measure.

'Yes, he's a hit wherever we go,' Annorah said in reserved agreement. She didn't want to give Redding the impression she was open to conversation or open to anything with him.

Redding didn't take the hint. 'You're a generous woman, then. I don't know that I'd be open to sharing someone so dear to me, especially if they attracted so much attention.'

She did not care for the leer in his gaze or the tone in his voice. 'What are you implying?' The chagrin she felt over the suggestion was very real in spite of the fiction of her arrangement. There was something surreal about defending the fidelity of a paid escort.

'Your fiancé is a handsome man. Women will

be interested in him wherever you go. But perhaps you intend to have a casual understanding
with him?'

She'd had enough of this conversation. Redding had separated her from the group and it was
making her nervous. 'Our private lives are none
of your concern,' Annorah answered sharply, an-
gling to move away, but Redding wasn't done.

'What do you suppose he sees in you, Annorah? Pretty isn't enough for a man like him. He
can have pretty any day of the week. Of course,
your kind of pretty comes with pound notes behind it. Perhaps you can hold him with your
money. That can be a convenient leash at times,
quite the effective way to keep him tied down.'
He winked. 'Do you suppose he'd like that or
does he prefer real ropes?'

'You've overstepped yourself,' Annorah
warned. That was putting it mildly. If she was a
man, she'd have recourse in a duel for this vul-
gar talk. As it was, she had no option other than
to listen until she could walk away.

'What you call disgusting, I call honest. There'd
probably be a lot more happy marriages if someone had told people the truth from the start.' He

moved closer and she stepped back. 'As for truth, there is some of that between us already. We have a history between us. We understand one another. You are not a green girl any more. I've not stopped thinking of you in all the years we've spent apart.'

'You've had two wives, sir,' Annorah scolded. She wouldn't let him see the fear he raised in her. Surely no harm would come to her. They were surrounded by people and Nicholas was here somewhere.

He shrugged as if the others were of no consequence. 'Place holders for you, my dear. It's always been you I've wanted. I've waited quite a while for you and now you're engaged to another man. I am sure there's something we can do about that.'

'No!' Annorah said fiercely, her fear for herself transmuting into fear for Nicholas. 'Don't you dare lay a hand on him.'

'Or you'll what?' Redding snorted. 'How can you possibly protect him? He doesn't know, does he? He doesn't know about you and me.'

'There was never any you and me. There was

you bullying a young girl into a very compromising position.'

'Nuance.' Redding smirked. 'Shall I ruin him? Would you have him then? Every man has a weakness. I'll find his and then where will you be?' He leaned close. 'I know about the deadline, Annorah. Are you willing to lose everything over him?' He stepped back. 'Think about it. I am willing to cut you a very good deal to save him and save your fortune. You only have your body to bargain with, but fortunately, that's exactly what I'm after.'

'Good day, Mr Redding.' She no longer cared how rude her departure looked or how it sounded. She wanted to reach Nicholas's side with a single-minded determination. She should have told him. She'd not thought Redding would go after Nicholas, but she should have. It seemed so obvious now in hindsight. She was not the only one on a deadline. He was, too. He stood to lose if she slipped away from him again.

Her emotions must have been written all over her face. Nicholas broke away from his group and came to her. He slipped his hand around hers with no questions. 'Come on, let's go. We've an hour before lunch is ready. No one will miss us. There's a little path just to the right. We can walk quite a way and still be in plain sight, but out of hearing. Now, whatever is the matter? You look like you want to destroy something.'

'Not something, someone.' Her voice trembled with emotion.

'Redding? I saw you with him. I was trying to keep an eye on that,' Nicholas surmised, running his thumb over the back of her hand in a soothing gesture. 'What did he say?'

'He hates you.'

'Because I have you,' Nicholas supplied.

'In part. I think he'd hate you anyway,' Annorah said with a flash of insight. 'I don't think he likes attractive men.'

Nicholas cocked an eyebrow. 'That's probably for the best.'

Annorah laughed for the first time that morning. 'That's not what I meant. He tried to convince me what an awful husband you'll make and, when that failed, he threatened to harm you.'

A contemplative look crossed Nicholas's features. 'I find that extremely interesting since your aunt spent most of last night trying to convince me what a terrible wife you'll make. Why do you suppose that is?' Nick tipped her chin up to meet his gaze. 'What haven't you told me, Annorah?'

Chapter Seventeen

'I don't know,' Annorah stammered, her eyes falling away from his face, a sure sign she was hiding something. A cold knot formed in his stomach. Her aunt Georgina's words rushed back along with Westmore's speculations and the fears of the night rose. What was she using him for? The defence he'd given Westmore on her behalf last night seemed feeble when confronted with this confession from her. How could he be so wrong about someone? Usually, he was a good judge of character. He could size up a person, moral code and all, with astonishing accuracy.

Nicholas stepped away from her and folded his arms. 'I think you do. Why don't you start talking and we'll figure out the truth from here?'

Her eyes flashed at that. 'I have not lied to you!'

He did believe that to a certain degree. 'You have not twisted the facts or distorted them, but I think you've conveniently left out some inconvenient truths.' He had her there. Her shoulders slumped and she put her forehead in her hand, rubbing at the space between her brows.

'Please, it's not like that.'

'Yes, it is. It is exactly like that.' He stepped forwards and pulled her hand away from her face, his voice softening. He dropped a kiss on her forehead and ran his hands down her arms. 'Don't let them see you upset. They'll think we've had a quarrel. I'm not sure that's what we want.' A thought came to him. 'I'd hate for them to think we could be so easily divided and conquered in the space of a day.' It was a shot in the dark.

Annorah lifted her head, her green eyes sparkling with wet tears, and his heart lurched. He was mixing that business with pleasure Westmore had warned about. 'They would like that.'

'Then tell me, what I am really doing here? I can't help if I don't know how. What is Redding to you? You know him from before don't you? Your aunt said "Do you remember Redding" yesterday when she introduced him.'

They started walking again, her arm back in his. Nicholas tried not to think of how right she felt beside him or how used he'd got to having her there. He needed all of his brain to follow her story.

'Redding courted me years ago. He was my aunt's choice. They had struck an alliance between them. She'd pave the way to courting me and he'd reward her once we married with generous access to the family fortune, which would fall under his purvey as my husband.' Annorah shrugged. 'Let us just say Redding was in earnest.'

Nicholas felt his anger rise. He knew very well what 'earnestness' meant in this context. 'Did he force himself on you?' Obviously, Redding had been unsuccessful. He'd been Annorah's first lover. Knowing this, he took extra pride in the fact that it had been at her request and he'd done his best, far better of an encounter than any she would have had with Redding.

'The worst of it was that it was my fault.' Annorah shook her head. 'At first, I believed him. I thought his sentiments were true, that he did care for me. He was a neighbour. He wasn't like the other suitors, who were strangers I'd met at dances for the first time. At the time, I thought he was attractive enough. One day, I went out walking with him. He had been calling on me most of the summer and my aunt felt such privacy was acceptable for us. When we were out of sight, he kissed me. I let him. I confess to being curious. But he didn't let it stop there. He wanted more than kisses.'

He could see the memories pained her. He absolutely despised men who didn't know their limits. He'd like to call the bastard out. 'You don't have to say anything more,' Nick assured her softly.

Annorah stopped walking and turned to face him. 'But I do. He's mean and he's vindictive. You have to understand how ruthless he is. He threatened to ruin you if I didn't come to him.'

'I can take care of myself, Annorah. He wouldn't be any worse than any other jealous husband,' Nicholas said grimly.

'I can't allow it.' Her face was pale, her concern tangible in her green eyes. 'I release you. I shouldn't have dragged you into this. I should have told you about Redding so you could have made a better decision. I didn't think he'd come after you. I thought he would leave it as a battle between the two of us.'

'And I can't allow that,' Nicholas said sternly. 'I agreed to be in this and I don't want out now.' He could not leave Annorah to face this ghost from the past by herself. He knew how potent those ghosts could be and hers were in the flesh.

They began climbing the slope up to the prospect. 'You don't want to get messed up with me, Nicholas. You might think I'm perfect, but I'm not. Redding wasn't the only suitor I refused, just the last. My aunt and uncle would not let this pass. When I told them about his advances, they said it was no more than I deserved for leading him on. A man was entitled to his urges.'

He was going to shoot the bastard and then he was going to shoot Aunt Georgina with her wandering hands. But he understood Annorah better and what had driven her to write that letter, what had driven her into seclusion in the first place. Bartholomew Redding wasn't the first suitor to abuse her finer sentiments, but he'd been the final piece of evidence she needed to believe she was worth nothing to any man but her bank account.

'That's when you went back to Hartshaven?' Nicholas prompted. All the pieces were fitting nicely now. Annorah would not have been more than twenty-one, maybe twenty-two. It was a young age to run an estate that size on her own. It was also a young age to shut oneself away from the world.

'Yes, and each year I was there, I had less and less use for the social world beyond the village. My aunt and uncle could feel their access to the Price-Ellis fortune slipping away.'

Nicholas saw where this was going. 'Hence, the summons to the house party.'

Annorah picked at the flower petals along the walk. 'Exactly.'

They'd reached the top of the hill. Annorah gave a small smile and studied the view. They were high enough to afford them a prospect of the land. Below them, the picnickers looked small, nothing more than a colourful group of people out for an enjoyable afternoon. 'Everything looks a lot less harmless at a distance. One would never guess what a viper's pit it really is down there and that's not even counting Mr Westmore.'

Nicholas shrugged. 'Westmore is nothing to

us.' That didn't mean he wasn't a pain in the backside, but he posed no harm to the ruse and that was Annorah's biggest concern. 'He's with the agency, but he's not here working. He's not going to expose us.' He saw relief cross Annorah's face. He felt some relief, too. If there was going to be trouble with Redding, Westmore would be good backup.

'Well, that's one less thing to worry about, thankfully, because my aunt and Mr Redding are enough trouble to manage without a third party interfering.'

Nicholas wanted to correct her on that point. He'd never said anything about Westmore *not* interfering. The man had raised plenty of interfering questions last night. Some of those had been allayed today. Every story had two sides and now that he'd heard Annorah's side, he could return to his initial assessment of her character. Annorah had the misfortune of being a woman used for her money. She'd chosen to protect her principles by withdrawing from the social field, a choice which had drawn the wrath of her relatives. Her choice had been a difficult but admirable one and his regard for her rose another notch. She'd taken the high road even though it had cost her. There had been no such high road for him.

'I suppose we should go back down. They're setting out the picnic blankets.' Annorah turned her head in a swift movement and he stepped back just in time to avoid being swatted with the wide brim of her hat. The new leghorns were pretty, but dangerous. A man had to be on his toes to avoid being hit. He had to be on his toes, too, if he wanted to steal a kiss beneath one. Nicholas wanted. He wanted it with a shocking amount of urgency, too. He kissed a lot of women because it was expected, but seldom did he *want* to.

'Wait.' Nicholas tugged at her hand, drawing her to him. 'We aren't leaving until I do this.' He cupped her cheek with a hand and took her mouth with his in a sweet, lingering kiss. 'It has been far too long since I've done that.' Only a day, in truth, but it felt as if eons had passed since those lazy mornings lying abed at Hartshaven, or the long afternoons, or the passionate nights. Just as shocking as his need to kiss her had been was the sudden stab of longing for Hartshaven. He wanted to be back there, with her. He wanted it to be just the two of them living in their own world without conniving aunts and arrogant asses of suitors.

'How soon do you think we can leave?' Nicholas murmured carelessly. The words slipped out before he could rethink the wisdom of them and their underlying assumptions—the most important assumption being that she'd want him to return to Hartshaven with her.

'After the ball. It's tomorrow night. We could leave the day after.' Her words brought them both up short. The careless conversation had backed them into a corner where they'd be forced to talk about the future and how to proceed with their sham engagement.

Annorah straightened and stepped back out of kissing range. Her hands smoothed her skirts in an anxious fidget. '*Can* you come back?'

Nick thought of Channing's concern over Burroughs on a rampage. 'My time is my own for a while.' Nicholas reached for her hand and kissed it. She had enough to worry about without worrying about his problems, too. 'Perhaps I'll find a place to stay in the village, so I am not under your roof.'

She smiled, relaxing. 'Thomas would like that.'

'He would indeed.' Nick laughed. The future was taking care of itself. This would do for now. He tucked her arm through his.

She was about to say something else and he feared he knew the words. He didn't want to hear them. Nicholas moved in quickly, silencing her with a rough kiss. The speed had surprised her. But that had been his intention. He did not want to hear her say the words *'I will pay you.'*

As they walked down the hill towards the picnickers, Nicholas struggled with the knowledge that this had stopped being about getting paid. He wasn't sure when that had happened. Maybe it had happened gradually since the arrival of Channing's note. Maybe it had happened all at once after Westmore's inelegant challenges to Annorah's suitability. It was quite possible, too, that this had all been brought on by an extreme fit of stubbornness on his part. He never had liked being wrong and he did tend to dig in his heels when confronted with a contrary opinion. Perhaps he could blame Westmore for that. This shift had happened because he was being contrary.

But that was the easy answer. The harder answer was that in enacting a facsimile of love for Annorah Price-Ellis, he'd actually fallen for his own fantasy. Too bad for him. Those were thoughts he'd have to keep to himself. There was no question of telling her. A real relationship would require he tell her other things, too. What would the point of that be? Eventually, this would all be over. Walking away when it was done was not optional. It was a requirement. He had to whether or not his emotions came with him. One of the primary tenets of the agency lay in the belief you were always better as a memory.

Annorah squeezed his hand as the picnic meadow came into view. 'Promise me you'll be on your guard?'

Nick gave her a laugh. 'I'm more worried about your aunt's hands than Redding. Yes, I'll be careful.' But he wasn't being careful and he knew it. His emotions were exposed and his feelings engaged and that possessed its own kind of danger. He would embrace the danger and let it run its course, consequences be damned.

It did run its course throughout the warm afternoon. There were cold ham sandwiches to eat, midsummer strawberries to pick and a few golden stolen moments to rest his head in Annorah's lap and look up into her green eyes. Most of all, he did enjoy it just as he'd promised himself, right up to the point where they returned to the house, stepped into the hall and were met by Uncle Andrew with the ominous words, 'As my niece's fiancé, I think it's time you and I had a talk. If you would step this way, Mr D'Arcy?'

Nicholas shot Annorah a quick look of reassurance, letting her know she had nothing to fear from this interaction. As for himself, he could only cling to the old adage forewarned was forearmed.

Good God, the girl was rich! Nicholas's head was reeling from the figures her uncle had tossed around when he emerged from the study two hours later with barely enough time to change for dinner.

After seeing the numbers, it was no wonder her coming out had been plagued with disappointments. It wasn't a gentleman's fortune, to be sure. It was a fortune earned in trade and through investment, a dirty fortune in the eyes of the *ton*, perhaps. Then again, when there was enough of it perhaps it didn't matter as much where a woman's fortune came from. *It hardly matters to you if it came from mucking manure. You aren't really her fiancé. You won't see a penny of it*, came the cold reminder from his conscience. *You have your two thousand pounds and you'll be thankful for it.*

'How's the old father-in-law?' Westmore stepped out of the shadows at the top of the landing. 'The two of you were closeted away for quite some time. There's only one reason for that. Settlements.'

'It's the natural course of things,' Nicholas said slowly, trying to assess what Westmore wanted. 'How is it going for you? Anyone catch your eye?' He opted for the old trick of deflection— more about Westmore, less about himself.'

'Maybe.' Westmore was vague and the trick didn't work. 'I'm worried about you. Deveril didn't send me to keep an eye on you, but I'm glad I'm here to do it.'

'There's nothing to worry about. I have it all under control,' Nicholas said in a low voice. It would all be under a little less control if they were overheard in the hall.

'No, you don't. You've got pound notes dancing in your eyes. You're starting to think you could kiss it out of her and make the ruse real.'

'That is ridiculous. I've squired around plenty of wealthy women and never once has that thought crossed my mind,' Nicholas growled.

Westmore merely chuckled. 'Most of them have been married. You've never liked one of them as much as you like her. I admit, your Miss Price-Ellis is quite lovely and fresh. She's not one of your London jades. That freshness can be appealing, especially when you know you were her first. I bet you're feeling protective and honourable right about now, at least that's what you're telling yourself.'

'You can stop right there.' The man was a damned mind reader, certainly about the latter. He did want to protect Annorah. She was strong in her own right, but he didn't want her to have to be strong on her own, not when he could stand beside her.

As for the former, he didn't want to confess to any feelings about the money. He'd rather not have known the specifics. It was one thing to know vaguely that she was wealthy. That had always been a known factor. To know *exactly* how wealthy did change things. It was impossible for it not to. But not in the way Westmore thought. The money didn't draw him. It pushed him away. There'd been moments when he'd thought she needed him as more than a man in her bed. He'd begun to believe he had more to offer her than his prick. The settlements, seeing that enormous mass of money, reminded him he did not.

Nicholas pushed past Westmore. He wished the subject of money had never been brought up, which, when one thought about it, was a very odd wish indeed for a poor man with debts to pay and a family to feed, a certain sign of just how upside down his world had become.

Chapter Eighteen

The world had gone crazy and Annorah was doing a poor job of distracting herself from that fact. She was supposed to be getting dressed for dinner, but all she could manage was pacing the length of her room and wondering about Nicholas and the money. What would he think of it all? Would he be angry that she hadn't offered him more once he saw all the wealth laid before him? Or would he be too dazzled? Would the money lead him astray? Would it tempt him into offering to make the engagement real? She feared the idea. She wanted him to be different.

Annorah picked up the brush from her vanity and began to comb through her hair, vetting it for any errant leaves or twigs from the picnic. She brushed with vigour as if hard strokes could banish the uncomfortable thoughts from her mind. How could she want him to be different? She didn't know him, not really, and she *couldn't* know him. The money would always get in the way, it already had. It was tempting even her. Perhaps *she* could use it to persuade *him* to make the engagement real.

Was that what she wanted? Marriage to an illusion of a man? Was the man she saw each day really Nicholas or a façade? Had she fallen in love with a man who was nothing more than an illusion created for her pleasure or had she fallen for the man himself? She didn't know what was worse: loving an illusion of someone who never was or loving something that could never be. With Nicholas it was hard to tell.

And yet, on the hill today, she'd felt there'd been moments that he'd been as real as he had with the children in the village, as he'd been at the summer house; that his regard was genuine, and that his concern for her outpaced the promise of her pounds. Annorah put down the brush and rang for Lily, desperate to get away from her thoughts. Hiring Nicholas was supposed to have been easy. It was supposed to have solved her problems and curiosities while avoiding all the complications of a real relationship; there'd be no doubt over money, there'd be no emotional attachments because it was all temporary. It was just supposed to be about sex. And it had been, until it wasn't. She was no longer sure when that point had been reached, only that it had been passed.

She dressed carefully with Lily's help, selecting an aquamarine chiffon that was all summer and light. She let Lily put up her hair, threading a strand of pearls through the artfully twisted tresses. She would need her strength to face Nicholas regardless of the outcome of her uncle's talk.

He was waiting for her in the hall before entering the drawing room as he'd done the previous night, but guests, *female* guests, were too impatient to wait for his appearance there so they'd joined him out here. He looked up at her with a winning smile and Redding's words stabbed at her heart. To have him would never be enough if he didn't want her, too. Rich women could always have a trophy. It was the reason she hadn't married before now, the very principle that lay at the heart of the current situation. She had never wanted the trophy any more than she'd wanted to be someone else's trophy, a thing no more meaningful to them than a silver cup displayed on a shelf, taken down and shown off on occasion.

She slid on to his arm, acutely aware any woman in the little circle would take her place if they could. Tonight she would show them they couldn't and maybe she'd show Nicholas he wouldn't want them to for reasons that had nothing to do with the pounds attached to her name, even if it was an exercise in futility.

This was most interesting. From his end of the table, Nicholas watched Annorah dazzle the gentleman to her right. Couples had all been split up tonight for the seating chart at dinner. While it gave him a respite from her aunt's wandering hands, it also took him away from Annorah. Still, it was enlightening to watch her at a distance. She was much changed from the woman who'd met him in the hall of her home with hands clasped nervously at her waist. The change was for the better. Then, he'd thought her quietly pretty. Tonight, she positively sparkled. Some of that sparkle was literal; she wore tiny diamonds at her ears, nothing as big as what a London ball required, but not too ostentatious for the country either. A matching bracelet at her wrist gave off fiery sparks in the candlelight. He could catch the faintest trill of her laughter and every once in a while he would catch her eye. It was tantalising and he had the vague idea she was flirting with him in this long-distance fashion of hers. It must be working because he was more than slightly aroused and a great many of his thoughts revolved around getting her to bed by the time cheese and fruit was served.

She caught his eye as she plucked a strawberry from the tray and bit into, licking the juice from her lips with a quick flick of her tongue. That did it. He was rock hard and racing through potential excuses for departing the company early when the women rose to leave the gentlemen.

Nicholas smiled. He had his plan. He'd feign a headache after a few sips of port and make his escape. She would note he was missing from the group when the gentlemen rejoined the ladies and she would come to him. Actually, that was the best part of the plan. She wouldn't have to.

* * *

Nicholas was waiting for her when Annorah came up an hour later. Not just waiting, but on-her-bed waiting, his banyan loose about him. He wouldn't give her the chance to go back on the implicit promises she'd been making over dinner. She wanted him for dessert? Very well, she was going to have him.

She jumped a little at the sight of him and he laughed. 'Were you expecting someone else?'

'No, of course not.' Annorah shut the door behind her and locked it. 'Anyone could have walked in here and seen you!'

'But why? This is your room. Only *you* should have been walking in here.' Nicholas chuckled. He got off the bed to help her with the buttons on the back of her dress. He nuzzled her neck. 'I've missed this.' He had. It was absolutely true. He'd not liked being parted from her last night, one more errant feeling in his world turned topsy-turvy. She smelled of lemons, tangy and sweet all at once, eternal summer. He would not be able to smell lemons again without thinking of her. Westmore would laugh at him for such sentimentality. But Westmore would be sleeping alone to-night.

He pushed the dress down, undergarments following suit as his eyes feasted on the expanse of bare back. 'Come lie down. I have a surprise for you,' he whispered, his voice hoarse. He'd meant to seduce her with his hands. Now, he wondered if he would last long enough to do it. 'On your stomach, Annorah, I want your back.'

He straddled her then, rising up to remove his banyan. He pulled a vial from its pocket and pulled out the tiny stopper. The scent of lavender and thyme filled the air around them. 'Breathe deep, Annorah. Lavender is for relaxing.'

She wiggled beneath him while he poured oil into his hands, her buttocks brushing against his sac. 'What are you doing?'

'I am warming the oil.' Nicholas blew on the liquid pooled in his hands.

'Oil? What for?' She tried to roll over, but Nicholas held her firmly between his thighs.

'Have you ever had a massage?' He began to rub, starting at her shoulders, relishing the feel of her skin, supple and firm beneath his hands.

'No.' Annorah laughed. 'Aside from our treasure hunt, where do you think I would have encountered such a decadent experience?'

'Decadent? Good, then I must be doing it right.' He swept his hand down to the small of her back, kneading the muscles there. Her muscles were tight, a sign of the strain the house party had put her under. 'According to eastern practices, a massage has both medicinal and sensual purposes.' He leaned forwards to reach her ear. 'I prefer the sensual.' His phallus was at full mast now, proof that a massage could be just as arousing for the giver as the receiver.

He cupped her buttocks, sliding down to kiss each one before moving on to massage her legs.

'Mmm, this is nice,' Annorah murmured. As if on cue, she rolled over and reached for him, drawing him over her. He settled between her legs. The massage had done its work. She was relaxed and ready for him. They could take their time with this joining. For tonight, that was what he preferred—a long leisurely goodbye, one that would imprint itself on his memory.

He kissed her and moved into position, but she halted him with her eyes. 'Perhaps we should talk about this afternoon first? I meant to ask you in the hall before dinner, but we were surrounded by so many of your admirers.'

'It was an eye opener. I understand better now what you were up against. You're no mere heiress.' He'd been overwhelmed by what was to be conferred upon her husband after marriage. But more than that, he'd been overwhelmed by what that must have meant for her as a young woman coming out. She would have been hounded by people seeking her hand for the purpose of accessing her fortune. His heart had gone out to her. He just couldn't be that man.

'Do you see now why I have to be the one to pick my husband?'

Nicholas nodded. Her aunt would pick a suitor who would be happy to funnel the funds her direction as a thank you for putting a rich wife in his path. If Annorah chose, she could negotiate that privately before the husband even saw the settlements, as she'd done with him.

'Good.' Annorah shifted beneath him, raising up on her elbows and staring him in the eye, all seriousness. 'Now that you understand, I want to ask you something else.'

Nick held his breath, not liking where the conversation was headed. 'You can ask me anything.' But that wasn't true. There were at least three or four things he didn't want to answer.

'Is it always like this? This thing between you and me? This passion, this pleasure, this craving like I'll never get enough?'

That was one of them. He definitely didn't want to answer that, but he wouldn't lie. He shook his head. 'No, it's not.' He paused to gather his thoughts. 'I suppose it's usually fun, but how do I explain it? The layers aren't always there.' He rolled to his side. His erection was going to have to wait for satisfaction. 'If you're asking me how it is with other clients…' he winced, hating the use of the word. Annorah was so much more than a client '…it's not like this. And I don't think it would necessarily be like this for you with someone else, if that's what you want to know.' He hated thinking of her with another.

'Thank you, Nick,' Annorah said softly. She levered up to look at him, a finger drawing circles on his chest. 'Did you think about making the engagement real today after you saw all the money? Because I did.'

'Oh, Annorah.' This was another thing he didn't want her to ask.

'Why not?' She warmed to her subject and Nicholas felt his heart sink. 'You just said we suited one another in bed at least. You need the money and I think we could make each other happy if we tried. I have to marry someone, Nick, now or in a year. Why not you? You might be the best choice I've come across in fifteen years.'

Nicholas sat up, dislodging her hand. 'No, Annorah. You don't want to marry me. I promise you I'm not your best choice.'

She sat up, too, her hair falling forwards, her cheeks flushed with anger. He would not be making love to her tonight, he just knew it. 'Tell me. Tell me why you are not my best choice?'

Nick got out of bed and shrugged into his banyan. He might as well put it on now. 'What do you think will happen when we go to London? We can't help but meet former clients and not all of them are nice, Annorah. They will be catty and someone will say to you, "I've been in bed with your husband". Worse, they might even start unpleasant rumours. Rumours travel. Can you imagine the look on your vicar's face?

On Thomas's face when the news reaches Hart-shaven about what I really am? You will not think I'm the best choice for you then, Annorah.'

'You should let me be the judge of that,' Annorah said quietly, but it was clear he'd shocked her. He hated doing it, but it was what must be done to make her see reason.

'That's just the start. There's the money, too—rumours will spread I only married you for the wealth. After a while you might start to believe them. They'll say I kissed it out of you, that all I had to offer you was my prick.'

She threw a pillow at him. 'Don't be crass. I hate it when you do that, when you think you're nothing but a sex object. I can listen to all of your other arguments, but not that one. You're a fine man, Nicholas D'Arcy. I wish you could see it, too.'

That humbled him. His hands stalled where they tied the sash of his banyan. She would think differently if she knew his secrets, of course. If she knew how one stormy night he'd failed his family, his father dead because of it, his brother paralysed. 'I'll honour our agreement, Annorah.

Not because you've paid me, but because I want to. But that's all. I can't marry you.'

Her jaw set, stubborn and determined. 'There's more, isn't there? It's not just the money, or the scandal. Will you tell me?'

'It would be better if you didn't know.' But Nick knew there would be no escaping it. The way to his freedom lay in the telling of the tale. She would either despise him and let him go because she could not bear to be associated with him, or she would accept him, flaws and all. The last was too great to hope for.

'Let me be the judge, Nicholas,' she whispered, reaching for his hands and drawing him to the edge of the bed. 'What happened?'

Nicholas started to talk. He'd not told anyone, not even Channing, about that horrible night. 'During a storm, lightning split a tree, a giant oak, near the stables. It came down and tore right through the stable roof. My father and Stefan were inside, trying to calm the horses down. The storm had set them off something terrible. I was just a minute behind them. When I arrived they were already inside. I saw the lightning strike the tree, I saw the tree split and I knew what was going to happen. It was all in slow motion like a bad dream. I ran and I shouted, but I didn't run fast enough, didn't shout loud enough. The tree went down, straight through the roof, and I couldn't reach them.'

Annorah squeezed his hand. 'It wasn't your fault.'

He gave a hoarse laugh. 'You are absolutely wrong there. Do you want to know why the roof fell? Do you want to know why I wasn't there?' This was the worst part of the story. He could have accepted that tragic accidents happened. But this was more. This had been accident of his own making.

Annorah was looking at him expectantly. He forged on. 'I was supposed to have been working on reinforcing the support beams that week. But I'd taken a self-appointed holiday that afternoon to meet a girl I'd become fond of.' He could feel the tic in his cheek working. 'I left the last beam unfinished, never dreaming there'd be a summer storm that very night. I spent the afternoon with her in an old woodcutter's cottage on the property. I was still there with her when the storm came up.' He shook his head. 'Maybe if I'd been home I could have warned them the beam wasn't steady. But I had a half-mile to run to reach them.'

He drew a deep breath. 'You can't say it wasn't my fault. It was. My father died instantly. Stefan was caught under the beam. I pulled him out, but it wasn't enough. He was paralysed. He still is. He's trapped in a wheelchair because I wasn't where I was supposed to be and they paid for it.'

He watched her jaw soften and she reached out an arm towards him. 'It's a terrible story, but you have to forgive yourself. I might not know exactly what you feel, but I do know what it's like to feel guilt.'

She did, he realised. She was faced with the guilt of how her decisions would affect her remaining family. There was solace in that. Perhaps she of all people did understand a little of what he felt.

'There is no question of going back to Hart-shaven with you now. But I will still honour the engagement if you want me to,' Nick said softly. He rose to go, but she held him fast with a hand about his wrist.

'I want you to honour more than the engagement, Nick.' Her eyes were full of unspoken words. She wanted him in her bed one more time and he could give her that, he could give himself that. Nicholas placed soft kisses over each of her eyes. They had a day and a night. Surely that would be enough time to store up the memories, to imprint the feel of her on his body, starting with this sweet, slick slide home as she closed around him and held him like she'd never let him go.

This was going well, was the one thought running through Bartholomew Redding's mind. Others might disagree. To the outsider, he might appear to be the passed-over suitor, a most pathetic position to be sure. But he knew better.

Redding whistled to himself, rocking back on his heels as he looked up from the gardens, trying to discern which room was Annorah's, not that it took a lot of thinking. At the middle window the light was out, the only room entirely in the dark. Other rooms on that side of the hall remained lit, mostly because everyone was still engaged in the drawing room or playing billiards. Georgina Timmerman's staff made a practice of leaving a lamp lit in everyone's rooms until they fell asleep.

He doubted there was much sleeping going on in that room. He'd been with the gentlemen when D'Arcy had pleaded a headache and left early and he'd been with the entire company when Annorah had quietly departed the evening games. It didn't take much of an imagination, just a lurid one, to know what sort of nightcap she'd find waiting in her room. She'd been a bold piece of baggage at dinner, flirting the length of the table. He doubted D'Arcy was the only man who'd gone hard when she'd mouthed the strawberry.

Redding fingered the folded letter in his pocket. He'd give them this night of peace. He could afford to be generous when victory was close at hand. Besides, he wanted Annorah to get her money's worth out of her investment.

Oh, yes, he knew it all now. His connections in London had known just where to look for the information he wanted. What amazed him was why he hadn't guessed sooner. The story was a little too pat. A truly cynical mind would never believe Annorah, who'd managed to stay unengaged for ten years, would actually show up with a fiancé in tow after five years of those ten in virtual seclusion. To have that fiancé be dashing, handsome, well mannered and devoid of any backward socialisms was far too suspicious to go unremarked.

The Timmermans had seen the development as an obstacle. He'd seen it as a mystery and that made all the difference. They had not stopped to question the authenticity of her claim. But he had.

The next question was how to use the information and when? Because the news was going to come out and when it did, Miss Price-Ellis would be desperate for a proverbial port in the storm. In the attempt to recover some decency from the scandal, she'd be glad enough to marry any man who offered that protection, even him. And that was the plan, of course.

Redding drew out a cheroot and lit it, the flame of the match flaring in the darkness. He took a deep, satisfied puff. Coupled with what he knew now, her bit of boldness at the table came as no surprise. Shrinking violets didn't hire petticoat-mongers. But Annorah had. It made a man wonder what other prizes she might have in store for him given the right inducement.

Chapter Nineteen

Nothing was going to ruin tonight! Annorah was nearly as giddy as a school girl at her first ball in an oyster gown of summer silk, the skirt with its embroidered hem of tangerine-and-turquoise flowers belling about her ankles as she swept down the staircase.

Nearly nothing, anyway. She couldn't quite erase the reality that the last night with Nicholas was here. It was a moment that had been inevitable since she'd sent the letter, but one she'd refused to linger on in sadness today. There would be time enough for sadness afterwards. It was far more efficient to focus on the joy that existed in the time remaining.

Her breath caught as she stepped inside the drawing room, which had been pressed into service as a ballroom for the night. It had been transformed for the evening into a midsummer night's wonderland. The carpet had been taken up and all the furniture relocated to other rooms, hallways or simply lined against the wall for seating. Fresh flowers and candles were everywhere, the ceiling draped with billowing swathes of dark, glittery cloth adorned with brillantes to give the image of a summer night's sky. On the far side of the room, the bays of French doors stood open so that guests might feel the illusion of not knowing where the outdoors began and indoors finished. It was masterfully done. Regardless of her feelings towards her aunt, Aunt Georgina knew how to give a party.

'It's beautiful, isn't it?' she breathed as Nicholas approached. It was a marvel to her how he knew the minute she was in a room and was unerringly at her side.

He swept her a bow. 'A beautiful setting for a beautiful lady. You don't deserve less. Tonight you will be my Titania and I will be your Oberon.'

Annorah laughed. 'Don't they quarrel? Aren't they plagued by mischief?'

Nicholas shrugged and led her into the depths of the room. 'That's merely details. More importantly, they are the king and queen of midsummer in the forest.'

Sets were forming for the first dance, a traditional quadrille, and they joined a group close to the open doors, where a cooling breeze served to keep the room comfortable. 'I like your version better,' Annorah said as they took their places.

'I do, too.' Nicholas flashed her an impish grin more reminiscent of Puck than Oberon and the dance was underway. The quadrille was a long dance, full of coming together and parting patterns and he teased her with little bits of conversation designed to leave her wanting more.

On the first pass he said, 'When I thought of midsummer, I never imagined myself in a place like this.'

'Where did you imagine yourself?' she asked, only to recognise there wasn't enough time for him to answer as they moved on to new partners.

'If I was in London, I'd be in Richmond at Lady Hyde's midsummer masquerade.' Again they parted, but with more anxiety on her part. Who would he have been with? What would he have been doing? She would have preferred he'd not shared that bit of information if it was going to lead to such disclosures. She didn't want to picture him with another, laughing, smiling, talking.

The dance ended and a lively polka began immediately, taking away a chance for more talk in its whirlwind. Nicholas was superb at the country dance and Annorah felt like she was flying as he wove them about the floor, weaving in and out of other couples effortlessly. With another partner, she might have worried about an inelegant crash as the result of such careless passes, but with Nicholas the thought never crossed her mind, not when there were so many other things to think about: the graceful power of his body as he led them through the steps, the warm press of his hand at her back, the firm grip of his hand on hers, his blue eyes laughing down at her as they whirled. Whatever doubts his comments had raised were abandoned in the dance. He was having a good time.

They were both breathless afterwards and Nicholas led her through the opened doors into the garden. It was strung with paper lanterns and already peopled with couples taking advantage of the mild summer night.

'I haven't danced like that in ages!' Nicholas said with breathless enthusiasm.

'Don't they dance like that in London?'

'Not really. We have our waltzes and polkas, certainly, but it's a slightly more sedate pace. Maybe we think we're too sophisticated to indulge our passions so publicly.'

We. Our. She heard it in his vocabulary. It wasn't meant maliciously, but he was moving away from her a little bit at a time. Maybe that was what tonight was about, too, a weaning of sorts. He was remembering his other life, his *real* life. Why shouldn't he? She had already planned how she was going to spend the first hours away from him. Her mind had raced ahead, making lists of things to do at Hartshaven when she returned. It was a defence mechanism against wandering the halls and missing him. Perhaps he was doing the same.

'Do you miss London so very much, then? I know you've been gone longer than you anticipated. I do appreciate it, though.' She thought of the letter he'd received at Hartshaven. He never had disclosed the contents, but it had been from London. She thought, too, of the newspapers he'd read regularly with breakfast. He'd seemed hungry for news. He'd read methodically as if searching for something. It all spoke of a strong connection with the city. His life was there, his social ties were there.

They halted their walk near a rose arbour covered in tiny pink buds. Nicholas reached out his free hand to pluck a pink bloom. 'That's a harder question to answer than you might think, Annorah.' He checked the rose carefully for thorns and tucked it behind her ear. 'When I think of London, I think of all the things I'd like to show you there. It's a fabulous city if you give it a chance.' He made a slashing gesture with his hand. 'I don't mean the usual, like Astley's Amphitheatre or the Tower. I want to show you my London.'

Annorah smiled. 'Like your Norwegian fisherman and his lutefisk.'

'You remembered.' The comment seemed to please him. Of course she remembered. Silly man, didn't he know she remembered everything he'd ever said to her, ever did with her?

'There are other places, too. I want to show you

Soho. It's like a little Europe full of immigrants who have made new lives for themselves in London. Soho is full of their restaurants and foods.'

Annorah could imagine it. Nicholas's London would be like the man himself: vibrant and alive, claiming the joy of each moment. She wanted to see that London. 'I think your London would be wonderful,' was all she could manage. To say more would be awkward. There was no question of him showing her his London any more than there was a question of her going to London. The ruse did not extend that far.

'What will you do when you get back?' she asked quietly. They both knew he couldn't stay at the inn near Hartshaven forever. It hurt to ask, but in the long run perhaps she'd be glad for the knowledge. It would give her a way to picture him, a way to keep him with her a little longer. Their façade did not require he be with her for the year. It was possible he'd go to London and never come back when he tired of Hartshaven. At least this way, she could look at the clock and say to herself, *It's six o'clock, Nicholas will be getting ready for the dinner party. It's eight o'clock; Nicholas will be going on to the opera.*

'I don't know.' Nicholas's answer made her feel more than a bit guilty. He'd be at loose ends in London because of his arrangement with her. He wouldn't be working.

'Well, whatever you do, I don't think you'll miss Westmore.' Annorah laughed.

'Westmore? It's not that I don't like him, it's that he's a hard man to know. His circumstances are a bit different than the rest of us.'

'The rest of us.' Annorah felt the statement should speak volumes about Nicholas and the agency, but she couldn't unravel it, she didn't know enough to understand the reference, a glaring reminder that Nicholas was not all he seemed, or was that more than what he seemed? He had another life. 'Are you going to tell me what that means?'

'I'll tell you this much. Most of us have fallen from grace. Westmore is climbing up to it.'

'Will you ever tell me about your fall, Nicholas?' It was the one thing she wanted to know about him. Who was he and how had he arrived at this point? What drove him? There was more to it than the accident. She was sure all those questions could be answered if she knew the whole of his story.

'I'd much rather kiss you.' Nicholas tipped her chin up, catching it between his thumb and forefinger. His mouth claimed hers as if it were the most natural thing in the world and, as always, his kisses swept away any ability for cogent thought, all need to know his story replaced with an entirely different need.

'There's a bower just beyond the boxwoods,' Nicholas whispered. 'We'll have privacy enough.'

One last time. It would be a wicked memory to treasure; she and Nicholas out of doors at a ball, with a risk of discovery. Not that anyone would care too much since they were 'engaged', but her aunt would care a little. All those elements combined made it all that more delicious.

They slipped stealthily from the path, sliding into the bower's shadowy depths, where the lantern light didn't reach. There was a bench and Nicholas had her on his lap with lightning speed, her skirts bunched about her thighs, the evening air on her silk stockinged legs. His hand worked the trouser fastenings at his flap. His member sprung free, hard and hot against her core while his hand fumbled in his coat pocket for a French letter.

'Are you always this prepared?' she teased, blowing lightly against his ear as he fitted the sheath over himself.

'Not prepared so much as hopeful, Annorah,' he whispered against her throat. 'I hoped we'd have a chance to be together. I didn't want that chance to go to waste.'

There was a rustle at the bower's entrance. She felt the intrusion in the clenching of Nicholas's arms about her, protective and defensive.

'Sorry to ruin your fun, then,' Westmore's gravelly tones broke in. 'But I think you'd better get back to the ballroom. Redding is about to make trouble. He may have already made it. It took me a while to find you.' The last was said with a bit of accusation. 'I can't watch your back if I don't know where it is.'

Nicholas helped her to her feet, standing in front of her to give her a moment's decency to right herself, never mind that Westmore had probably already seen far too much. She had the feeling she'd become *de trop*. The conversation had turned from love words to guns. Westmore asked Nicholas if he'd brought his pistols.

'I have mine, too, of course,' Westmore said to Nicholas's affirmative response. 'You needn't worry on that account.'

Nicholas had pistols with him? He'd been with her all this time and he'd come armed?

'What do you suppose Redding knows?' Nicholas was all efficient business as he tucked in his shirt tails and readjusted his trousers. Gone was the easy expression he usually wore, replaced by something far grimmer.

Annorah held her skirts in one hand and struggled to keep up with the men's long-legged, urgent strides. She'd been conveniently forgotten just as she'd suspected. She might as well have stayed back at the bower and redone her hair for all the attention they paid her. Nicholas had said he wasn't close with Westmore and now they were acting like bosom bows.

'It can only be one of two things or both,' Westmore supplied. 'Either he knows about the agency or he knows about Lord Burroughs's wife. I don't have to tell you it would be better if it were Burroughs.'

She watched the back of Nicholas's head nod in agreement. 'Then the scandal could all fall on me without jeopardising the agency and everyone in it.'

Burroughs's wife? What was *this*? Horror after horror raced through Annorah's mind. She found a burst of speed, her slippers sliding on the wet grass of the lawn. The shorter route back meant forgoing the pathways. She pushed in between them. 'Burroughs's wife? Whatever do you mean? What's going on?' She shouldn't have been surprised. She knew what he did and who he did it with. Yet, being so bluntly confronted with it was entirely different in practice than theory.

Westmore shot her a look of impatience reserved for dealing with idiots. 'His last client's husband got a bit jealous and the man has been tearing London apart looking for him ever since he crawled out of Burroughs's town-house window. What did you think Nick was doing here?'

Annorah felt sick. She could hardly breathe. 'Nicholas, is that true?' She grabbed the sleeve of his coat, forcing him to stop. She wished she hadn't. She searched his face in the light of paper lanterns, looking for denial but she found only pity. Pity for her, the poor rich girl who'd bought herself a lover and was now suddenly stunned that her lover had a history.

'Yes, it's true, but I can explain, just not now. We have to get back, we have to see what can be salvaged.'

Salvaged. It was a nice way of saying he had to wait and see what happened in order to plan his next strategy, a strategy that probably involved her. What would he have to tell her? What would she believe? What would she need answers to? Annorah fell back, letting the men go on ahead.

This should not come as a surprise, but saying it over and over did not make it better. She'd known nothing about him. He'd wanted it that way and she'd let him keep his secrets, thinking it would make no difference. Maybe it didn't make any difference. All this still would have happened.

Or maybe not. Maybe she would not have asked him to come, would not have risked exposing him to more people. Annorah sank down on a low stone bench, outside the ballroom, her mind working at rapid speed. All the pieces were coming together, all the things she should have paid attention to, but hadn't. She'd been caught up in his kisses, caught up in the pleasures he bestowed on her.

But the clues had all been there: the newspapers, the letter, the quick acquiescence to the extended stay. In hindsight, she could see the answers. He'd read the newspapers, looking for mention of his scandal, looking for an indicator it was safe to go home. The letter had been such an indicator, only it had brought the opposite of what he hoped. The letter must have told him to stay away. On the heels of that warning, her invitation to the house party, plus another thousand pounds, had probably looked like manna in the wilderness.

For all she knew, he'd changed his mind about returning to Hartshaven because he had news he could return to London. She'd been an absolute fool and she could only lay part of the blame at his doorstep. Part she had to lay at her own. Nicholas had warned her on more than one occasion of what could happen if she associated with him. She'd simply not believed it or that it could be as bad as he had made it out.

He had not lied to her. It was every bit as bad

as he'd cautioned and that wasn't even the worst of it. She'd fooled herself into the most dangerous illusion of all: believing someone loved her. Again. It was the one thing she'd thought she'd be safe from with Nicholas. She'd felt safe too soon and now she was rewarded with the darkest of betrayals. Her mind began to slow and her body felt numb. Her world had fallen apart. Somehow, she'd have to get up from this bench and carry on. There would be fall out, and there would be scandal and decisions she had no idea how she would make.

A noisy group of young men exited the ballroom, everyone talking at once. 'There's going to be a duel!' one of them said in loud tones, exclaiming to the others. 'I can't believe it!'

'Well, not yet,' another argued. 'It's not official.'

'Redding's done everything but call him out!' said another.

'He called him a petticoat-monger, if you can countenance it. No man can bear that label without fighting,' the first young man spoke up brashly. 'If Redding had called me that, I'd have

shot him on the spot. D'Arcy has to issue a challenge.'

Nicholas to fight a duel? She wanted to believe
such a claim was ridiculous, but it wasn't. He'd
almost fought another man in London. Duels
were part of the Nicholas she didn't know, but
that didn't change the role she'd played in this
débâcle. She'd brought him here, she'd built up
a fantasy that had put him at risk. Annorah rose,
sticking to the shadows. She didn't want to go
into the ballroom, but she had no choice. This
was her fault. She had to go in there and protect
Nicholas even if her heart was breaking. What
did it matter now if she retreated to the cottage
in the north? The fight was lost. Perhaps it had
always been lost. Surely, this was the darkest moment of her life.

Chapter Twenty

Protect Annorah. Protect Westmore. Protect Channing. Protect the agency. But above all protect Annorah. The best way to do that was to follow Channing's protocol for difficult situations: isolate and defuse. These were the thoughts running through Nicholas's mind when he entered the ballroom with Westmore at his back. The others had defence mechanisms built in for such an occurrence. Annorah did not.

She'd looked positively ill when they'd left her trying to digest the pieces of information Westmore had callously flung out in his haste to reach Redding. Westmore wasn't known for his sensitivity and Annorah had paid for it. She hadn't followed them into the ballroom. Perhaps that was for the best—out of sight, out of mind. The further he could keep her from the scandal that was about to break, the better, and it was going to break, just like a summer deluge, immediate and fierce. The only control he had was *where* it would break.

Already, groups gathered near the Timmermans and Redding fell silent when he passed, likely having overheard Redding's early allegations. Andrew Timmerman looked thunderous. Redding, that skinny weasel, looked triumphant. Georgina didn't know quite how to look. Her chance to win access to the fortune was still intact, yet her niece was once again the victim of a nasty relational turn of events.

'I want a word with you, Mr D'Arcy,' Timmerman began, his face florid with barely contained emotion.

'Not here,' Nicholas answered tersely, taking the first opportunity to shape the conflict to his liking and right now he'd like a little privacy. *Isolate.* The first rule of managing a difficult situation was to keep it contained. Privacy could do that. Airing dirty laundry to the entire ballroom could not. If Timmerman's head was so hot he couldn't see that, Nicholas would see it for him.

'He's right,' Westmore put in. 'Whatever is going on is not a public matter until things are sorted out. Let's adjourn to your study.'

Timmerman began to see the wisdom of the idea. Some of the colour began to recede from Timmerman's features. Nicholas would have taken it as an encouraging sign, but Redding stepped forwards, seeing his advantage slipping away. Information was only powerful if people had access to it.

'He wants to hush it up, Timmerman. Can't you see his ploy? It's as good as an admission,' Redding sneered. 'If there was nothing to worry about, he'd want to publicly clear his good name where everyone could hear.'

'Have you already slandered it?' Nicholas ground out. 'It doesn't take a brave man to spread rumours about someone not present to defend themselves.'

'Easy now,' Westmore muttered.

But there was every need and Nicholas pushed Redding a bit further. 'The privacy isn't for me. It's for Annorah, who should be your first concern.' He fixed Redding and Georgina with individual stares. 'Unless your plan is to see her publicly ruined so you can sweep in and claim her from the rubble.' It didn't take deep intelligence to understand how a man of Redding's calibre operated. 'That would work out nicely for you both, wouldn't it? You'd have your money and you—' he glared at Redding '—would have a fortune at your disposal.' An extraordinary fortune from what he'd learned this afternoon.

His barb had struck home as he'd intended. Georgina paled and Redding stepped back. Good, let them have a taste of their own petty strategies. They no more wanted their personal motives and finances discussed in public than he did. Let them also realise he was not the only one here with something to be risked. Self-righteous bastards like Redding often forgot their own transparencies in the heat of the moment.

'Perhaps now you'd like to adjourn to your study?' Nicholas offered to Timmerman. Timmerman was staring at his wife and Redding. Nicholas's deflection had worked. Timmerman's anger was now directed at the pair of them. Only, it had worked too well.

'Redding, you are here solely on my wife's sufferance, not mine. I want you packed and out of my house within the hour for the trouble you've brought it.'

No, no, don't do that. Nicholas wanted to cringe. They'd all been about to go to the study and defuse. But not now. Redding would not tolerate being ousted. Beside him, Westmore straightened his stance in confirmation. He could almost count down to Redding's eruption in his head. *Three, two, one...and oh, yes, definitely make it loud enough for everyone to hear.*

'You're the fool, Timmerman. You are harbouring a petticoat-monger under your roof and kicking out a legitimate landowner and a neighbour. He's nothing but a fancy, paid whore who's come sniffing after your niece's fortune. You might want to ask yourself how he got here. Is he here because he smells the gold or did your precious niece invite him?' Redding's thin lip curled up. 'I use the term invite very loosely. Perhaps she hired him.'

That was outside of enough. Nick exploded. 'How dare you challenge a woman's honour?' A thick crowd had pressed around them. There was no more privacy. This had now become a public event, the very thing he'd wanted to avoid. He had to tread carefully here. The danger with public events is that it put a man's bravado on trial in front of his peers. Men did and said things that could not be undone. Still, he might be able to work it to his advantage if he was quick. He could publicly protect Annorah, perhaps publicly exonerate her.

Redding knew he had the upper hand for a moment. 'A woman's honour, but not the other?' He turned to Timmerman. 'Don't you find the grounds interesting on which D'Arcy issues the challenge? We have no denial of his true self.'

'Remember your place, Redding. You and I are men,' Nicholas recited almost from rote. 'We may settle our grievances in our own fashion. A woman has no such recourse but that which her male supporters allow her.' It was one of the primary lessons Channing preached at the agency. He heard a stifled cough from Westmore. At least Westmore could take back news he'd made an admirable defence of the code.

'You haven't answered my question. He's stalling, Timmerman. But he can't bluff his way out of this.' Redding held up a folded sheet of paper. 'My acquaintance in London writes that there is rumour Nicholas D'Arcy is a high-paid courtesan of the male variety.' Redding snickered. 'My friend has a more polite vocabulary than most.' He glared at Nicholas. 'That issue is settled. The only real one remaining is how you got here. Did Miss Price-Ellis pay you?'

A gasp circulated the ballroom on a rising tide of whispers, then a collective hush fell. No one wanted to miss this. There was a rustle in the stillness, the sound of skirts, the shuffled movement of people stepping aside. No, he did not want it to be Annorah, not right now when all she could do was make everything worse. Annorah would think she could save him, that she *should* save him by taking the blame. She would do it, too. She was far too literal of a creature to think beyond the moment. The moment demanded sacrifice and she would give it without thinking of the long-term damage that truth would do. Nicholas would not have it. He had nothing against the truth, but it was a powerful weapon that must be used sparingly and with great caution. He slid his gaze sideways to Westmore, the one ally who would understand. Westmore moved stealthily, falling back into the crowd to remove Annorah.

She would not like it, but Nicholas would have to trust Westmore to explain the reasoning on his behalf. He would not see her again. He would have no chance to say goodbye and definitely not in the fashion in which he'd planned.

Certain that Annorah had been safely removed from the ballroom, Nicholas squared his shoulders. If he could not defuse the situation, he could deflect it. 'Miss Price-Ellis did not pay me to attend this house party. My choice to accompany her was entirely voluntary.' It was true on both accounts. He had decided to come on his own volition after receiving Channing's note. Furthermore, Annorah had not yet paid him. He'd officially taken no money from her at this point for this aspect of their association, nor would he in the future. If she should send a deposit to the agency, he would have Channing send it back.

Timmerman's posture seemed to ease a bit at his niece's name being cleared of any complicity. The crowd seemed to deflate a bit. The scandal wasn't as astonishing as it could have been. It was good that people were starting to think Redding had been all smoke and mirrors with his insinuations and letter from London, but Nicholas knew there was one more hurdle. The sooner Redding threw it out, the sooner this could be over.

'Does she know what you are?' The last hurdle did not come from Redding, but from Timmerman. This was the most damning of all the questions, the most dangerous. A lie was thin protection for Annorah. Nicholas didn't want an ounce of this sordid scandal touching the beauty of Hartshaven. All it would take would be someone travelling to Hartshaven to unearth the truth, that he'd been there all week and that he was no librarian. They hadn't looked at a book once.

'She does not know all that I am, sir.' Nicholas met the older man's gaze evenly. 'We did meet by correspondence and I do hold her in genuine regard, but my past has not been a detailed subject of discussion between us. You cannot blame her for this. None of you can.' This last bit was meant for the audience at large. 'If you want to blame anyone, blame Redding for having the indelicacy to air his concerns publicly instead of addressing them to me privately. You can even blame me for having the audacity to reach above myself by coming here and pursuing her. But do not blame her.'

She is beautiful and fun, and alone because people like you, every last one of you in this room, have forced it upon her with your narrow ideas about what a woman with a fortune can and must do with her life and who she must do it with. Well, it's no wonder she came looking for me.

Nicholas was gone and most of the guests with him. Annorah sat with Westmore in the study, watching the hours of the early morning tick away on the long-case clock. The ball had broken up not long after the confrontation had ended, not that she'd seen it or had any first-hand witness to what would surely become gossip legend in this part of Sussex. Westmore had hauled her from the ballroom and her uncle had come a half hour later to inform her that Nicholas had gone. Then he'd returned to seeing off the guests with her aunt as if nothing unusual had happened.

There'd been footsteps in the hall as other guests made their way upstairs to their rooms and the house had eventually fallen silent. Servants would rise early to clean up the clutter. 'Would you like to go upstairs?' Westmore asked at one point. 'You must be tired.'

Annorah shook her head. She wasn't tired, she was numb. There was a difference. Her aunt and uncle came in once everyone was seen to. She hoped they wouldn't stay long, but she had no luck left. They both took seats, signalling the beginning of a longer conversation. Perhaps it was better to get it over with.

'Annorah, Mr D'Arcy dealt most unfairly with you and we are sorry for it,' her uncle began. 'He did not disclose to you all that he was. His life in London was questionable, to say the least.' Her uncle shifted in his chair, decidedly uncomfortable with the discussion. 'He was not fit company for you or for any gently bred woman.' He spread his hands on his thighs, studying his fingernails. 'I will not force you to listen to the details.' He tossed a pleading glance at her aunt. *Tag, you're it.*

To her credit, Aunt Georgina *did* look worn out by the events of the evening. Her face was pale and, for the first time, Annorah saw the discreet signs of age upon her. 'My dear, you've had such horrid luck with these things. You should know by now that you need to be guided by those who know better. If you had, you would have been married. But now all is about to be lost.'

'Not quite. I don't think it's that's dire yet.' The voice drew Annorah's gaze to the doorway. Redding stepped inside, confident and commanding. 'There's still a way out of all of this.'

Annorah froze. Her aunt and uncle turned eager, hopeful eyes his direction as he laid out the plan she was certain he and her aunt had intended to spring all along before Nicholas had arrived.

'We've been neighbours a long time. Perhaps I could offer myself as a husband? Annorah and I could marry in time to satisfy the lawyers and save the family fortune. You needn't suffer.'

Annorah blanched. This was the horror she'd fought so long to avoid. Now, despite all her machinations, it had found her anyway. Perhaps it was true, perhaps no one could outrun their fate. It had caught up to her and she was alone to face it, just as she'd always been. Her aunt and uncle were already making grateful noises for the offer.

But she still had one quiet and forgotten ally.

Grahame Westmore shifted in his chair, drawing all eyes away from Redding to himself. 'There is still the little issue of the standing engagement. The announcement ran in *The Times* today and I believe Mr D'Arcy signed the betrothal agreement.'

'You did what?' Georgina flew at Uncle Andrew. For a moment Annorah pitied her uncle.

'You were the one who was so eager to secure proof we had an engagement in time,' Andrew responded, leading his angry wife to the door of the study. He gave her a sharp look when she would respond. 'We will discuss this upstairs.'

Redding had discreetly melted back into the hallway after that domestic tantrum, leaving Annorah with Westmore. Annorah stood up and paced the room, some of the numbness over the evening and Redding's latest offer wearing off. She wasn't entirely sure all of it would wear off ever. She trailed her fingers over the knick-knacks lining the edge of her uncle's wide desk. 'Nicholas has left without saying goodbye.' She'd thought earlier that the devastation she'd felt on the terrace had been her darkest moment, but it had been superseded in short order by Nicholas's vanishing act and then again by Redding's offer. It just went to prove the old adage that things could always be worse. She wondered if she'd struck bottom yet. Probably not, there was still Hartshaven to turn over to the charities.

'He had no choice,' Westmore answered, crossing his legs and settling back deep in his chair. 'Your uncle couldn't allow Nicholas to stay. Your uncle had to think about saving face for himself, too. If this evening's events had been done in private, your uncle would have had more latitude to decide.'

'I could have saved him if you had let me speak,' Annorah challenged.

Westmore scoffed. 'A noble but foolish sentiment, Miss Price-Ellis. What would you have said? Yes, you'd hired him for five nights of pleasure at the going rate of a thousand pounds? How exactly would that have exonerated you or him? That would only have condemned you both. He worked too hard to protect you in there. I could not let his efforts go to waste, all undone in a gallant moment of unnecessary sacrifice.'

Annorah shook her head. 'You don't understand. I told him once that I'd be proud to stand beside him in any drawing room. The first chance I had to prove it, I ran, even if I was forced to it. I should have found a way.'

She was gaining no leverage with Westmore. He was a rugged, practical man by appearance and apparently by temperament, too. He had no empathy for sentiment, something he'd evinced on three occasions this evening. Make that four. His next comment affirmed it just in case there'd been any room for discrepancy.

'Why is that something you'd want to prove?' Westmore cocked his head and arched dark brows in query. 'I think your sentiments speak well of you, but they are misdirected. You won't want to hear what I have to say, but you should listen. Nicholas is a handsome, charming man, much more charming than I'll ever be. There isn't a woman in London who would turn him from her bed, paid or not. He is the stuff of dreams. So, let him tell you that he loves you and all of that foolish romantic drivel that goes with it and then let him go, because that's what we do with dreams. We wake up from them and we go into the day, if we're smart.'

'Or if we've been hurt,' Annorah snapped.

Westmore was right; she didn't want to hear a single word of what he offered. 'I've been hurt before, sir, by men who would use me for my money, Redding the worst among them. But you have been hurt far deeper and you've refused to recover. That's the difference between us.'

A dark shadow passed over Westmore's face, giving his features a menacing cast. Annorah feared she might have gone too far with this man she didn't know beyond Nicholas's recommendation. He took a step towards her. 'You call hiring a paid escort for sexual pleasure recovered? I call it cowardly. You thought it would be a safe playground in which to indulge your curiosities—all the benefits of an intimate relationship without any of the costs. You wouldn't be the first to do so, but that doesn't mean you've recovered.'

Through the sheer panels draping the window Annorah could see signs of early light. She could be away. 'I do not care for your insinuations, Mr Westmore.'

'My insinuations or me? Let's not mince words, Miss Price-Ellis.'

'Perhaps both, to be fair. Please excuse me. I am going to call for my carriage.' She was determined to make a dignified exit and she almost did, too, but Westmore had the last word just as she reached the door.

'The worst lies are the ones we tell ourselves.'

Annorah shot him a hard look, opting to let silence speak for her instead of words. She was going home to Hartshaven, where she could separate the débâcle from the beauty of these past two weeks and put herself back together. She just hoped all the pieces would be there when she was done.

The thought sustained her as she woke Lily and saw her trunks loaded and the carriage rolled down the gravel drive of Badger Place as the sun peaked over the horizon. She would never come back here again. Annorah laid her head against the padded side of the carriage and gave into weariness, secure in the knowledge that when she awoke she'd be at Hartshaven where everything would be as she left it.

Chapter Twenty-One

'You did not stay where I left you.' Channing steepled his hands and leaned back in his chair in his office. A newspaper lay open on the desk. Nicholas didn't need three guesses to know what he was reading.

'You told me not to come back to London, to stay in the country.' Nicholas was surly. He hadn't slept in nearly two days.

'I can see that you didn't take those instructions either. Instead you went and got engaged to your latest client,' Channing scolded. 'This is serious, Nicholas. Burroughs is after your hide and you were less than circumspect at the Timmermans' house party. It's not just you on the line here, although that alone should have been enough to warrant some caution from you.'

He'd never encountered Channing quite so angry before. Nicholas pushed a hand through his hair. 'What do you want me to do? I'll duel with Burroughs if that will make things right.'

'Dear God, do you ever listen to yourself?' Channing exploded out of his chair with frustration, pacing the room. 'How do you think a duel helps *anything*? A duel is as good as an admission. The league is all but exposed. We can't afford that.' People might know or highly suspect what each of the individuals who worked for Channing did, but no one knew they worked through the same agency or that Channing Deveril, son of an earl, coordinated it all. It was a business built on secrecy. Clients had a need for discretion as much as Channing's gentlemen.

'What do you want from me, then?'

'I want to know what happened in Sussex.'

Nicholas stared blankly at Channing. How could he explain it to Channing when he couldn't quite explain it to himself? He did have an explanation for it, but the explanation seemed improbable and, even if it were true, it merely created an impossible situation. 'It's complicated.'

'It sure as hell better be.'

'I assure you it's a regular Gordian Knot,' Nicholas replied drily. Just like the knot in his stomach. He couldn't sleep, couldn't eat, couldn't do much of anything except think about Annorah. Had Westmore taken care of her? Was she raging mad at him? Had she forgiven him? Probably not. Two days was not long when it came to a woman's wrath.

Channing rolled his eyes. 'I'm sure that's a mythical reference from a book I've never read.' Channing was smart like a fox, not a scholar. 'Can you try at least?' Channing's tone softened, his anger receding.

'Nothing out of the usual. You know how these long-term arrangements can be.' That arrow would hit its mark even if Channing's expression gave nothing away. Channing had done an extended assignment over the Christmas holidays and hadn't been the same since. Nicholas highly suspected something had or perhaps hadn't happened. He moved the conversation swiftly forwards. 'I'll be fine.' *Doubtful, but why admit to it? That made it too real.*

Channing gave him a sceptical look. 'And the engagement? Will it be fine? Forgive me if I doubt it. You look like hell. I can't imagine the engagement will fare much better.'

'It will last a year. It was what was agreed upon,' Nicholas said staunchly. It was the last bit of loyalty he could show Annorah.

Channing blew out a breath. 'I suspect this means you won't be working. It would be awkward for an engaged man. What will you do with yourself?'

Nicholas shrugged. Annorah had asked the same. He had no ideas. 'London is an entertaining city. I am sure I'll find something to do.'

'Burroughs will hear you're back,' Channing warned. 'Have you thought about going home? It would be safer.' He reached into his coat pocket for an envelope. 'Miss Price-Ellis has sent the money for the engagement.' Channing waved a thick envelope.

'I can't take it.' But lord, it was hard not to, hard not to salivate over the pound notes and what they represented. His mind was already spending them: care for Stefan, dresses for his sisters, relief for his mother. But he owed Annorah more. She would have her engagement, but if rumours travelled to Hartshaven, the engagement would be covered in scandal after the house party.

Channing tossed the envelope to him. 'Then you can send it back yourself.'

Nicholas took himself upstairs to the private chambers, where each of the league had their own bedrooms. The rooms were not for work. This wasn't a brothel after all. The rooms were for privacy. Most of the men Channing employed had nowhere else to go. They needed a roof over their heads and food in their bellies. He certainly had needed both when Channing had run across him in the East End.

Nicholas unpacked his trunk, putting his shirt studs and cravat pins in a small box on his bureau. He'd come a long way since then. When he'd first come to the city, he'd not had a single cravat pin to his name. Anything he'd had of value he'd sold and sent the money home while he tried to make a living wage, clerking for a shipping firm on the docks.

Nicholas put his carefully pressed shirts into a dresser drawer. Those days on the docks had been a rude awakening for a gentleman's son used to the outdoors and the freedom of his own hours. He'd been twenty-one at the time and had only recently fallen from the standard of living that had sustained him during childhood. But he'd set aside his pride and gone to work, scraping together whatever he could for his mother and two sisters. He'd lived over the fisherman's shop and shared their meals, learning with shocking clarity how the rest of the world survived. Channing had met him when he'd been assigned a delivery to Deveril House in Mayfair. Within a week, he'd taken Channing's offer to join him at his business on Jermyn Street.

That had been six years ago. Now, he lived comfortably under Channing's standard and, thanks to Annorah, he was debt-free, something he wouldn't be if he'd stayed on the docks. He'd not once regretted his decision. His work was not much different than what his social life might have been had his father lived. He'd have come up to London and done many of the same things on occasion. The only discrepancy was that he was doing them every night, all year, instead of just during the Season. Channing had not forced him to make the jump from escort to intimate partner for hire. That had sort of evolved on its own and he'd not minded. Until now.

Until Annorah had come along and reminded him of other pleasures, that life could be more than moving from one activity to another. Nicholas put his valise of sexual enhancements in the closet. He was unwilling to unpack it and risk unpacking his memories as well. They'd made good use of the items: the massage oil, the treasure hunt, the silken ropes, his sheaths. He thought about their last real conversation the night before the ball. Did she understand the interest had been mutual? Did she know he'd lost himself in the fantasy, too?

Nicholas caught sight of himself in the mirror over his dresser. Channing was right. He did look like hell. At least that was easily cured with a bath and cucumber rings. He rang for one of Channing's footmen to bring up hot water. It was William who answered the bell. He was eager to please, another person who owed their financial surety to Channing. The footmen who populated Argosy House were often young boys Channing had rescued from the streets in Seven Dials. He trained them up here, letting them learn the skills

of running a big house and the skills for valet-
ing. When they turned eighteen, they were given
a reference from Channing and offered a chance
to go into service.

'I'm glad you're back, sir.' William dumped in
the last bucket of hot water. 'Did you have good
time? I have your cucumbers here, too.'

Nicholas sank into the warm suds. 'Yes, I had a
good time and thank you for the cucumbers.' He
shut his eyes and opened them again, sitting up.
'William, one more thing before you go. There's
an envelope on the bureau. Can you see that it's
posted back to the woman who sent it?' He slid
down in the water once more, placing the cucumbers over his eyes in hopes of blocking out
thoughts of all he had given away. It wasn't working.

It hadn't worked. Annorah stared out over the
gardens of Hartshaven, hands gripping the stone
balustrade of the veranda. Nicholas was simply
everywhere. It had been weeks and she'd not succeeded in purging Hartshaven of his presence.
There were memories wherever she looked or
went. She couldn't walk in the garden without

recalling his audacious talk of stamen and irises. She couldn't stand on this very veranda without remembering his first kiss, or eat at the table without recalling their long conversations.

Those places weren't even the worst. Her bedroom had become uninhabitable. She'd moved out of her bedroom under the pretence of wanting to redecorate and taken up residence in a guest room. She was pretty sure the staff was growing suspicious since she had yet to order any paint or wallpaper or fabric samples.

Oh, she had tried to forget him. She'd thrown herself into the ladies' circles in the village, doing more than usual. She'd cleaned out the attics and donated old furniture for a refurbishment project the vicar was undertaking. She continued with the summer school for the younger children in the village to encourage literacy. She had enjoyed that the most, although it was full of memories of Nicholas. She loved it when the little ones would climb on her lap to hear Bible stories or when they'd show her their attempts at printing on their chalk slates. In the autumn, she vowed to spend more time with them. There was much to do in conjunction with the vicar's schooling efforts and she could do it.

'Miss, there's a letter for you.' Plumsby came out on to the terrace with the salver.

Annorah picked it up, a little thrill running through her at the thought of contact at last. Even a letter, a brief thank-you note, would be something from him. But the thrill was quickly replaced by anger.

The letter was her own. He'd not taken the money. She turned the envelope over in her hands, her temper rising. Why? Was this because he wanted nothing more to do with her and this was his way of letting her know his job was done, or because he was making good on the truths he'd told to protect her in her uncle's ballroom? Westmore had told her Nicholas had proclaimed he'd taken no money to accompany her to the ball.

In the end, Nicholas hadn't been all that different from her other romantic débâcles. He'd simply been the worst. They'd wanted her for her money at least. Nicholas hadn't even wanted that.

That's not fair! her heart cried out against the cruel judgement. Maybe there was yet a third option: Nicholas had returned the money because he'd *wanted* to accompany her, not because he needed to. That was a slim hope indeed. She knew very well circumstances had prevented him from returning to Hartshaven, but it was difficult to accept. She wasn't believing that line of reasoning as much as she was understanding her anger.

She would honour their agreement even if he wouldn't. He would not redeem payment on his own, he was proving to be stubborn. But it would be more difficult for him to refuse cash in front of him. An idea began to grow. Annorah tapped her fingers on the balustrade, the plans coming fast now. She would go to London and give him the money herself. No one returned a thousand pounds for a job they'd been hired to do without significant reason. She would see him one last time and know once and for all if there was anything real between them.

Annorah fully acknowledged the answer might hurt. She knew she was going to London to present him not only with payment, but with herself as well. She would stand in front of him and she would challenge him to refuse her heart and her money.

When Nicholas D'Arcy had awakened her, he'd awakened a tiger. For thirteen years, she'd passively dealt with her situation. She'd waited for lawyers, waited for her aunt, waited for suitors, waited for the inevitable. Perhaps she'd even waited for this moment when there was nothing else, no one else, but herself to stand between her and her destiny.

She slapped the envelope against the palm of her hand. It was up to her. 'Plumsby, tell Lily to pack my things. I am going to London for paint and fabric samples.'

Chapter Twenty-Two

London thrummed with the pulse of life everywhere she looked. It was almost overwhelming, and that was just the view from her hotel room. Annorah did not recall the city being so busy the last time she'd been here, but she'd managed. Anger was an amazing energy source. She'd become a whirlwind of efficiency, of doing things now, not later. She had rooms at Grillons, an appointment with a dressmaker and one with a prestigious warehouse on the docks that carried fine fabrics. It had taken the better part of her first day in town to secure those arrangements. Now it was four o'clock and she had a decision to make.

Annorah pulled out a card from her reticule and thumbed the corner, debating. Common sense dictated she should go down to the restaurant and take tea like the other ladies staying here, or she could go to the agency. The address on the card stared back at her, daring her to do it. Perhaps she should send word ahead and make an appointment for tomorrow?

Anger fuelled her response. No, she could not wait. What if he refused to see her? Advance warning would give him that choice. She would lose the element of surprise, but she'd retain her dignity. If he didn't want to see her, the agency wouldn't be forced to slam the door in her face. There would be a polite note and a refusal wrapped in equally polite euphemisms about busyness and genuine regret that he could not connect with her.

She would not tolerate such a response. That would not solve the issue with the money, nor was it truly what she'd come here to do. If she'd braved this crowded, stinking city in July, she was not going to settle for half-measures of sitting in a hotel and sending a note. She had money to give him, money that was rightfully his and she had to do it in person. He'd left her no choice when he'd returned her letter unopened. And Annorah Price-Ellis was tired of being left with no choices.

Annorah called for Lily, who was just in the bedchamber beyond the sitting room. 'I need the blue carriage ensemble. We're going out.' There, she'd publicly proclaimed her intentions. She couldn't back out now.

'We? Do I get to come, too?' Lily's eyes were wide with excitement. She'd never been further than the village.

'Yes, Lily. I will need you very much.' Annorah smiled at the girl's enthusiasm. 'A well-bred lady goes nowhere without her maid in the city.' The maid was supposed to act as a chaperon and lend a sense of decorum to a woman out and about in the city, but Annorah thought it would be the other way around. She'd be more of a chaperon to Lily than Lily would be to her.

Still, London set great stock by the rules. She knew she was pushing the boundaries of decency by calling in person. It was beyond the pale for a single woman to go to a gentleman's abode. She knew enough about the neighbourhoods to know Jermyn Street was known for its more expensive bachelor quarters. Annorah hoped the presence of a maid and her more mature age would compensate for whatever else the call might lack in decency. Besides, it wasn't as if she was going to a home *per se*. This was a business.

Only it didn't look like a business. Annorah was rethinking that last argument for decency an hour and a half later. She peered out of the carriage window once more and then back at the card in her hand to make sure she had the address right: 619 Jermyn Street. This was the place, but it appeared to be a town house. In its defence, it was a well-kept town house. The only difference between it and the other residences lining the street was that this one didn't give the appearance of having been converted into apartments. This one looked like a fully intact home.

'Is this the place?' Lily asked in awed tones, craning her neck to see outside.

'I think so.' Annorah gathered up her courage, her heart beating fast. There were so many reasons for that rapid pulse beat—what would she find at the door? Would she be turned away? Would she be admitted? Would that be worse, actually going inside? Would he be there? She'd never know the answers to any of those questions if she didn't forge ahead. 'Wait for me, Lily. I may be a while.'

At the door, a black-and-bronze plaque announced this was indeed Argosy House, but nothing more. There was no indication this was the offices for the agency. She raised the knocker, a thick, bronze lion head, although she was sure anyone inside would have already heard the pounding of her heart. The knocker seemed superfluous.

The door opened, answered by a butler just like any well-run home would be. Annorah had her own card and rehearsed speech ready. 'Good afternoon, I am hoping to speak with Mr D'Arcy.' She passed the butler her card.

'Right this way, miss, I will see if he is at home.' The butler ushered her in and she drew a breath of relief. She had not been left standing on the step. Not that anyone in the city knew her or would have recognised her, but there was something unnerving about being left to wait on someone's front steps while the people inside decided if one was worthy to grace their halls.

The butler led her to a small sitting room just off the main hall. 'Would you like tea?'

Annorah shook her head. 'No, thank you.' She took the offer as a hopeful sign, though. Surely he would not have offered tea if Nicholas was not at home. Tea took effort to prepare, too much effort if she was to be merely turned away.

The butler left and she entertained herself by studying the room. It was warmly done in striped wallpaper of cream on cream, the subtleness of the striping lending elegance to what might otherwise have been plain. The matching sofa-and-chair set was upholstered in dark-blue floral chintz and a vase in Chinese blue graced the cherry side table, filled with colourful summer blossoms.

Fifteen minutes passed. No one had come. Perhaps she should have rethought the offer for tea. A horrid thought came to her. What if he was with someone? Would he have already forgotten their agreement? Annorah closed her eyes and willed the thought away. She would not think like that. Yet she had to be realistic. He'd come back to London. He'd gone back to work. It was what he did and she *knew* that. She had to keep her mind focused on her goals. She tried to summon her anger.

She was here to give him money. She was here to see him one last time because she wanted to bring the whole matter to an end, not because she was harbouring any impossible fantasies about mutual love. She could admit she'd fallen for him, as long as she understood what that meant and what it didn't mean. It did not require that he had fallen for her, that her fantasies had been reciprocated. There were footsteps in the hall, purposeful steps on the hardwood. He was coming! Annorah looked up and stood, her eyes fixed on the doorway where they were promptly met with dismay.

It wasn't him.

The man who entered the room was nothing like Nicholas. He was tall, but that was where any resemblance ended. This man was gracefully slender and had the purest gold hair she'd ever seen. He also had kind eyes. 'Miss Price-Ellis, what a pleasure. I apologise for the wait. I'm Channing Deveril. Welcome to Argosy House.' Those eyes matched his tone, making it easier to swallow her disappointment.

'Please be seated. I have tea on the way.' He took the chair and crossed a leg over one knee. 'How can I be of assistance?'

'Will Mr D'Arcy be joining us?' It didn't sound as if he would if this man was offering his assistance.

'I'm afraid not. Mr D'Arcy is out this afternoon, but I am more than happy to convey any message you'd care to leave or answer any questions you may have.'

The tea tray came and Annorah busied herself with serving, trying to gather her thoughts. What did all this mean? Was Nicholas upstairs right now, avoiding her? Had this Mr Deveril been sent as his emissary to politely dispose of her? Or was Nicholas simply out and Mr Deveril spoke the truth?

'Cream, yes, thank you.' Mr Deveril took the tea cup from her. 'Please, Miss Price-Ellis, you can talk to me. I know Mr D'Arcy thought highly of you. He'll be sorry to have missed your call.' It was a practised, rote kind of response. This probably wasn't the first time he'd had to intervene.

'Do you have to do this often, Mr Deveril, console Mr D'Arcy's clients?' Annorah smiled over the rim of her tea cup to mitigate the sharpness of the comment.

'I usually let Nicholas do that by himself.' It was a neatly worded assurance. Nicholas was indeed absent from the premises. Irrational jealousy stabbed. Was he out with another woman even though he'd promised not to be?

'I've come because he and I have unfinished business. I owe him payment. I have reason to believe he will not take the wage if I merely leave a note for the bank.'

Mr Deveril's eyes lit with understanding and with reserve. 'Ah, yes, the payment for the ill-favoured house party and the engagement. I appreciate you bringing it, but I hope it was not your sole reason for coming to town. He will not take it. He cannot. He's been very clear with me on his position.' He would not tell her any more than that. They both knew he was walking a careful line between assisting her and protecting his employee's privacy.

Annorah put the envelope full of money on the table between them. There was nothing like the actual sight of a thousand pounds all in notes to sweeten any pot. Tangible money was so much harder to refuse than theoretical. 'I hope you can see that he gets it at some point. You don't have to give it to him directly. Maybe you know the state of his finances and can apply it towards any obligations on his behalf?' Deveril seemed to hesitate. 'I know he has family—perhaps I could convey the money to them.'

The comment got Deveril's sharp attention. 'Has he spoken to you of his family?'

Victory at last, a very little one but still the polite ice of this tea party was starting to thaw. She grabbed on to the offering. 'He told me of his brother, Stefan, and their summers hunting for hidden treasure. I believe his family is in Stour.'

Deveril gave her a long, considering look. 'Did he now? I find that very interesting. Nicholas is an extraordinarily private person. There's much he doesn't even tell me.' He reached for a little cream cake from the tray, but Annorah was not fooled by the casual gesture. He was probing for something. 'What else did the two of you talk about?'

There was no malice in the probe. Deveril could be trusted and she had to trust him. He was the only key to Nicholas she had right now. 'Lutefisk. We talked about lutefisk.' She wrinkled her nose. 'He mentioned he once lived with a Norwegian fisherman and his family.' A moment's insight hit her. 'Are you the reason he left them? Did you offer him something better?'

Deveril nodded. 'He would not have lasted long on the docks. Clerking was not for him. He's too alive to be buried in a clearing house.' He set down his tea cup and rose, scooping up the envelope. 'I'll see to it that his family gets this. Is there anything else?'

This was her cue to leave. Annorah followed his lead and rose, too. 'Thank you for sending him to me. I care for him greatly. He is a good man.' She saw Deveril take a breath. He was going to say something conciliatory, something polite and generic he probably said to all the broken-hearted women darkening his door hoping for a glimpse of Nicholas D'Arcy. She held up a stalling hand. 'Please, you can think what you like, but for me this is no passing infatuation. I wish things could be different. We made each other happy. I know the value of that. Thank you for your time, Mr Deveril.'

She made to move past him, but he fell into

step beside her. 'I hope you enjoy London. Will you be staying long?' He seemed hesitant, as if he were weighing a decision in his mind.

'No, I don't have much use for London. I come as seldom as I can.' Annorah laughed. 'I have rooms at Grillon's for this stay.' She paused and decided to be completely honest. 'I came specifically for Nicholas.' After this visit, she doubted she'd have reason to come again for a long time. How could she come, knowing Nicholas was in London, somewhere, and not accessible to her? It would be a type of torture. Better to stay at Hartshaven and take out her memories one by one. Still, a type of torture, but far less dreadful.

Deveril drew a breath. 'I told you the truth when I said he wasn't here.' He took her by the elbow and drew her aside in a little antechamber by the front door. 'Before he came to you, there was some business involving a duel. London is not safe for him at the moment. More than that, he means to honour the year of your supposed engagement. He could not do that and remain in the city, as I'm sure you understand. Since he has spoken to you of his family and because of your extenuating circumstances, I will tell you this in the strictest of confidences. Nicholas has gone home.'

Then she was going after him. She'd come to London. She could go to Stour.

Chapter Twenty-Three

It wasn't working. Nicholas had to acknowledge the truth of it after three weeks. Being home didn't erase the loss of Annorah. Neither did it make facing his ghosts any easier. Not even hard work, like roofing the stable in the heat of July, seemed to help. Nick stopped, laid down his hammer and wiped his brow. It was as hot as Hades up here. He reached for the water he'd brought up and drank. It might have helped if everyone wasn't being so damn nice to him. His mother, his sisters, even Stefan had welcomed him home like a prodigal son.

Stefan had been so glad to see him, so willing to pick up where their relationship had left off years ago. They'd always been close, but Nick had not expected Stefan's reception to be warm.

After all, it was his fault Stefan was paralysed. But Stefan did not see it that way.

As for his sisters and his mother, they'd been so happy to see him, too, so eager to show him all they'd been able to do with the money he'd sent home over the years. He wondered what they would do if they knew everything they said simply riddled him with more guilt. For them, he felt guilty over the money he hadn't taken from Annorah. He felt guilty for hiding his London life from them. He felt guilty every time he looked at Stefan and knew he was responsible for his brother being confined to that chair.

Nick went back to work, hammering in a shingle with unnecessary force. Annorah was wrong, he wasn't good. He'd been very bad and these were the rewards for his sin. Even when he tried to do good, it turned out poorly. Wasn't Annorah proof of that? He should have stuck with what he knew: sex and women, not matrimony. He'd brought scandal to her when he'd stepped outside his boundaries, no matter how noble his intentions had been. He hoped she was weathering it all well, that life at Hartshaven hadn't been compromised.

'Nick, we've got company!' Stefan's call interrupted his thoughts.

Nicholas looked down to see his brother wheeling himself towards the stable. It did amaze him how proficient Stefan had become with the chair since he'd last seen him. In those days, Stefan had been pasty and thin, an invalid who had been confined too long to the sick room. The man who had met him on his return was robust and tanned, his arms muscled and strong from the exertion of wheeling himself around.

'Who is it?' Nicholas asked, climbing down the ladder.

'Don't you know?' Stefan teased him with a grin. 'Isn't this your big surprise? I was wondering when she would show up.' When Nicholas said nothing, Stefan went on. 'Your fiancée? The one we've read about in the London papers? Surely you remember her?' he jested.

It was all Nick could do to stay upright. Annorah was here? Stefan *knew* about his supposed fiancée? 'How do you know we're engaged?' Nick asked hesitantly.

'We might live in the country, but we're not entirely out of touch. When you left for London and started writing these fabulous letters home, Mother decided we'd better take a subscription to *The Times* so we could keep up with you. She feared you'd find us dull dogs when you came home. We saw the announcement. We've been waiting for you to say something.'

A knot of dread began to form in Nick's stomach. How much did he need to tell them? 'Stefan, what else does the family know?' How could he tell them the engagement was not real? Was Annorah already in there, laying out his latest sins to his mother? Or was she in there creating false hope? His mother yearned for him to marry. She would have been over the moon about the engagement. Part of him dreaded walking into the parlour and facing Annorah in front of his family and part of him wanted to race up to the house.

Stefan touched his arm. 'I know you're not a clerk in a shipping firm,' he said quietly, confirming the worst.

'Mother and the girls? What do they know?'

'Mother knows you're quite the ladies' man. She sees the references in the society column. I think that's all she knows. She knows about your latest scrape with Lord Burroughs. She was frightened for a week that you'd be duelling. I have tried to shield them from a bit of your reality.' Stefan smiled. 'All has ended well. Perhaps you will tell me about it some day.'

There Stefan went again, assuming they were close once more, brother-companions roaming the land in search of adventure as they had in their boyhood, but there was hurt mingled there, too, ever so subtly. Stefan *wanted* to be part of his life. It hurt him to be pushed away as much as it hurt Nick to be included. His throat thickened at the realisation. Annorah would tell him this was the gift of a family and a home, these relationships; people who loved you and cared for you no matter what.

But that made accepting those gifts even more difficult. He didn't deserve Stefan's goodness. All these years, Stefan had covered for him when he should have stood in shame. 'It hasn't ended all that well, Stefan. The engagement isn't real. It's a ruse to protect her inheritance. I'm not sure why she's come, actually.' He could guess. Annorah would not have liked having her money returned. That opened up another question. How had she discovered he was here? Only Channing could have told her. He'd have a bone to pick with Channing next time he saw him.

'She's come a long way for something that isn't real,' Stefan remarked as they began the slow trip back to the house. 'I liked her. I only spoke with her for a few minutes before Mother sent me out after you, but I liked her. She's kind. She knew who I was right away.' Stefan paused. 'She's wearing Mother's cameo, too, which makes me think that you lie, Brother.'

'I *can't* marry her, Stefan.' Nick picked up a pebble and threw it, releasing some of his pent-up frustration.

'Can't or won't? The engagement might be a façade, but your feelings aren't. She means something to you and I think you mean something to her. I know you, Nick. You're very private. You don't talk about yourself to just anyone, yet you talked to her about your family.'

'It's complicated, Stefan. There's no time to explain. She's wealthy and if I ask her to marry me now, to make the engagement official, she'll always think it's for the money. There are people who will say I kissed it out of her.'

Stefan seemed to contemplate that for a moment. 'Is that the only reason you won't marry her?'

'I'll drag her down. She runs a school in the village.She's goodness personified.'

'Wait, you're not still blaming yourself for the night of the storm?' A tremor of anger ran through Stefan's tones.

'It's my fault,' Nick answered sternly. 'I wasn't where I was supposed to be. Father died and you were injured.'

Stefan placed a firm, restraining hand on Nick's arm. 'I've never blamed you for that. Tragic accidents happen. Don't let the past hold you back from the future, Nick. If anything, you saved me that night. You pulled me out.' They'd reached the steps, where a ramp had been constructed for Stefan to access the house. 'Go on—' Stefan motioned '—I'll be along shortly. Go in there and tell her why you won't marry her and let her be the judge.'

That was the problem. He'd already told her the worst and it still hadn't been enough. She'd simply not been driven away. Instead, she'd hunted him down. Nick heard her before he saw her, her laughter drifting out into the hall as she and his mother talked. She was precisely the kind of woman his mother would want for him, he realised. He'd never stopped to consider it before. There was no need to. But now, suddenly, there was every need. He could see her here with his family, could see her starting a summer school like she had at Hartshaven and his heart nearly broke.

She looked up the moment he entered the room. She looked fresh, dressed in white, her hair in a neat chignon at her neck. Even the July heat could not cause her to wilt. He should have changed, should have washed off at the pump. He would look dirty to her. Her eyes met his, betraying her nerves. She wasn't sure of the reception he might give her. She understood how bold this unannounced arrival was.

'Annorah, you're here.' Nick stepped forwards, taking her hand and raising it to his lips like he had that first day at Hartshaven. 'You've met everyone. Stefan is already out singing your praises.'

'You should have told us she was coming, but it's a delightful surprise,' his mother interjected. 'We've been waiting for you to say something,

Nick.' She turned to Annorah. 'We read about it in *The Times*—we get a subscription you know. But we wanted Nick to tell us in his way, when he was ready.' She beamed at them. 'And now he has.'

Annorah merely smiled and flashed him a look. He needed to get Annorah alone before she and his mother started naming their first-born. 'Mother, if you'll excuse us, I'd like Annorah to myself for a moment.'

'Of course, I'll go and see about something cold to drink.'

Nicholas shut the door behind her and faced Annorah. She was so beautiful, all he wanted to do was look at her. How had he survived three weeks without the sight of her? Her eyes sparkled in earnestness and Nick knew what she would say before she spoke. They would be the words he longed to hear, giving him absolution, giving him the future he'd thought was out of reach, a chance to marry, to have a family. His very own fairy tale. But happy ever afters didn't happen to him. That's when he knew he had to refuse whatever it was she was going to offer. 'So, Annorah, what brings you to Stour?'

'That's not exactly the welcome a woman wants to hear.' Annorah smiled, gathering her courage and overlooking the chilly welcome. Even hot and sweaty and dirty he was a sight to behold. She took out the envelope. 'I came for you, Nick. You won't take my money, but maybe you'll take me.'

'Stop, Annorah.'

But she would not relent, not on this—it was far too important for both of them. 'I've heard the worst. I know your secrets and it's not enough to drive me away. I've had time to think and my conclusion is that you take too much on yourself. What happened was unfortunate, but it wasn't your fault. You can't keep punishing yourself.'

Annorah reached for his hands. 'What could you have done? Run fast enough to do what? To catch the tree? To stop it from falling? To hold back the lightning itself?'

'I've always wondered if I should have moved Stefan that night. If by doing so I caused worse damage to him. All I could think of was getting him out of there in case the rest of the roof went, or a horse got loose and trampled him.'

'You can't blame yourself. You did all you

could in those moments.' She wanted to free him, wanted to give him absolution. This was the place he went when he withdrew from her, this haunted place full of half-formed memories and doubts.

'You don't know, you weren't there,' he began to protest. She would not have it. She knew all too well how this defence mechanism worked to let people stay shrouded in their grief.

'You're right. I wasn't there. But I was somewhere similar. Look at me, Nicholas.' She stared at him until he was forced to look up. 'When my parents died from the fever, I wanted to die, too. My whole life had been taken from me. I was angry with my mother for having gone down to nurse the sick, angry with my father for letting himself go, and I was angry with myself for not getting sick and dying, too. Why me? Why did everyone around me get sick, but not me? I still don't have that answer and I probably will never have it. The point is, you and I were spared. We get to carry on.'

It was her turn to look down. 'Can I make a confession, too?' This got his attention. She swallowed and met his gaze. 'Until I met you, I hadn't done a very good job of carrying on. I'd convinced myself it was enough to just survive. But you've shown me it's not, not even close to enough.' She paused and gathered her courage. 'I went to London to find you and when you weren't there, I came here not just to make sure you took the money.'

'Then why did you come?' Nicholas's voice dripped like thick honey in the autumn, his eyes dark with desire. Damn him, he was going to make her risk it all on a single throw of the dice.

'I came for you. I want you, Nicholas D'Arcy, but you have to want me, too. I can't be like those women in your past. I don't want to have only your body. I need to have your mind and your heart because those are the things I love about you most. Can I, Nicholas? Can I have those things?'

'Haven't you been listening to anything I've said? Haven't you looked around here?' Nicholas began to pace. 'I have a family to support: a mother, two sisters and a crippled brother. You've met them. They will always need me. And scandal will always follow me, I fear.' These were paper dragons indeed. He was vacillating. He wanted to accept. He wanted to be selfish and take all that she was offering. It wasn't about the money, it was about her. He wanted her. She could have been poor and he'd have still wanted her.

Annorah rose and met him toe to toe, her eyes fiery emeralds. 'I was listening, but were you? I don't care about a title and money. I have all the money we'll ever need and in the end it's all ours anyway. You can build your brother a whole hospital if you want, but from what I've seen, he doesn't need that. And you're wrong. You can give me something. You have a family. I would love to have a family again. I will gladly share yours with you at your home or at Hartshaven if you want to bring them. All I need to know is the answer to my question. Can I have you, body and soul, Nicholas D'Arcy?'

Annorah held her breath, every fibre of her being tingling and alert. She felt alive, something she'd not thought to feel six weeks ago when all this had begun. Back then, she'd thought she'd only had a month to live, really live. Now, the possibility of a lifetime loomed before her. She watched his face, searching for signs. It started in his eyes. They began to crinkle, the blue depths firing with a spark, then his mouth, his kissable mouth, turned up into his trademark smile, the one that warmed her to her toes.

'Why, Miss Price-Ellis,' he drawled, 'is this a proposal or a business proposition?'

She smiled, relief pumping through her. He had saved her— not the fortune, not Hartshaven, but *her*. 'Neither, Nicholas. This is forever.'

'Then I accept.' He grinned and drew her to him.

Epilogue

The wedding was small, held at Nicholas's parish church, attended by family and a few close friends of the D'Arcys. There were fresh flowers and pretty dresses for Nick's sisters and the bride. It was a simple affair because, as Annorah was fond of noting, love was simple when one got right down to it.

The sensationalism of it in London was far larger than the actual ceremony itself. No one could believe Nick D'Arcy had actually wed, and to an heiress to boot! Jocelyn Eisley wrote an entirely inappropriate poem to commemorate the event and Grahame Westmore led the boys of the league in a toast to Nick's good health in the drawing room of Argosy House.

Everyone wished Nick happiness in his new

life. Well, almost everyone. Lord Burroughs certainly didn't. He remained staunchly determined to seek revenge, a revenge that was turned more towards the rumours of the existence of a League of Discreet Gentlemen of which Nick was supposed to be a part. But these worries and well-wishers were far from Nick's mind as he lay with his bride up in the hills in a cave above the Stour River specially appointed for their wedding night.

It was one of the caves he and Stefan had explored in their youth. He'd gone to great lengths to have it fitted out with the splendour of a bridal suite. There was food and champagne, fire and flowers and a soft bed. Annorah had loved it on sight. Fishing rods were propped against the wall. They would spend a few days up here, exploring the caves and fishing in the river. But all that could wait. Right now, he wanted to make love to his bride and revel in the knowledge that she was his.

He got out of bed to pour more champagne, feeling Annorah's eyes follow him across the space, then they moved past him. He'd lost her attention. He turned to follow her gaze. 'What are you looking at so intently?' he joked. 'Besides me, that is.'

'That crack at the back of the cave,' she said, missing his humour entirely. 'It doesn't look like the rest of the room.' She was out of bed, wrapping a sheet about her and picking up a lamp. 'I don't think one would notice it in the daylight without the variance in light to show the differential.'

'We can explore tomorrow. Come back to bed.' Nick laughed, but Annorah was determined.

She set down the lamp and began feeling along the seam. He had no choice but to join her. When Annorah had her mind set on something, she didn't relent. He was proof enough of that and gladly so. She hadn't given up on him. He would be forever thankful she hadn't.

Together they pulled and tugged, prying the seam loose. She was right. This crack was artificially made. Someone had cut into the stone, making a crude door of sorts, which meant there would be a hollow space behind it. Nick gave a final tug and the crack crumbled away to reveal a space and his heart leapt with excitement.

'You look like a schoolboy.' Annorah laughed.

Nick looked down at himself. 'A rather well-endowed schoolboy, I would hope.'

'What do you think is in here?' She was excited, too. He could hear it in her voice. They were down on their knees and Annorah cast the lamplight over the opening.

Nick reached in a hand, coming into contact with soft, worn leather. 'I've got something!' He pulled out a sack. It had weight to it. He fumbled with the string around the neck of the bag.

'Do you think it's…?' Annorah didn't finish her sentence. He poured the contents into her cupped hands, gold coins spilling on to the floor.

'The gold,' Nicholas finished for her. 'The pirate's gold, the Jacobite treasure, the king's ransom, whatever you want to call it.' He reached in for the other bags, thirteen in all. 'I can't believe after all these years it was here all along. Stefan and I must have explored this cave a hundred times.

Annorah laughed. 'You just needed to see it with new eyes. Shall we tell them? It's not too late in the evening to ride down with the news.'

Nick looked at her with mock seriousness and then down at himself, drawing her gaze with him.

'Yes, it is, far too late.' He was fully aroused, not by the sight of the money, but by the sight of his wife dressed in a bedsheet, the lamplight shining in strategic places. 'The treasure will keep, but I'm not sure I will.' Then he whispered the three words he knew she loved to hear. 'Come to bed.' And she did.

* * * * *

Discover more romance at

www.millsandboon.co.uk

- ❤ WIN great prizes in our exclusive competitions

- ❤ BUY new titles before they hit the shops

- ❤ BROWSE new books and REVIEW your favourites

- ❤ SAVE on new books with the Mills & Boon® Bookclub™

- ❤ DISCOVER new authors

PLUS, to chat about your favourite reads, get the latest news and find special offers:

- Find us on facebook.com/millsandboon

- Follow us on twitter.com/millsandboonuk

- ❤ Sign up to our newsletter at millsandboon.co.uk